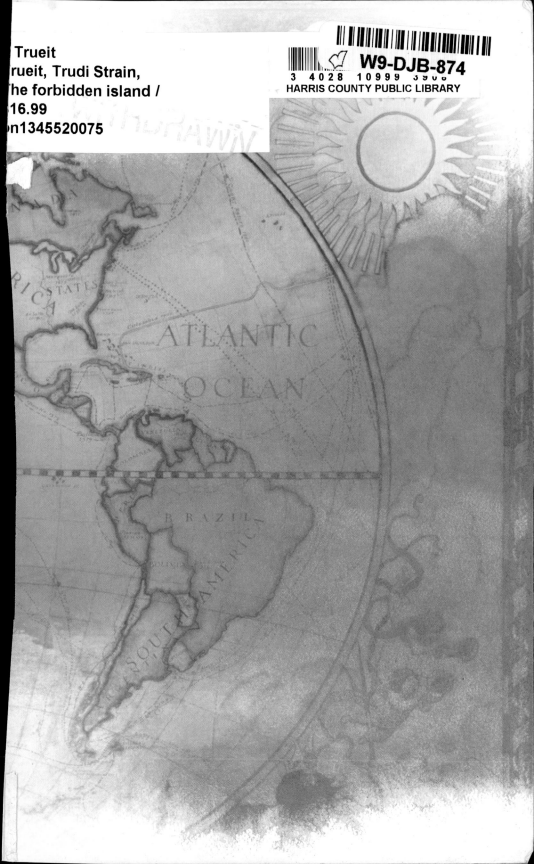

ATLANTIC

OCEAN

BRAZIL

SOUTH AMERICA

EXPL◉RER
ACADEMY

THE *FORBIDDEN ISLAND*

TRUDI TRUEIT

UNDER THE *Stars*

NATIONAL
GEOGRAPHIC

FOR BECKY AND JEN, MY TEAM COUSTEAU —TT

Since 1888, the National Geographic Society has funded more than 14,000 research, conservation, education, and storytelling projects around the world. National Geographic Partners distributes a portion of the funds it receives from your purchase to National Geographic Society to support programs including the conservation of animals and their habitats. To learn more, visit natgeo.com/info.

For more information, visit nationalgeographic.com, call 1-877-873-6846, or write to the following address:

National Geographic Partners, LLC
1145 17th Street NW
Washington, DC 20036-4688 U.S.A.

For librarians and teachers: nationalgeographic.com/books/librarians-and-educators

More for kids from National Geographic: natgeokids.com

National Geographic Kids magazine inspires children to explore their world with fun yet educational articles on animals, science, nature, and more. Using fresh storytelling and amazing photography, *Nat Geo Kids* shows kids ages 6 to 14 the fascinating truth about the world—and why they should care. **natgeo.com/subscribe**

For rights or permissions inquiries, please contact National Geographic Books Subsidiary Rights: bookrights@natgeo.com

Designed by Eva Absher-Schantz
Codes and puzzles developed by Dr. Gareth Moore

Hardcover ISBN: 978-1-4263-7339-8
Reinforced library binding ISBN: 978-1-4263-7433-3

Printed in Hong Kong
22/PPHK/1

PRAISE FOR THE EXPLORER ACADEMY SERIES

"A fun, exciting, and action-packed ride that kids will love."
—**J.J. Abrams,** award-winning film and
television creator, writer, producer, and director

"Inspires the next generation of curious kids to go out into our world and discover something unexpected."
—**James Cameron,** National Geographic
Explorer-in-Residence and acclaimed filmmaker

"…a fully packed high-tech adventure that offers both cool, educational facts about the planet and a diverse cast of fun characters."
—*Kirkus Reviews*

"Thrill-seeking readers are going to love Cruz and his friends and want to follow them on every step of their high-tech, action-packed adventure."
—**Lauren Tarshis,** author of the I Survived series

"Absolutely brilliant! Explorer Academy is a fabulous feast for mind and heart—a thrilling, inspiring journey with compelling characters, wondrous places, and the highest possible stakes. Just as there's only one planet Earth, there's only one series like this. Don't wait another instant to enjoy this phenomenal adventure!"
—**T.A. Barron,** author of the Merlin Saga

"Nonstop action and a mix of full-color photographs and drawings throughout make this appealing to aspiring explorers and reluctant readers alike, and the cliffhanger ending ensures they'll be coming back for more."
—*School Library Journal*

"Explorer Academy is sure to awaken readers' inner adventurer and curiosity about the world around them. But you don't have to take my word for it—check out Cruz, Emmett, Sailor, and Lani's adventures for yourself!"
—**LeVar Burton,** actor, director, author, and host
of the PBS children's series *Reading Rainbow*

"Sure to appeal to kids who love code cracking and mysteries with cutting-edge technology."
—*Booklist*

"I promise: Once you enter Explorer Academy, you'll never want to leave."
—**Valerie Tripp,** co-creator and author
of the American Girl series

"…the book's real strength rests in its adventure, as its heroes…tackle puzzles and simulated missions as part of the educational process. Maps, letters, and puzzles bring the exploration to life, and back matter explores the 'Truth Behind the Fiction'…This exciting series…introduces young readers to the joys of science and nature."
—*Publishers Weekly*

"Both my 8-year-old girl and 12-year-old boy LOVED this book. It's fun and adventure and mystery all rolled into one."
—**Mom blogger,** Beckham Project

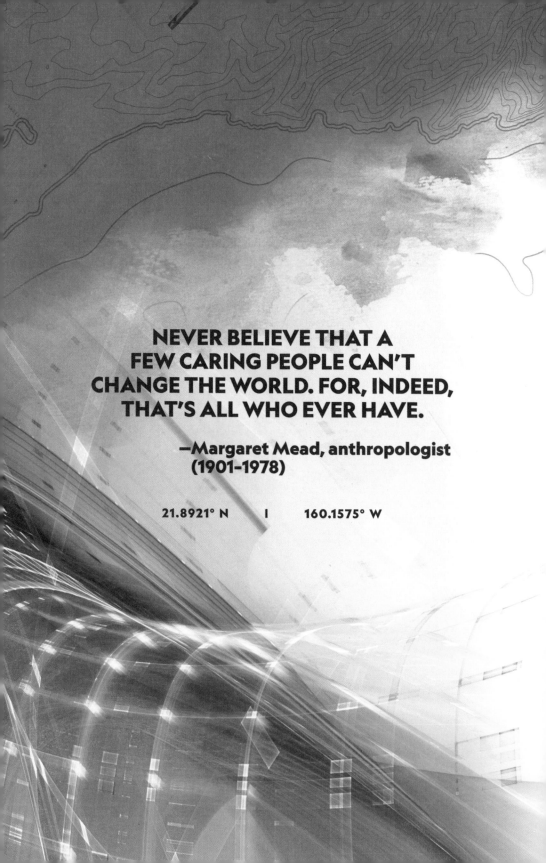

NEVER BELIEVE THAT A
FEW CARING PEOPLE CAN'T
CHANGE THE WORLD. FOR, INDEED,
THAT'S ALL WHO EVER HAVE.

—Margaret Mead, anthropologist
(1901–1978)

21.8921° N | 160.1575° W

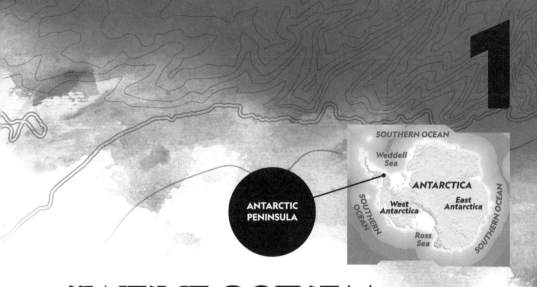

"WE'VE GOT 'EM this time!"

whispered Bryndis. She was squeezing Cruz's hand so hard his finger-tips were turning white. "We're going to beat Team Magellan!"

Things *did* look promising. Heads shook and hisses flew as Ali, Zane, Kat, Matteo, Yulia, and Tao huddled up. For nearly an hour, the four explorer teams had been battling it out in *Orion*'s CAVE. Cruz was frazzled. He could tell his teammates were, too. Lani's cheeks were flushed and shiny, a chunk of Sailor's ponytail had escaped its band, and Emmett's emoto-glasses resembled a couple of chocolate doughnuts left in a car on a hot day. Dugan shifted like a goalkeeper ready to defend against a penalty kick. However, this was no soccer match. This was a brain-busting, heart-hammering, take-no-prisoners geography bee.

Each team had 30 seconds to answer a question from Professor Modi that might or might not include a holographic element. Get the question right, and their teacher moved on to the next team. Get it wrong, and you earned a strike. Three strikes and your team was out.

Galileo was the first to be eliminated, followed by Earhart several rounds after that. Cousteau and Magellan had fought on. Back and forth they'd gone in the virtual reality chamber, tossing out facts about cities and countries, bodies of water, deserts, mountains, parks, and monuments. Cruz had lost track of the number of rounds. Now both teams had two strikes. Cruz's team had already answered their question correctly. If Magellan couldn't do the same, Cousteau would be crowned geography bee champion.

The prizes were worth the torture. The winning team would get first pick on their next mission. Every member would also be awarded 100 bonus points. Finally, each would get a high-definition ultra-sensitive ingression analysis upgrade to their Portable Artifact Notation and Data Analyzer (PANDA) device. Cruz wasn't exactly certain what that meant, but it sounded good.

Standing in a holographic forest of aspen trees with golden leaves, Cruz drew in a hopeful breath. He wanted the rewards, sure, but he also needed to win at *something*! He'd been pretty down the past few weeks, since discovering that the seventh piece of his mom's cipher was not genuine.

"The angle of the top inside edge on this one *is* different," Emmett had proclaimed after carefully examining the black marble fragment through his magnifying emoto-glasses. "You have to get really close to see it, but your mom was right. It's not one of hers. The pieces must have been switched."

"Switched? How can that be?" Sailor spun to Cruz. "I thought as long as you have it around your neck it's protected by your bio force field."

"It is, but I don't wear it *all* the time," Cruz reminded her. "I have to shower, you know. I also take it off when we scuba dive . . ."

"Jaguar!" accused Sailor. "The explorer spy took the seventh piece."

"Maybe," cautioned Emmett.

"What do you mean 'maybe'? Dr. Vanderwick was Zebra, and she's no longer a threat," she argued. "It *has* to be Jaguar."

Emmett shook his head. "Not necessarily. The switch could have happened before we found the dragon's blood warrior."

"Why not check it against the first photos Cruz took of the piece?" suggested Lani. "That should at least tell us *when* it was swapped. Cruz, could you ask your dad to send it back?"

Each time Cruz found a new piece of the cipher, he'd immediately snap a couple of pictures and message them to his father. He would then delete the photos from his tablet and run a program to record over the data so the images could not be recovered from his computer's trash bin. "Uh-oh!" moaned Cruz after opening the file on his tablet. "I didn't overwrite the photos. After we left the museum in Xi'an ... in the car ... I called Bryndis to update her, and I—I guess I must have forgotten ..."

"We know, head in the clouds," teased Sailor.

She'd made light of it, but everyone knew it was a costly error. Cruz had opened the door for someone to hack into his tablet, nab the photos, and create a fake piece to trade for the real one. Lani was right about the picture, though. If the edge of the stone in the image matched the one Cruz wore now, then the exchange had occurred *before* they'd ever made it to the Terra-Cotta Army museum. If not, the piece had been swapped *after* they'd found it, placing Jaguar as their prime suspect. Cruz sent the photo to Emmett, who spent forever studying it. When, at last, Emmett glanced up, gray beads bounced through the emoto-glasses. "It's not the same."

To Cruz, this was the best scenario possible, given the situation. If Jaguar had the cipher, there was a chance it was still on board *Orion*. Cruz had sent his honeybee drone, Mell, on a shipwide search for the stone. Of course, there were places even a bee couldn't go, like inside a drawer that was shut tight or a zippered backpack. There were also some places she didn't dare go, such as the galley. Chef Kristos would have lost his top if he'd have found an insect in his kitchen, robotic or otherwise. Still, the MAV was able to sweep *most* of the ship. She'd found nothing. Was Cruz too late? Was the seventh cipher already in Nebula's hands? He could only pray that it wasn't.

In the meantime, as *Orion* sailed east, Cruz worked to advance his mom's journal to unlock the final clue. He'd patiently explained the situation to his holographic mother. He'd asked for her help. Begged. Sulked. Demanded. Yet, no matter what he said or how he said it, her response remained the same. She calmly refused to unlock a new clue. It had left Cruz with only one option. By bedtime tonight, he would know if his last resort would work.

"Fifteen seconds!" Professor Modi's pronouncement jolted Cruz back to the present.

Cruz looked up at the white-barked aspens, their autumn leaves fluttering against a vivid blue sky. This place was beautiful, but he had no idea where they were.

"Magellan won't get it," Lani said quietly to Cruz. "I only came across it while reading about how trees communicate."

She was kidding, right?

Lani caught his look. "It's true. Trees can communicate with each other using fungus filaments known as mycelium. See, the mycelium grows into the tree roots, allowing some trees to connect using chemicals and electrical signals. One tree can tell others when it's in pain, or warn of dangers, like insect infestations or drought."

She *wasn't* kidding.

Cruz was still a bit skeptical. "You're telling me trees talk to one another?"

"They do more than that." Her eyes brightened. "They take care of each other, too. Older trees will send water and nutrients to saplings through the system to help them grow. It's called the mycorrhizal network. Professor Ishikawa says there are miles of mycelium in just a teaspoon of forest soil. It's kind of like nature's fiber-optic cable. They even nicknamed it the wood-wide web. Cool, huh? Professor Ishikawa told me we'll be studying it in biology next year, but I'm not waiting. I'm trying to speak 'tree' now."

Of course she was.

"Time!" called Professor Modi. "Zane, I'll need Magellan's answer."

"Uh ... uh ..." Zane swallowed hard. "We're gonna say ... Utah?"

Professor Modi lifted his tablet. "Pando is a grove of more than forty-seven thousand quaking aspens spanning a hundred acres that share a single root system ..."

Cruz elbowed Lani. "Hey, I bet they have great conversations."

She rolled her eyes.

The professor was still talking: "... is one of the oldest and largest organisms on our planet. It's located in the Fishlake National Forest in *Utah.*"

Team Magellan cheered. Team Cousteau groaned.

"Crikey!" Sailor did a facepalm. "Will it *ever* end?"

"It will, and soon," declared Professor Modi. "We have five minutes left in class, just enough time for a final tiebreaker to decide the winner."

The CAVE erupted in applause, with Teams Earhart and Galileo clapping the loudest. Since being eliminated, they'd had to sit and watch Cousteau and Magellan go toe to toe.

"The category is a place on the map," said Professor Modi. "I will begin listing clues. General at first, then more specific. The first team to buzz in and correctly identify the location I am describing will be declared the winner of this year's freshman geography bee."

A red buzzer on a stand materialized in front of Dugan.

"Teams, a reminder to confer before you answer," said their teacher. "I can only accept your *first* response."

Cruz felt a breeze cool his forehead. The smell of fresh grass tickled his nose. A carpet of green grass rolled under the soles of his shoes. The meadow headed for the wall behind their professor, ending at a rocky coastline. Beyond the shore was a wide blue sea. To his left, Cruz saw steep, jagged cliffs, and on his right a dirt road cut through the rolling hillside. A lazy train of cottony clouds chugged across a late-afternoon sky, their shadows trailing on the ground below. Cruz swiveled his neck. The wall behind them was still a blank canvas. Interesting.

"Clue number one," said Professor Modi. "You are on a tropical island that measures sixty-three square miles. A trio of volcanoes, now extinct, is responsible for forming its triangular shape."

Team Cousteau circled up. They threw out a few possibilities, like Jamaica and Vanuatu, but nobody was certain.

"Better to wait than make a wild guess," advised Lani.

Magellan wasn't hitting their buzzer, either. Cruz saw that the wall behind them was still black. *Odd,* he thought. Shouldn't it be part of the scenery, too?

Emmett had noticed it as well. "Must be a malfunction," he muttered.

"Clue number two," continued Professor Modi. "The original Polynesian inhabitants called this island Rapa Nui, but we know it by a different name, thanks to a Dutch explorer who landed here on a particular day in 1722."

"Polynesia!" Sailor grinned at Lani and Cruz. "We're in the South Pacific."

"Could it be Kaho'olawe or Ni'ihau?" Cruz named the smallest islands in the Hawaiian chain.

Lani bit her lip. "Kaho'olawe *is* triangular, but—"

"The landscape's wrong." Cruz realized his mistake. "I don't think there's this much grass there, and the soil is red."

"Ni'ihau isn't triangular," noted Lani. "The terrain is likely similar to Kauai's, but I'm not completely sure. I've sailed around the island but never set foot on it. You?"

Cruz shook his head. Ni'ihau was a private island. You needed permission to visit.

Professor Modi was clearing his throat. Neither team had answered, and he was ready to give the next hint. "Clue number three: The island is known for its *ahu* and *moai*."

"Ahu?" Dugan rubbed his chin. "Isn't that sushi?"

"You're thinking of ahi," said Bryndis. "Tuna."

Moai. The word sounded familiar to Cruz. He started to ask Lani if it could be a Hawaiian word when she blurted, "The big heads! You know, the stone statues on—"

"Easter Island!" piped Sailor.

That was it!

"Does everyone agree?" asked Dugan. When all hands shot up, he smacked their red button.

Zooooooooonk!

It blared through the CAVE. Cruz saw that Zane had his hand on Magellan's button. Oh no! Both teams had buzzed in at the same time!

Kwento moaned. "Another tie."

"Cousteau was first," said Weatherly.

"No, Magellan," countered Femi.

Voices filled the CAVE as the rest of the explorers ventured their opinions.

"Hold on, hold on!" Professor Modi was typing on his tablet. "I'll check the replay."

Lani glanced at Cruz. "There's a replay?"

He gave Monsieur Legrand's usual response: *"Tout est vu."*

"Everything is seen," said Lani's translator.

"While you're waiting," remarked their teacher, "it might interest you to know that for the past twelve years a member of the winning geography bee team has *also* received the North Star award."

Cruz nudged his roommate. "It's gonna be you. You're gonna win."

"Nah," said Emmett shyly, though he couldn't hide the yellow-and-pink strings pulsing through his glasses like kite tails in a brisk wind.

"Got it!" called Professor Modi. "The first team to ring in was…"

A hush fell over the room. Cruz felt his heart beating in rhythm to the word that pulsed in his brain: *Cousteau. Cousteau. Cousteau.*

"Magellan."

Cruz crumpled. They'd lost.

"Team Magellan, I'll need your answer," said Professor Modi, but it was merely a formality. Magellan would get all the great prizes and bragging rights. And boy, would Ali and Matteo brag. Cruz stubbed his toe into the grass.

"Christmas Island," said Zane.

Cruz's head shot up. He locked eyes with Lani. Her jaw dropped. So did his.

"That is incorrect." Their teacher shifted his gaze. "Cousteau, you now may—"

Dugan pounced. "Easter Island."

"Correct." Professor Modi smiled. "Congratulations, Team Cousteau!"

Cruz slapped palms with Lani, Sailor, Emmett, and Dugan. When he got to Bryndis, he grabbed her hand. She held on, curling her fingers around his. They'd done it. They'd won the bee!

Professor Modi was gesturing to the wall behind the teams. It was no longer blank! The hillside the explorers stood on now continued up to a U-shaped volcano, its cone long since blasted away. A giant stone head materialized only a few feet from Cruz. The rough, charcoal-colored statue was as tall as the second-floor apartment and attic of the Goofy Foot surf shop! A few yards to the right, another gigantic head appeared on the grass slope, then another and another, until a dozen or so moai were scattered across the meadow. Each carving had similar geometric features: prominent foreheads, deep-set eyes, large noses, and stern mouths. Only one head stood straight. The rest, some with shoulders peeking above the ground, were either tipped forward or backward or leaning to one side.

"You are standing at the base of Rano Raraku volcano," explained Professor Modi. "This is the main quarry where

the Rapa Nui mined tuff to carve these moai. The statues were part of their religious rituals. There are more than eight hundred of these completed monolithic carvings on the island, ranging from six to thirty feet high. Each one weighs as much as a school bus. The term *ahu* that I gave in the clue refers to the shrines and platforms beneath some of the moai."

Several explorers had their hands up.

"Questions will have to wait until tomorrow, I'm afraid," said their teacher. "We're already running over time. Again, congrats, Team Cousteau."

The lights were dimming in the CAVE. Cruz felt a cold ping on his head. The chubby white cumulus clouds of a moment before had become ominous dark cumulonimbus thunderheads. The sky tumbled and churned like a stew boiling over a pot. A zigzag of light flashed.

Boom!

It began to hail. Shielding their heads, the explorers raced for the

exit. The ice pellets bounced off Cruz's head and arms. They stung!

Weatherly was waving her OS band in front of the scanner at the door. "It won't open!"

Others also stepped in to try, but the sliding partition did not move. The hail was coming down harder and faster. The chunks of ice were getting bigger, too.

"Ow!" yelped Lani when a jawbreaker of a hailstone smacked her shoulder.

"Take cover!" yelled Professor Modi. He motioned to a long, horizontal bulge of rock jutting out of the side of the volcano. "I'll try to stop the program from the main panel." He ran for the console in the opposite corner of the CAVE, while the explorers scrambled to safety under the ledge. Cruz was on the end, closest to the professor, yet could hardly see him through the white curtain of hail. Their teacher was frantically typing on the keyboard, but the weather was only getting worse.

Cruz hit his comm pin. "Cruz Coronado to Fanchon Quills."

"Fanchon, here," came the reply. "Hey, shouldn't you be in class?"

"I am!" he cried. "We're in the CAVE, and we need—"

"What game are you playing? It sounds like you're dropping marbles on a tin roof."

"No game ... We're in trouble ... We've got hail the size of tennis balls coming down in here. Fanchon, we need—" Cruz's jaw fell open.

It was white. And huge. And coming right at him!

"Cruz?" shouted Fanchon. "CRUZ?"

▶ CRUZ SAW A SWISH of blond

hair, then an arm, and before he could blink again, a missile of ice the
size of a watermelon was smashing into the ground. It shattered into
thousands of crystal shards. Bryndis stood between Cruz
and the broken hailstone. She whirled around, fists
clenched and eyes blazing. "You okay?"

Cruz managed a nod. "Yeah-huh."

"Nice spike, Bryndis," crowed Dugan.

"Look out!" warned Sailor.

Dodging another melon of a hailstone, Bryndis shoved Cruz back
under the ledge with the others.

"That was crazy," said Cruz,
his heart wildly thumping.
"But thanks."

"I know."
Bryndis
pushed her
hair out of her
face. "And you're
welcome."

"Cruz, are you

there?" It was Fanchon on his comm link. "Come in! What's going on?"

"We're trapped in the CAVE!" Cruz yelled above the drumming ice. "The door won't open, and it's hailing ice bigger than cannonballs in here."

"Get to the control panel—"

"Professor Modi is trying, but it's not working!"

"Hang tight," said the tech lab chief. "I'll see what I can do from here."

Cruz glanced at the line of explorers under the rocky ledge. Kwento had blood on his fingers. Zane was rubbing his elbow. Femi was leaning against Sailor, her foot raised.

Emmett tugged on Cruz's sleeve. "Something's wrong."

Cruz gave him an annoyed look. "Ya think?"

"No, I mean, *really* wrong." He looked at Professor Modi. "The emergency override should have kicked in. And this"—he gestured to the supersize hail bombarding them—"doesn't just happen."

"You mean—"

"Nebula," mouthed Emmett.

"But why? We're *all* here, including the spy."

"Exactly. Two birds. One stone."

He saw Emmett's point. Cruz was one bird. Jaguar, the other. If Nebula was in possession of the seventh cipher, it might feel it no longer needed an explorer agent. And there was only one way to make sure a spy *never* spilled any secrets.

A shiver racked Cruz's spine. He'd figured now that Dr. Vanderwick, aka Nebula Agent Zebra, was out of the picture, the ship was relatively safe. He should have known better.

The cauldron of clouds was beginning to sink, flattening into a gray sheet. The hail was letting up. In its place, lacy white tufts began to fall.

"Snow!" exclaimed Weatherly.

"I'll take snow over hail any day," said Dugan.

"That's probably what Fanchon thought, too," surmised Cruz.

The explorers gingerly stepped out from beneath the overhang. Kwento showed Cruz a three-inch scrape on the side of his hand, but it wasn't bleeding. Zane and Femi didn't seem to be seriously hurt, either.

Professor Modi, still next to the control panel, looked more at ease. He wasn't talking quite so fast over his comm link.

"Weird." Emmett had knelt. He sifted snow through his fingers. "It's not cold."

Everyone was slowly making their way down the gentle slope to the exit door, which was still closed. Dugan had his head back, trying to catch flakes on his tongue. Other explorers were doing the same. Some had stopped to take selfies with the moai, now wearing frosty white wigs. After the earsplitting barrage of hail, Cruz was just glad for the peace.

Bryndis was beside him. "Smart of Fanchon to turn the hail into snow."

"Oh, it's not snow," said Dugan.

"It's not? What is it?"

Dugan was too busy trying to get under a big flake to answer. Giving Bryndis a what-have-we-got-to-lose? look, Cruz tilted his head back, too. He lined up his mouth with the biggest snowflake he could see drifting toward him. He felt softness on his tongue. Emmett was right. It wasn't cold at all. It was . . . sweet?

Through the flurry, Cruz caught Sailor's eye. "Is this . . . ?"

"Fairy floss!" she snickered.

"We say 'candy floss' in the U.K.," said Weatherly.

"Sugar thread," chimed Matteo.

"Ghost breath," said Kwento, earning a chorus of "Ohhhh!"

Sailor twirled. "Who cares what you call it, just catch it!"

The CAVE went silent as 24 explorers tried to snag as many cotton candy flakes as possible before the weather changed.

AT PRECISELY EIGHT O'CLOCK THAT EVENING, a sharp rap on the door of cabin 202 brought Cruz out of his trance. He'd been staring at their 3D printer for a half hour. Waiting. Hoping. Praying.

Tearing himself away from the machine, Cruz went to open the door. Sailor swept past him. "Is it done baking?"

Not turning from his computers, Emmett let out a snort. "We're not making a pie."

"You know what I mean."

Closing the door, Cruz returned with Sailor to the 3D printer in the opposite corner of the cabin. "Actually, she's not wrong. To form rock, you *do* need heat..."

"And pressure." Sailor bent to look through the postcard-size window. "So, when is slice number seven going to be finished pressure baking?"

"Soon," answered Emmett.

"He's been saying that ever since we got back from dinner," groaned Cruz.

Sailor let out an exasperated sigh.

"I'd say that's pretty good considering we're managing to do in twelve hours what it took nature millions of years to accomplish," said Emmett.

"Guess I'm just anxious," said Sailor.

Cruz was, too. Since he didn't have the original seventh cipher, making, or rather faking, a piece was the only way he could think to advance the journal. They'd already had a trial run. When Nebula had kidnapped Cruz's dad, the trio had crafted a decoy stone to use to ransom him. However, Cruz had felt that the plan was too risky and had not given the decoy to Nebula. This time, though, their homemade chunk of marble couldn't merely resemble the real thing. If they were going to fool Cruz's mom's holo program, the stone had to be identical.

Cruz, Emmett, Lani, and Sailor had devoted every spare minute of the past two weeks to working on the project: doing calculations, inputting data into Emmett's design program, gathering minerals and supplies, and equipping their 3D printer to create a duplicate of the seventh piece. At precisely 7:28 that morning, Cruz had pressed the start icon on the touchscreen of their 3D printer to begin forming the rock fragment. It should be done . . . well, soon.

Cruz joined Sailor in staring through the little window of the printer. They couldn't see much. The engraver was in the way, hovering over the stone. Sailor began to hum. She lightly rapped her fingers on the side of the machine. Cruz began to copy her beats, then tapped out a short rhythm for her to repeat. On they went, taking turns drumming to fill the time.

"You both ought to know watching a printer won't make it go any faster," said Emmett, still engrossed in his work.

"We're not watching." Sailor gave Cruz a sideways grin. "We're performing."

A knock at the door interrupted their concert.

"That's Lani," said Cruz, moving to open the door.

But it was Aunt Marisol, not Lani, who breezed past him. "Is it done yet?"

"Soon," said Sailor.

His aunt's face fell. She gave a frustrated tug on a scarf with a neon-pink-and-yellow abstract art print she'd loosely wrapped over her sweater. It was a Christmas present from Cruz's dad, who liked bold colors and wild prints even more than Aunt Marisol did. Cruz could only look at the bright geometric shapes and sharp lines for a few seconds before his eyes started to go wonky.

Sailor admired the scarf. "Sweet as!"

"Thanks," said Aunt Marisol. "Hey, I heard about the rogue storm in the CAVE. Is everybody okay?"

"Yeah." Sailor lifted her tablet. "Want to see the highlights?"

"Absolutely."

Cruz shot Sailor a warning look, but she was too busy queuing up the video to notice.

"Goodness!" cried Cruz's aunt, watching the playback. "I heard it was bad, but . . . !"

"And my mum and dad are scared that I'll get hurt on a mission," chortled Sailor. "Forget missions; it's the geography bees you have to worry about. Here comes the good part. See, this ginormous block of ice was hurtling toward Cr—"

"And thank you, Sailor!" Cruz clamped a hand over her screen.

This time, Sailor caught on. "Um ... right. No big deal, Professor Coronado."

Lani showed up as Cruz was reaching to tap his comm pin to call her. "I would have been here sooner. I was trying to fix the lock on my door," she explained.

"You were?" Sailor munched on her lower lip. "I stopped by your cabin on my way, but you weren't there."

"That's because the problem was my OS band." Lani held up her wrist. "This is a new one. Fanchon can't get around to repairing mine right away. She's backed up in the tech lab. I hope she gets a new assistant soon."

"One that isn't a Nebula agent would be nice," remarked Aunt Marisol.

Cruz knew she was still upset about their close call with Dr. Vanderwick. After all, *Orion*'s assistant tech lab director had nearly destroyed the ship! His aunt believed Dr. Hightower should have uncovered the fact that Sidril Vanderwick was a spy. But Cruz didn't blame her. He put the blame squarely where it belonged: on Hezekiah Brume.

Cruz had been doing research on the president of the pharmaceutical company. The articles he'd read described Mr. Brume as a shrewd yet reclusive businessman. Brume was almost never seen in public. Cruz could not find a single photograph of him. He wasn't surprised. Brume's teenage daughter, Roewyn, was also pretty secretive, though she had dared to step out of the shadows to help Cruz more than once. In Petra, she'd even saved his life. Cruz knew it took guts for Roewyn to side with him, and he was grateful.

"I thanked Fanchon while I was there," recounted Lani. "She said she was going to have it snow *real* flakes, but with the climate controls out of whack, she worried it would either get too cold and we'd freeze or too hot and we'd flood. CCC seemed like a safe choice."

"CCC?" asked Aunt Marisol.

"CAVE cotton candy," decoded Lani. "See, when the CAVE program went berserk, Fanchon couldn't shut off the precipitation order. She could, however, change it to anything she wanted. *Anything.*"

Aunt Marisol's eyebrows inched upward. "You're saying she turned hail—"

"Into spun sugar," said Sailor. "Want a look?"

Aunt Marisol definitely did. They were halfway through watching the recording for the second time when they heard it. *Ping!*

"Pie's ready." Emmett finally turned from his computers.

"Lani hates pie," joked Cruz.

"I'm making an exception today," she retorted.

Everyone gathered around the machine. Emmett opened the top door, reached inside, and removed the triangle of black marble. "It's still warm." Emmett carried it to his desk as if it were a priceless vase. Cruz, Lani, Sailor, and Aunt Marisol were right behind him.

Emmett had already set out his tablet. On the screen was Cruz's photograph of the original seventh cipher. He placed the new stone on the screen to the right of the piece in the photo. Emmett held out a palm to Cruz, who took the lanyard from around his neck and handed it over. It contained the six pieces that Cruz's mom had confirmed were genuine. Cruz had not reattached Nebula's phony piece. It remained in his dresser drawer. Emmett placed the six interlocking stones to the left of the photo. "We already know the composition of ours is identical to the real thing," he explained. "Now we need to check that everything else is, too: color, shape, engraving, and surface, including all the *edges*." Emmett took a seat, while the others bunched in to peer over his shoulder. They nervously watched as Emmett compared the new piece to the one in the photograph, then to the actual wedges themselves. Once this was done, he moved to connect the new piece to the sixth stone.

Cruz held his breath. If it didn't fit . . .

Click! The stone easily snapped into place.

"Perfect," breathed Sailor.

It was a good start. Several tense minutes later, Emmett raised his head. The emoto-glasses were a golden blizzard. "It's a match."

Cruz slapped palms with Lani and Sailor and gave his aunt a quick hug, though they weren't out of the woods yet. The ultimate test awaited.

Detaching the new piece of marble from the others, Emmett dropped it into Cruz's palm. "We can't tell the difference. Let's hope your mom—the program, I mean—can't either."

Emmett had purposefully corrected himself. He knew Cruz was uneasy about the plan to fool his mother. "You won't be tricking any-one," he'd argued. "It's a program, not a person. Besides, your mom's wish was for you to find all the pieces of the cipher. You can't do that unless you advance the program, and you can't advance the program without a little—"

"Deceit?" clipped Cruz.

"You've tried everything else," said Emmett gently. "Your mom would understand."

But would she?

The five of them gathered around the short, circular table in the center of the cabin, and Cruz activated the holo-journal. Waiting for the biometric identification scan to finish, Cruz began to feel hot and prickly.

Moments later, his mother's image appeared. "Hi, Cruzer."

He never tired of hearing it.

"Hi, Mom."

He never tired of saying it.

"Cruz, do you have the seventh piece of the cipher?"

"I do." Cruz held out the stone, unable to keep his hand from shaking. He was afraid to look at her, afraid his expression might give away the truth. She could always tell when he was lying—when she was alive. Would it be any different now?

Cruz heard the tinkling of Aunt Marisol's charm bracelet. She had to be wringing her hands. Out of the corner of his eye, Cruz saw Emmett's

glasses turn into worried half-moons. Cruz's mother was still examining the stone. She was taking longer than usual. After a few minutes, she lifted her head. The verdict was in. Cruz's heart thumped hard against his ribs.

Gray-blue eyes met his. "I'm sorry. This is not a genuine piece. You have not unlocked a new clue."

Cruz felt the last drop of hope drain from his body. Many times, he'd heard his mother say this, especially recently. Yet something about this rejection was different. Her tone was softer. Sadder. It was as if she knew he was struggling, as if she wanted to help. He was being silly, of course. This was a holo-video, a preprogrammed image with limited responses. She could not feel or know or want anything. It was all in Cruz's imagination—in his head, or maybe his heart, longing for things he could never have.

Cruz stood there, bewildered, as his mother vanished for what he feared was the last time.

▶ON THE FINAL quarter mile of a

five-mile run along the River Thames, Thorne Prescott felt his heart buzz. He stopped under a tree, unzipped the chest pocket of his nylon tee, and took out his phone. The caller ID read Swan.

He answered with a simple "Yes."

"Out for a jog, huh, Cobra?" asked a voice that Prescott was positive belonged to Oona Mosshaven, Hezekiah Brume's executive assistant. "It's a beautiful morning. Taking the Chelsea Embankment route along the Thames?" Swan, of course, already knew the answer to the question she asked. Nebula always knew where you were. Prescott gazed out at the muddy waters sloshing against the retaining wall. "Yeah," he said, still catching his breath.

"I have instructions," she said. "Lion wants you standing by. Orion is in Antarctica but will be sailing north soon up the east coast of South America. I don't have a port yet."

"Is it . . . Jaguar?"

"Yes . . ." There was a long pause. "And no."

What kind of answer was that? Either Emmett's time was up, or it wasn't. Prescott wiped the sweat from his brow. "Swan, what's going on?"

"I . . . I . . . shouldn't . . . I was only supposed to let you know you would be needed."

"And you've done that. But if there's an issue, I've got to know that, too. I need to be prepared."

"Lion is having some trouble—"

"Hold on," broke in Prescott.

A group of tourists was coming down the sidewalk. Prescott turned from the river to face the two-lane road that ran next to it. He waited for a break in traffic, then sprinted to the other side of the tree-lined street. He stepped into the shadow of a grand, Victorian-era granite drinking fountain, then cut through a break in a short hedge. He stopped in front of a statue of Thomas More next to Chelsea Old Church.

The Renaissance statesman was seated on a stone platform. More's head and limbs were gold, a stark contrast to his black robes and flat hat. The gold only served to emphasize his hands, tensely folded in front of him. Prescott knew his English history. Once one of King Henry VIII's most trusted advisers, More fell out of favor with the ruler after refusing to support the king's decision to break with the Catholic Church. Henry wanted to divorce one woman to marry another, which was forbidden by church law. More refused to come around to Henry's way of thinking. His stand cost him dearly. He was convicted of treason and executed.

Prescott lifted his phone to his ear. "What's the problem, Swan?"

"The explorer spy has the seventh cipher, but . . ."

Prescott's mind spun with possibilities. He'd lost it? Damaged it? Sold it?

"Jaguar is refusing to give it up," said Swan.

Prescott let out a deep laugh. Emmett! He had to admit, the kid had fire in his belly. And ice in his veins. Very few people were bold enough to take on Hezekiah Brume. "Lion must be furious." Prescott tried to keep the glee from his voice.

"That's putting it mildly."

Prescott could only imagine. Brume often lost his cool when he thought he was losing ground. Zebra's untimely death and now an uncooperative teen? The earth under Brume's feet was definitely shaking. "Why don't I see what I can do to move things in the right direction?" he offered.

"You mean, talk to Jaguar?"

"Yes."

"That's impossible—"

"It's also too late," confessed Prescott. "When things went dark with Zebra, I had no choice but to contact Jaguar." Hearing her groan, he continued. "Let me try. Lion doesn't need to know. If it works, problem solved. If it doesn't, we can do things his way."

She sighed. "I . . . I suppose."

"That's what I like. Confidence."

"I do appreciate it. I can give you twenty-four hours to get Jaguar to come around. After that, Lion is going to take care of things himself."

"I understand."

"Thank you, Cobra."

"Thank you . . . Oona." He waited for the tiny gasp before hanging up.

It gave him a small sense of satisfaction to surprise her. Nebula wasn't the only one who knew things. Not that it mattered. Lion was in control. He had supreme power and would not hesitate to use it.

Prescott glanced up into the grim face of Thomas More. No one was safe from Nebula. Not even the most loyal servant.

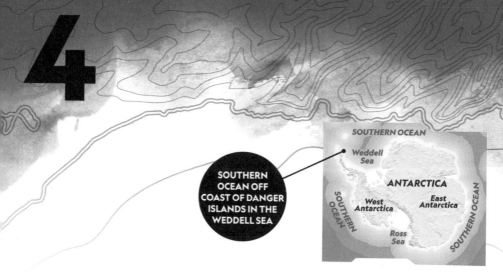

SOUTHERN OCEAN OFF COAST OF DANGER ISLANDS IN THE WEDDELL SEA

SOUTHERN OCEAN

Weddell Sea

ANTARCTICA

SOUTHERN OCEAN

West Antarctica

East Antarctica

SOUTHERN OCEAN

Ross Sea

▶ EHH. EHH.

Emmett didn't move.

Ehh. Ehh.

Still no sign of life from the bed across from Cruz's.

"Emmett?" rasped Cruz. "Your sloth is squeaking."

A recent gift from Emmett's aunt and uncle, the metallic green alarm clock shaped like an upside-down V contained hundreds of animal calls. Emmett could choose to wake up to the sound of practically any known creature on Earth, from the lawn-sprinkler clicking of cicadas to the slow-revving motor of a brushtail possum. Cruz's favorite was a new download: the deep, haunting song of the blue whale. Emmett, however, preferred the cute hum of a baby sloth, so that's what they woke up to most days. This morning, though, Cruz was up well before Emmett's sloth. He'd been watching the gentle rise and fall of a snoozing Hubbard next to him.

Cruz had slept poorly in the week since his mom's holo-journal program had rejected their homemade cipher piece—or, as Sailor dubbed it, the a-rock-alypse. At first, Cruz wasn't discouraged by the failure. Neither were his friends. Like him, Emmett, Sailor, and Lani were determined to find out what had gone wrong, correct it, and try again.

With *Orion* sailing southeast across the Southern Ocean toward the northernmost tip of Antarctica, they'd had plenty of time to go over their duplication process. Emmett had run a complete diagnostic scan of his design program. Sailor had verified the stone's components and measurements. Lani had pored over their calculations. Cruz had put the 3D printer through its paces to be sure it was functioning properly. However, despite their attention to even the smallest detail, they hadn't been able to find a single error, oversight, or problem. Everything had worked as it was meant to, producing a stone that *was* a duplicate of the original. So, until they could discover why Cruz's mother had rejected it, the explorers knew it was pointless to make another piece. They'd only get the same disappointing result.

"We'll figure it out," Lani had said to Cruz.

He appreciated the comforting words, but he had his doubts. Big ones. This wasn't a clue to follow, a puzzle to solve, or a code to crack. His mom had made it clear that to unlock the last clue he needed the actual seventh cipher. Nothing else would do. No, this wasn't something to "figure out." This, unfortunately, was a dead end.

Ehh. Ehh. Ka-donk.

Fumbling for the clock on his nightstand, Emmett had rolled out of bed and onto the floor.

Cruz leaned out over his mattress. "You okay?" he asked the lump.

Emmett sat up, rubbing his head. "Eh."

He sounded exactly like the baby sloth from the clock, which made Cruz laugh. "Since you're up, do you want the shower first?"

"You go," yawned Emmett before crawling back under his comforter. An arm came through the folds of the blankets. It stretched out toward Cruz, palm up, waiting.

Cruz carefully wriggled free of his covers so he wouldn't disturb Hubbard. He slipped the lanyard over his head and, on the way to the bathroom, dropped the circle of black marble into Emmett's hand. It was their new protocol. The stone cipher was not to be left unattended. Ever. If it wasn't on Cruz, then it had to be personally guarded by either Emmett, Sailor, or Lani. After dressing, Cruz fed Hubbard while Emmett took his shower. Cruz attached Hubbard's leash to the dog's collar. He tapped on the bathroom door. "Emmett, I'm taking Hub for his walk, then to Fanchon's."

"Okay. See you at breakfast."

On the way out, Cruz grabbed his tablet. Making a right turn out of the cabin, Cruz and Hubbard made a pit stop at the dog's meadow on the stern deck, then strolled down the explorers' passage into the atrium. Standing in the center of the inlaid-wood compass design on the floor, Cruz peered up through the top portholes of the dome. The glittering stars were inching past as if on a slow black conveyor belt. Captain Iskandar had decreased *Orion*'s speed to navigate the iceberg-filled waters off Antarctica. Over the past day or so, Cruz had heard crunching now and then as the bow cut through layers of ice. Where, exactly, were they going?

"*Mōrena.*" Sailor swept into the atrium from behind him. She was pulling her hair back into a ponytail. "These shorter and shorter days are making it harder and harder to get up. That's not right, is it? A day is *always* twenty-four hours. What I mean is the decreasing amount of sunlight we're getting each day is making it harder, and— Oh crikey, it's finally happened!" Sailor dropped her arms, and a wave of hair fell past her shoulders. "I've turned into Emmett."

Cruz snorted a laugh.

"Sunrise isn't until ten this morning," wailed Sailor. "Can you believe that? *Ten* o'clock! I checked the sunrise-sunset chart. It sets at two fifty-one p.m.—that's less than five hours of daylight. We only get *four* hours of light tomorrow. Three days after that, guess what happens?"

"The sun won't rise at all," boomed a voice. "Until September, that is." Professor Luben was coming across the atrium toward them. He wore a cranberry red button-down shirt with the sleeves rolled up to his elbows and black pants. As he approached, Hubbard inched backward to stand in Cruz's shadow. Cruz knew that Professor Luben wasn't much of a dog person, and he had a feeling Hubbard knew it, too. "It'll be polar night," said Professor Luben. "On the upside, you'll be able to view the stars and many of the planets during the day, when the skies are clear."

"Is that why we're here—to study the night sky?" asked Cruz.

Professor Luben lifted a finger. He cocked his head the way Hubbard did when he was listening. Something was different. Cruz felt it, too. It took him a second to figure it out. When their teacher glanced up at the atrium's ring of portholes, Cruz followed his gaze. Yep. The stars were no longer in motion. *Orion* had stopped. It could be because the ice was too thick to continue, or...

Cruz locked eyes with Sailor.

A mission!

"Professor Luben—"

Their teacher was already climbing the grand staircase. "Patience, explorers," he tossed over his shoulder. "Have a good breakfast. You'll need it."

It *was* a mission! The second that Professor Luben disappeared into the lounge at the top of the stairs, Sailor tapped her GPS pin. "Display *Orion*'s location, please."

Her pin projected a holo-map of the curving arm of the Antarctic Peninsula. A red dot appeared off the northeastern tip of the peninsula. Sailor used her thumb and index finger to zoom in. It showed that the ship was about 20 miles southeast of the Joinville Island group near the northwest mouth of the Weddell Sea. Sailor and Cruz exchanged puzzled looks. What could they possibly be doing here?

In the dining room, they found that the other explorers were asking the same question. What was going on? At precisely eight o'clock, everyone was in their seat in Manatee classroom, anticipating Professor Luben's arrival. Two minutes passed. Then five. Then ten.

"Should one of us call him?" asked Tao.

"He probably overslept," said Felipe.

"Only if he went back to bed," clipped Sailor. "Cruz and I saw him in the atrium a half hour ago."

Bryndis half turned in her chair. "It's like orientation when 'Welcome to the Academy' was written on the screen in the library. It took us forever to figure out it was a clue."

"Some of us never did." Dugan slapped an embarrassed hand over his eyes.

That day was forever burned into Cruz's brain. It was how he'd met Bryndis. Moments after he'd realized the message was a repeat of Taryn's greeting the day before, the two of them were racing down the halls of the Academy. Hand in hand, Cruz and Bryndis had led the rest of the explorers to the lobby. It was their first real test, and it was both thrilling and terrifying.

Bryndis had smiled at him then the same way she was smiling now.

"Did Professor Luben give you any clues?" Lani's head flipped from Sailor to Cruz.

"No," replied Sailor. "All he said was to have patience and have a good breakfast."

"A good breakfast?" echoed Lani. "Maybe we're supposed to go to the dining room."

"Or the galley," said Weatherly.

"Or sick bay," offered Emmett.

"Or maybe you're supposed to stay in your seats right here!" Professor Luben trotted into the room, a tablet under his arm. "My apologies for being tardy, explorers. Good morning!"

"Good morning!" came the enthusiastic reply.

Cruz raised an eyebrow at Emmett. "Sick bay?"

"'Cause it's where you treat *patients*."

"Oh! Good one."

"Time is of the essence, so I won't keep you in suspense," said a breathless Professor Luben. "You are about to embark on your next mission."

A cheer went up! Cruz and the rest of his teammates hooted the loudest. They had won the geography bee, so whatever they were about to do, Cousteau would be the first team in line to do it. Raising his bent elbows like chicken wings, Cruz bumped them with Lani and Emmett.

A holographic globe of Earth was appearing beside Professor Luben. By the time it was fully formed, the planet was easily three times the size of their teacher's head! The professor spun the holo-globe until Antarctica came into view. Just east of the peninsula, beyond the tip of the continent's curved arm, a red dot glowed.

"*Orion* is here, about seventy miles from the northernmost tip of Antarctica," said their teacher. He zoomed in to the Joinville Island group as Sailor had done with her GPS. Instead of stopping there, though, he kept moving inward to the archipelago's largest islands: D'Urville, Dundee, and Joinville. Soon, a cluster of tiny islands about 15 miles southeast of Joinville Island came into view. They hadn't shown up on Sailor's projection!

"We're anchored off the Danger Islands," continued Professor Luben. "Let me assure you they are well named. The unpredictable weather, thick pack ice, large icebergs, and rocky terrain of the islands make this one of the most treacherous areas in the world to explore. Few people have dared to attempt it." He gave them a devilish grin. "But that's exactly what you are about to do."

Cruz's heart jumped. This sounded exciting!

"For a short window of time, weather and tidal conditions are in our favor, so we are going to take advantage of the opportunity," said their instructor. "We'll break into teams. Three of the teams will be assigned an island to explore. They will travel on one of the two motorized inflatables or *Rigel*, the hovercraft. The fourth team will explore under the sea in *Ridley*."

Cruz loved diving in *Orion*'s submersible. Now that he'd gotten in his first dive as a pilot under his belt, he was eager to do it again. He swiveled to Emmett. "*Ridley?*" Lime bubbles of joy pulsed through the emotoglasses. Cruz hoped Bryndis, Sailor, Lani, and Dugan would want to go, too.

The holo-globe was disappearing, though Professor Luben was still giving instructions. "Each team will be accompanied by a faculty member, but you should know this assistance will be limited. This is *your* mission. It will be up to your team to decide what route to take, what equipment to bring, and what data to collect. I would remind you to use the technology at your disposal. The only hard and fast rule is that

you must be back on board *before* the sun sets at ... uh ..." He looked around for where he'd set down his tablet.

"Two fifty-one," called Sailor.

"Right," said the professor. "Once I dismiss the class, you'll have some time to plan with your team. Some of you will have less time to prepare but more time to explore. For others, it will be the opposite. Further details will be provided once you receive your assignment. Your field reports are due Friday before the end of the school day."

"Hey." Lani's whisper tickled Cruz's ear. "Is it me, or does this sound like more of a test than a mission?"

"It's a test, all right." He'd been thinking the same thing. The school year was winding down. There were only two missions left. Now was the time for the faculty to gauge how well the explorers could put into practice what they'd learned over the course of the year.

Cruz heard a familiar sound. He touched Lani's arm. "Did you hear that?"

She tilted her head. "Yeah. It sounds like ..."

"Water!" they cried together.

Behind Professor Luben, a huge wave was rising! The blue swell curled upward. The wall of water crested a few inches below the ceiling before violently crashing down over their teacher. Cruz saw foam. Heard screams. The startled explorers jerked back as the wave rolled outward. Cruz braced, too, though he knew it was an illusion. The tide quickly swept through the room, engulfing the lower half of the desks and the students in them.

"This is wild!" Lani had raised her tablet to keep it from getting wet, though of course it wouldn't. It couldn't!

Cruz watched the foamy ocean water swirl around his waist. It was a strange sensation, being in a holographic sea. Your brain was telling you one thing, your body another.

"Look!" Dugan was up out of his seat, the tide hitting his knees.

About a half dozen icebergs were surfacing next to Professor Luben. Hands on his hips, their teacher was completely dry. He waited for them to settle before continuing. "Here we have the six major types of iceberg shapes: wedge, block, dome, tabular, pinnacle, and drydock. For our purposes, these are a bit smaller than the real deal."

Fully formed, the holo-bergs began drifting between the rows. Cruz watched the drydock berg glide past Emmett's desk. Towering a good seven feet above them, it looked like a giant letter U. The middle of the berg had eroded, creating a submerged slot between two columns of ice. Next came the tabular berg, a thick, flat rectangular slab about half the size of the table in the conference room. Once the hunks of ice reached the back wall, they sank.

"Each team will choose one berg from those that remain," said Professor Luben. "The berg you get will reveal your faculty guide, mode of transport, and destination. Your order of selection will be determined by your place in the geography bee. As the winners, Team Cousteau gets to select first."

What?

Cruz thought they were going to get to choose their mission assignment, but this was being first in a luck-of-the-draw game. Some prize! Exchanging frowns with Emmett, Cruz knew he wasn't the only one who felt they'd been shafted. Bryndis and Dugan had their heads together, as did Sailor and Lani. Everyone on Team Cousteau was grumbling.

"Bryndis, please choose an iceberg for your team," instructed Professor Luben.

Cruz couldn't believe it. Another surprise! And not a good one. Teams usually selected their own representatives, even when it came to games of chance. Professor Luben *had* said they were pressed for time, but still, this was totally unfair.

Bryndis watched the smooth, round dome berg bob by her desk. Next came the uneven, chiseled block. It was followed by the pinnacle. With its trio of pointed corkscrew spires, the ice reminded Cruz of drill bits. Only one hunk of ice was left: the wedge. It was a right triangle; one side had a straight edge while the other side was sloped. As the berg approached, Bryndis stood.

"You're picking the wedge," confirmed Professor Luben.

"Uh … no." Spinning, Bryndis pointed down the aisle. "Team Cousteau chooses the pinnacle."

"The pinnacle?" asked Professor Luben, as if she'd given an incorrect answer on an oral quiz. "Are you sure?"

"*Já.*" Her face red, Bryndis quickly sat back down.

Their teacher put his hands on his hips. "Yulia, please select for Magellan."

"We take the block," said Yulia without hesitation.

"Decisiveness," said Professor Luben. "I like that."

Earhart chose the wedge, which left Galileo with the dome. Once selected, the icebergs glided toward their respective teams like obedient robots. Dugan reached to pull in the pinnacle for Cousteau.

"*Bonjour!*" Monsieur Legrand's face appeared in the tallest of the berg's three spiraled cones. "We will be exploring Heroína Island in *Rigel*. Please report to aquatics promptly at ten thirty this morning for a ten forty-five launch. Wear cold-weather gear, and bring any tech equipment you would like to use. I will bring our food. We will be the fourth team to depart." His stare bore down on them. "Prepare wisely." The video ended, and the iceberg began to rapidly melt.

"Fourth?" whined Dugan. "This isn't right. We *won* the geography bee. We should be going first, not last."

"Should we say something?" asked Lani. "Call Professor Modi to straighten things out?"

"It wouldn't do any good." Emmett was reading his tablet. "Technically, Professor Luben *is* following the geography bee rules. It states here that the winning team gets first choice the next time teams are required to make a selection involving a mission. It doesn't say anything about what kind of selection it's supposed to be."

"So that's that." Dugan punched a chunk of holo-ice. "We're sunk like these icebergs."

"It's a setback, for sure, but we can handle it," soothed Sailor. "How about if we go to the library to plan our mission once we're dismissed?"

The holo-bergs were dissolving. In them, Cruz saw the faces of Professors Benedict, Ishikawa, and Luben. Had Bryndis chosen the wedge, they would have gotten Professor Luben.

Their teacher dismissed the class with a jubilant "*Fortes fortuna adiuvat!*"

"Fortune favors the brave, *not* the last," grumbled Dugan as they shuffled out of class.

Emmett brought up the rear. His emoto-glasses looked like a dying fire: charcoal gray trapezoids spitting flecks of orange. Cruz let the rest of the team go ahead. He fell into step beside Emmett, who was holding his tablet against his chest. "What's going on?" he whispered. "Is it something else in the geography bee rules?"

"No."

"Then, what?"

He turned the screen toward Cruz:

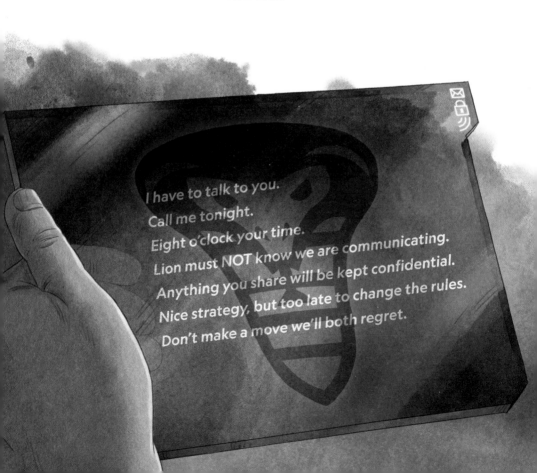

I have to talk to you.
Call me tonight.
Eight o'clock your time.
Lion must NOT know we are communicating.
Anything you share will be kept confidential.
Nice strategy, but too late to change the rules.
Don't make a move we'll both regret.

5

► "**"CHANGE THE** rules'? 'A move we'll both regret'?" Emmett wrinkled his forehead. "What's Jaguar up to anyway?"

"I don't know, but I'm worried," said Cruz.

The boys spoke in hushed tones, lagging behind the rest of their team.

"Why?" Emmett's frown faded. "Now that Jaguar's got the cipher, I doubt he's much of a threat to you."

"I didn't mean for me. I meant for *him*. Sounds like Jaguar wants out of the spy game."

"Could be," clipped Emmett, "but that's his problem."

"Actually, since Prescott thinks you're Jaguar, it's *your* problem."

"Oh, yeah."

They turned into the stairwell to go up two decks to the library.

"Look, having you pretend you were the spy to get more intel on Nebula seemed like a good plan, at first, but now…" Cruz paused. He took a breath. He knew the gravity of what he was about to say.

"Now… what?" pressed Emmett.

"I think we should tell Cobra you aren't Jaguar."

"Are you serious?" Emmett's voice ricocheted through the stairway. "Sorry. If we do that, we might never find out what happened to the seventh cipher." Aqua, teal, and royal blue waves created an ocean of determination within the emoto-glasses. "Cruz, this could be our *last* chance."

"I know." Oh, how he knew! "But you've been in Nebula's crosshairs for too long as it is. It's getting more dangerous."

"Let's see how it goes tonight," said Emmett.

"I...I don't know." Cruz's forehead felt tight. "If Prescott finds out—"

"He won't," insisted Emmett. "He's not that smart. I was onto him the second I saw him follow you off the plane in D.C. Well, maybe not *the* second but definitely when I spotted him in the café, so what was that— ten minutes?" He puffed up. "I was onto him in ten minutes."

"Onto him?" Cruz was confused. "How could you be? You and I had only just met."

The emoto-glasses flashed brighter. "Come on, Cruz. You're good at solving puzzles. Haven't you put the clues together by now?"

"Clues?" He was still lost.

Emmett sighed. "Didn't you ever wonder how we got to be roommates?"

"I guess..." But Cruz hadn't. Not really.

"What are the chances that a guy whose mom founded a top secret organization would be paired with another guy whose mom is the current head of that *same* org—" Emmett stopped mid-step. "Coffee."

"Huh?" said Cruz a second before the earthy aroma filled his nose.

Peering over the rail, the boys saw Captain Iskandar in the stairwell. He was coming up the steps, carrying a brown earthenware mug of steaming coffee. "Morning, gentlemen."

"Good morning," they answered in unison, and the trio continued up the stairs.

"Ready for your mission?" asked the captain.

"We will be," said Emmett. "We're going up to the library to plan."

"Make sure you're ready for the weather," he cautioned. "Do you know the signs of hypothermia?"

"Shivering, sleepiness, confusion, slurred speech or loss of coordination, reduced pulse." Emmett rattled off the list of symptoms they'd learned in Monsieur Legrand's survival training class. "Our OS bands will alert Nyomie to a slowing pulse rate or if anyone's core body temperature drops below ninety-six degrees. Plus, we'll be completely covered in Fanchon's bio-thermal fabric from head to toe. Even our GPS sunglasses are insulated to protect our eyes."

Captain Iskandar raised his mug. "Be sure to take along something to warm you from the inside out."

"Great idea." Emmett leaned toward Cruz. "Let's see if we can get some of Chef Kristos's peppermint cocoa to take along."

They continued climbing the steps, Emmett and the ship's captain discussing their favorite hot beverages, leaving Cruz free to mull over his conversation with Emmett before they'd been interrupted. Naturally, once Cruz had found out that Emmett's mom was the director of the Synthesis, he'd wondered if it was more than coincidence. Things usually happen for a reason, even if you can't see it. Or won't. So, if it was intentional, why *had* he been paired with Emmett? Cruz could think of only one reason, and it sent a chill through him that not even Chef Kristos's delicious hot chocolate was likely to warm.

Cruz slipped his left hand, the one closest to Emmett, into his pocket. He curled his fingers around Fanchon's wafer-thin brass virtugraph. Cruz brought it out and dropped his arm to his side. He pressed on the sleeping dove perched on the north end of the compass.

One . . . two . . . three.

The virtugraph was activated.

They'd reached the fifth deck. With a wave, Captain Iskandar strolled briskly down the passage to the bridge, while Emmett and Cruz headed the opposite way. Cruz glanced back. The door to the bridge was shutting. The corridor was empty.

The blood was pounding so hard in Cruz's ears he wasn't sure he'd be able to the hear the answer to the question he was about to ask. But he had to know. "Emmett . . . are you . . . a spy for the Synthesis?"

"*What?*" Emmett stopped in his tracks. "Are you joking? No, I am not a spy! Not for the Synthesis, Nebula, or anybody else."

Cruz turned his cupped palm upward. If the needle pointing toward Emmett inside the truth compass was black, his friend was lying. If it was red, he was being honest. Cruz took a deep breath before glancing down. It took a few seconds for his eyes to focus in the dimly lit hallway, but when they did, he saw...

Red.

Whew! The emoto-glasses confirmed it. They were turning dark pink, the color of truth. Dozens of tiny red beads ping-ponged inside the square frames. Uh-oh. Anger.

"I can't believe you'd ever think that!" snapped Emmett.

Cruz rushed to apologize. "I didn't mean to make you mad, but if you're not a spy, then why—"

"My mom thought you might be in danger from Nebula once you got to the Academy," said Emmett, the fiery balls bouncing inside his frames beginning to slow. "Dr. Hightower and Mom felt it would be a good idea

if you had a roommate who knew your history, somebody who could watch out for you and be on the alert for trouble." He shifted. "I . . . I know I haven't exactly done a great job of keeping you safe."

"Hey, I'm still alive, aren't I? Does Aunt Marisol know you're—"

"Not a real explorer?" Emmett dropped his gaze. "No."

"I was going to say protecting me. Of course you're a real explorer."

"I'm not," he said. "I wasn't officially accepted to the Academy. I didn't submit an application or get an invitation from Dr. Hightower."

"That doesn't matter—"

"It does, Cruz. It does. Don't you get it? Once we complete your mom's cipher and you're no longer in danger, then *my* mission is done. I'll go home, and you'll . . . well, you'll continue on *Orion* with the rest of our—your—class."

Was he kidding? This was crazy. Emmett Lu was the perfect explorer. He had been here from the beginning, and Cruz couldn't imagine life at the Academy without him. "Emmett, you can't . . . you can't . . . just . . . *go!*"

"Can. And will." The square emoto-glasses collapsed in on themselves, the red beads disintegrating. "It's okay, Cruz. Really. I know this is breaking news to you, but it isn't to me. I've known all along I couldn't stay. Oh, and you can't tell anyone about this, not even Lani or Sailor."

Stunned, Cruz dropped his head. It couldn't be true. Yet, the virtu-graph still clutched in his palm provided all the proof he needed. Cruz would have given anything to see the black needle pointing toward his friend.

But he saw only red.

"RED?" DUGAN SQUINTED at the satellite photo. "Red rocks? In Antarctica?"

"Weird," muttered Sailor.

Lani twisted her silver lock of hair. "And *pink* snow?"

"Even weirder," said Sailor.

"Can you zoom in?" asked Emmett.

Bryndis, who was at the controls, shook her head. "I'm in as tight as I can go."

Clustered around one of the computer map tables in the library, Team Cousteau was reviewing satellite images of Heroína Island. Cruz was only half listening. He was still rehashing his discussion with Emmett. Maybe his roommate hadn't been an explorer when the school year started, but he sure was one now. That's what counted, wasn't it? Emmett was an essential member of Team Cousteau. He was also the closest thing Cruz had to a brother. Emmett couldn't leave the Academy; he just couldn't. Not now. Not ever.

"Cruz?" Lani's hand was waving in front of his face.

"Sorry, what?"

"You okay?"

"Uh-huh. Just sleepy." He stretched his arms overhead. "Must be the shorter days."

"Actually, a day is always the same length," said Emmett. He was bent over the table, his nose an inch above the screen as he inspected the satellite photo through his magnifying lenses. "What you mean is the declining amount of sunlight we're experiencing each day is making you feel more tired than usual."

"That's what I meant." Cruz grinned at Sailor.

She looked up from her tablet to return the smile. Cruz knew she would be as upset as he was to learn that Emmett would not be coming back next year. It wasn't right. Cruz wished he could talk to her about it. He needed her to tell him that things would be okay, even if it was a lie.

"Guys, it says here that the Danger Islands are made up of igneous rock, mainly gabbro, formed during the Cretaceous period, and is similar to the formations located at the tip of the Antarctic Peninsula," said Dugan.

"Gabbro?" echoed Lani. "Isn't that black granite?"

"Yep." Dugan turned his computer to show them a picture of a dark gray rock comprised of black and gray grains. Cruz caught a few flecks of deep green, too, but not a speck of pink or red.

Emmett's head came up. "I see black dots on red rocks. That's it. Too far away. Sorry."

"Looks like we'll have to explore the mystery for ourselves," said Lani happily.

Cruz picked up his tablet. "I'll message Fanchon and see if our PANDA units are ready." Fanchon was uploading their upgrade from their geography bee win.

"Ask her to throw in a couple of SHOT-bots while she's at it," said Emmett.

"Okay."

"And ask about when she did the last software update on our MC cams."

"O-okay."

"And see if she can boost... Never mind." Emmett heard Cruz's sigh. "I'll message her."

"We should plan our travel route," said Lani. "Remember what Professor Luben said. Monsieur Legrand may be coming, but he won't be guiding us."

"I'll add a GPS overlay to the map so we can see *Orion*'s current position," said Bryndis. She zoomed out until the full island chain came into view. A moment later, a blinking red dot appeared a couple miles west of Heroína.

"Yeah!" Dugan's palm hit the edge of the table. "This is gonna be a snap."

"I wouldn't be so sure," warned Emmett. Using his index finger, he traced the perimeter of a large white mass hugging the west coast of the island. At first, Cruz thought it was a thick patch of fog, but as Bryndis zeroed in on that section of the map, he could see it was ice. Chunks in various shapes and sizes were shoved up against one another like a big logjam.

Sailor moaned. "Pack ice."

"It *is* the end of summer, so the ice might not be as thick as it was whenever this image was taken," noted Lani. "Might be good to plan a couple of routes."

"We've got less than an hour." Sailor nodded to the clock at the corner of the map table that read 9:40. "If we divide duties, we can get everything done in time."

"Emmett and I can pick up the tech gear," said Cruz.

"Lani and I can chart travel routes and landing sites," volunteered Bryndis.

"Dugan, do you want to help me research the island's history and check the exploration archives?" asked Sailor.

"Sure," he said. "Let's do our work, grab our stuff, and meet in aquatics at ten twenty."

The team broke up. Cruz and Emmett headed to the tech lab, where they were met by Fanchon Quills. She was wearing her pink periodic table *LAB IS FUN* apron over a red long-sleeved tee and jeans. Caramel-colored curls, the ends dyed purple, spilled out of a head scarf printed with yellow daffodils. The tech lab chief clutched a toaster-size black storage container under one arm. "Here are two SHOT-bots and your beefed-up PANDA units. I've sent each of you a link to the manual so you can familiarize yourselves with the upgrades. There's some important stuff there, so be sure to review it when you have time. Also, I've run a full diagnostic on your parachutes and flotation devices and boosted the signal on your comm pins. Can I do anything else for Team Cousteau?"

"Just one more thing," said Cruz. "Could you run a quick check on Mell and her remote? It's so cold outside, and—"

"Of course." Fanchon set the box on the counter. "It'll take about ten minutes."

"Okay." That still gave Cruz and Emmett plenty of time to stop off at cabin 202 for their gear, then get to aquatics to meet the rest of the team. Cruz took off the honeycomb remote, gently scooped Mell from his pocket, and gave both to the tech lab chief. Fanchon went into the second cubicle. While they waited, Cruz checked his messages. He had one from Aunt Marisol wishing him well on the mission and one from his adviser, Nyomie, reminding them there would be a cabin inspection this Saturday afternoon.

"Fanchon, are you getting a lab assistant soon?" called Emmett. "'Cause if you aren't, I was thinking maybe I could—"

"Job's filled!" called a man from somewhere in the compartment.

Cruz's head snapped up. He was almost certain he knew that voice! It belonged to—

"Jericho!" Cruz gasped as a lanky young man wearing jeans and a T-shirt beneath an open blue lab coat appeared. Seeing Jericho Miles on board *Orion* wasn't a shock, but finding him *here* in the tech lab was. Jericho was always well out of sight of the explorers, working in the secret Synthesis lab on the lowest level of the ship.

"Hi, Emmett and Cruz. It's good to see you," said Jericho. "Honestly, it's good to see *anyone*. I was starting to go a little stir-crazy below-decks." Sticking out his tongue, he made one green eye cross in and wiggle back and forth.

It was hard not to like Jericho when he was so . . . likable.

"So you're not with . . . you know . . . ?" asked Cruz.

Straightening his eyes, Jericho said firmly, "I'm with the Academy now." It was almost as if he was saying, *I'm on your side, Cruz.*

But was he? Cruz's mom had warned him about trusting anyone with the Synthesis. There was no telling who was friend or foe within the organization.

Fanchon stepped out of the nook. "I see you've met my new assistant. We'll be introducing him to all the explorers soon. Here you are." She presented Cruz with his remote and drone. "Your MAV is in tip-top shape. Mell is bee-utiful!"

Smiling at Fanchon's pun, Cruz reattached his pin and slipped the drone into her usual pocket.

Emmett tucked the box of tech gear under his arm, and the boys headed out of the lab. Emmett insisted they stop at the galley to get a big container of Chef Kristos's peppermint hot chocolate to share with the team. Their cocoa detour had put them behind schedule, so they raced back to their cabin to grab their equipment.

"Let's go!" Emmett was juggling his coat, pack, and cocoa, while holding the door open with his foot for Cruz. "It's ten twenty."

Cruz shoved his arms into his hide-and-seek jacket. "I'm right behind you."

"Sailor York to Cruz Coronado and Emmett Lu."

The boys slapped their comm pins. "Coming!"

"Don't bother. The mission is off!"

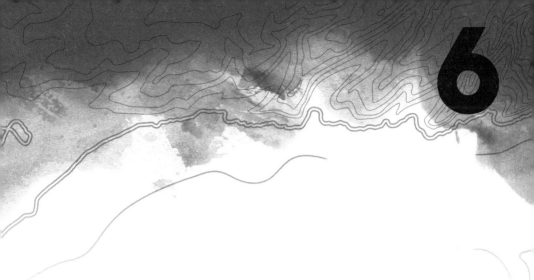

6

▶ **EVERY MEMBER** of Team Cousteau was hunched over *Rigel*'s open hull as if by staring at the broken engine they could magically fix whatever was wrong with it.

"What's wrong with it?" asked Dugan, his words muffled by his hood and face covering. It was 18 degrees on the launch deck. To protect them from the biting Antarctic air, everyone was bundled in their hide-and-seek jackets and bio-insulated masks, scarves, and gloves. They looked like six polar bears—seven if you counted chief mechanic Sunniva Tomaso.

"It's the solar thermal receiver." Sunny crouched next to the tender boat. "It's only functioning at thirty percent capacity."

"Isn't there anything you can do?" pleaded Bryndis.

"I could try to tweak the nano inverter," she answered. "It might get you where you're going, but I can't guarantee it would get you back."

"We'll take that chance," said Lani. She leaned to survey her team-mates. "Won't we?"

Five hoods nodded at her. They would. They definitely would.

"We will *not*," proclaimed a stern male voice. Monsieur Legrand was coming down the stairs behind them. "But thank you, Sunny. Sorry, Cousteau, your mission is officially canceled."

"Only for today, though, right?" asked Emmett, hopeful blue swirls swimming in his emoto-glasses. "We can still go tomorrow using one of the other boats."

"No," said their teacher. "A storm is on the way. We must leave the area by sunset. Captain's orders."

The explorers groaned.

Monsieur Legrand motioned for them to follow him back up to aquatics to collect their gear. Inside, Cruz shuffled to the corner of the bench where he'd hastily flung his pack. No one spoke as they peeled off their layers. Unwrapping his scarf, Cruz looked left, at the inner wall with its racks of water equipment: skis, paddleboards, and kayaks. To his right, four evenly spaced portholes on the outer starboard wall bathed the room in circular beams of sunlight.

"I know it's a disappointment," said Monsieur Legrand.

In a day full of them, thought Cruz.

"Remember, you learn far more from adversity than victory," said their teacher.

Yeah, yeah, they knew. Whenever you messed up in survival training, Monsieur Legrand was always there to rattle off his list of things that failure taught you: perseverance, courage, self-worth, good sportsmanship, humility, flexibility, resiliency. He meant well, but it didn't change the fact that the other teams were out there exploring and Cousteau wasn't.

Monsieur Legrand reached for the cooler of food. "I'll return this to the galley. The day is yours, explorers."

Free time was usually cause for celebration, but nobody was in the mood for it today. After Monsieur Legrand left, Dugan plopped onto the bench. Emmett took the seat beside him. Sailor began to wander aimlessly. No one was in a hurry to leave. Cruz glanced out the porthole next to Bryndis. A pale blue barge of an iceberg was drifting by, carried by a glassy cobalt sea. He couldn't spot a single cloud in the sky. Talk about a perfect day for exploring! The sun was inching above the jagged silhouettes of the Danger Islands. In the glare, Cruz thought he spied one of *Orion*'s inflatable boats to the south. He wanted so much to be *there* instead of *here*. From behind him, Sailor coughed.

"Hey, Lani," said Cruz, half turning. "Guess you have plenty of time now to talk to your trees."

"Guess so." Her voice was flat. Something was wrong.

"What's the matter?"

"I'm trying to connect with the mycorrhizal network, but I can't get past the research phase. I'm stumped."

"Nice one," said Dugan, catching her pun.

Cruz grinned, too, until he saw her gloomy expression. Lani really *had* hit a snag. "What happened?" he asked.

"I wish I knew. Professor Ishikawa has been helping me conduct experiments with some beech saplings in the bio lab. I've tried connecting with their root systems using water, simple sugars, phosphorus, nitrogen, potassium—all the nutrients trees need—but I've gotten no response. They're slow growers, I know, but they're not even growing in the direction of the food. It's like being ignored by the popular kids at lunch." Lani shook her head. "Trees are so middle school."

Sailor was clearing her throat again. "Uh … *guys!*"

Cruz spun the other way. Sailor was standing across the room, pointing up at—

"Kayaks!" cried Bryndis.

Cruz couldn't believe it. Talk about missing something right in front of your nose! Well, above it, anyway. Everyone made a beeline for Sailor.

Lani ran a hand along the bottom of one of the two-man boats. "Are they for us?"

"Who else?" teased Cruz.

"I mean, are we allowed to take them?"

"It's *our* mission," said Dugan. "Who's going to stop us?"

"Monsieur Legrand, for one," reminded Bryndis.

"We've only practiced in the CAVE with virtual kayaks," said Emmett. "If he doesn't think we're ready, he won't—"

"We'll have to convince him we are," argued Cruz. "Besides, aren't our teachers always saying 'Dare to explore'?"

"But are they serious?" Bryndis's blue eyes widened. "Do they really believe in us?"

"We are and we do!" Monsieur Legrand was striding toward them. He checked his watch. "Twelve minutes. I was wondering how long it would take you to come up with an alternate plan. Every problem has a solution. The challenge is to keep your emotions in check until you find it." He glanced from them to the kayaks. "So, are we going to drink hot chocolate all day or get these boats into the water?"

Team Cousteau jumped into action, while Monsieur Legrand went back up to the galley to retrieve lunch. When he returned, their instructor gave them a refresher lesson on how to sit in the cockpit of the kayak, hold the paddle, stroke correctly, and right the boat should it capsize. He also reminded them about the procedure for deploying the flotation devices contained in their uniforms in case someone went into the water. Once he felt they were ready, everyone loaded their gear. The food and tech equipment went into Monsieur Legrand's boat since he would be sailing alone. There wasn't room for their packs, but all they needed were their tablets anyway, and they were able to fit them in their large outer jacket pockets.

"Explorers, double-tap your comm pin and speak my name," reminded Monsieur Legrand. They did so, knowing the move would keep the comm link between all of them open until they double-tapped again at the end of their journey. "It's your mission, Team Cousteau," said their teacher, stepping aside. "Lead on."

Since Lani and Bryndis were navigating, everyone agreed they should be in the first boat. Dugan and Sailor got into the second hull, Emmett and Cruz took the third, and Monsieur Legrand brought up the rear alone in the fourth boat. One by one, the kayaks slipped smoothly and silently away from *Orion*. Sitting behind his roommate, Cruz felt his heart rev when it was their turn to cast off. Finally, they were on their way!

The four kayaks glided in single file through the icy labyrinth, the only sound the swish of paddles through water. Cruz enjoyed the easy windmill motion of dipping his right blade into the water, then the left blade, then back to the right again. With each stroke, it was as if he were leaving one world behind and entering another—a world painted

every imaginable shade of blue. The sky was vivid delphinium, the water deep indigo, and the icebergs glistened pale blue above the water and turquoise below it. Cruz did a double take when he saw a block of ice with dozens of white and dark teal vertical stripes!

"The bands are formed by seawater seeping into the cracks, then freezing," explained Monsieur Legrand over the comm link. "They aren't always blue. Stripes can be yellow, green, brown, or black, or a combo of colors. It depends on the algae, minerals, and other materials present in the water, as well as how the light is refracted from the ice. Does anyone know the terms for smaller icebergs?"

"Bergy bits and growlers!" Lani beat the rest of them.

"That's right," praised their teacher. "Bergy bits are usually between six and fifteen feet wide with more than three feet showing above the water. Growlers are under six feet wide and have less than three feet showing, so about the size of a grand piano."

"I get why they call it a bergy bit," said Dugan. "But growler?"

"As it melts, an iceberg releases air that's trapped inside, and sometimes that escaping air can sound like an animal growling," replied Monsieur Legrand.

Cruz made it a point to listen extra carefully from then on. Most of the chunks of ice they passed were flat with whipped-cream-like peaks that seemed to fit into the bergy bit category. Lifting his blade, Cruz saw a flash of gray to his right. At first he thought it was a seal, until the animal surfaced and he caught sight of grooved skin surrounding a dark eyeball!

Cruz couldn't breathe. "M-Monsieur... L-Legrand!"

"I see," came the cool response. "Alert your team."

"Um... ev-everybody," sputtered Cruz. "Cetacean sighting on the starboard side of kayak number... uh... uh..."

"Three." Emmett helped him out.

The dark gray whale rolled, showing Cruz more grooved throat pleats and an ivory belly. As it swam past, Cruz gauged that it was about half the size of the adult right whales they'd helped in the Bay of Fundy. His

MC camera identified it as an Antarctic minke whale and gave two pronunciations: one where the *e* at the end was silent, and one with a long *e*, making it sound like "minky."

"*Magnifique*," whispered Monsieur Legrand. "Minkes can be curious, but it's rare to see them this close. They're among the smallest baleen whales, and quite fast. A minke can scoop, strain, and eat krill in less time than it takes for a humpback to open its mouth."

The whale moved from one kayak to the next, much to the delight of the explorers. Cruz figured that once it reached Lani and Bryndis, the animal would continue on. He figured wrong! The whale made a smooth turn. It was coming back!

His MC camera under his hood, Cruz fumbled to get the eyepiece over his GPS sunglasses. When that didn't work, he tore off his sunglasses and dropped them onto the bottom of the boat. He wasn't about to miss getting pictures of this! Cruz began snapping away. The whale cruised toward him like a submarine, its curved periscope of a fin barely breaking the surface. It dipped, dived, and breached again;

however, this time, only its head came up out of the water. Cruz knew this posture. He'd seen whales and dolphins do it back home. It was called spyhopping, going almost vertical in the water so the cetacean could lift its head above the surface and see what was going on. The move gave Cruz a clear view of the ridge that ran down the middle of the whale's head from its twin blowholes to a pointed snout. An eye appeared out of the water. Cruz stayed as still as he could. The minke seemed to be studying him, maybe wondering about his strange yellow shell. Oh, to have Fanchon's Universal Cetacean Communicator now!

Whoooooosh! Air shot through the whale's blowholes. A second later, a powerful odor hit Cruz. It smelled like fish and farts.

"Peee-eww!" shrieked Dugan. Nobody needed a comm pin to hear him.

"Whale breath," gagged Emmett. "That's the smell of half-digested krill."

"That is one stinky minke," choked Lani.

Coughs turned to laughter. Waving away the odor, Cruz peered over the starboard side of the boat. He didn't see the whale. He swung to the port side. Still nothing.

Emmett's head was going back and forth, too. "Looks like he's gone deep. Minkes can remain underwater for twenty minutes at a time."

"It's nearly noon," reminded Sailor.

Less than three hours of daylight remained. They needed to move on. Team Cousteau picked up their paddles. As the kayaks closed in on Heroína Island, the pack ice became thicker. Cruz was glad they'd taken the time to review the satellite photos and plot a course. Lani and Bryndis were doing a good job of skirting south to avoid the densest section of ice. The most direct route would have taken them into the heart of the ice jam. While they might not have gotten stuck, they would have wasted precious time backtracking.

"Wow!" Cruz heard Lani cry, though he could not see her. The lead kayak had disappeared around the corner of a tall block iceberg.

Soon after the second boat navigated the same hunk of ice came Sailor's "Crikey!"

"Is everything okay up there?" asked Emmett.

"It's … you won't believe …" Bryndis was cutting in and out. "I've never seen so many … totally wild …"

He heard static.

"Bryndis?" called Cruz. "So many *what*?"

She didn't answer.

"Come on, Cruz," Emmett tossed over his shoulder. "Let's pick it up."

Cruz didn't need to be told twice. He paddled like crazy, shifting his weight left and using a short, sweeping stroke to help them take the corner of the mammoth berg. Once they'd cleared it, Cruz saw …

Penguins! Thousands and thousands of penguins. The black-and-white birds covered the bay's rocky shoreline, stretching up the hills and along the cliffs as far as they could see. Penguins even lined the icebergs, their little black heads turning to watch the kayaks glide past. Sailing into the inlet, Cruz felt like he was riding on a float in a parade. Should he wave?

His MC camera identified the birds as Adélie penguins *(Pygoscelis adeliae)*. Squinting, Cruz leaned to the port side of the boat. Were those bubbles in the water? It took him a minute to realize the penguins were porpoising, surfacing to breathe before diving again, but they were moving so quickly it looked as if the water were boiling.

Cruz spotted Sailor and Bryndis's kayak on the rocky beach. The girls were out of the hull, and Sailor was helping Dugan and Lani drag their boat up onto the shore. Bryndis stood a few feet away, waving to Emmett and Cruz to make their way to her. Cruz felt the kayak hit bottom. Bryndis waded out to hold the bow while the boys stepped out.

Cruz's senses were quickly overwhelmed—first by the sound of so many squawking birds, then by a powerful stench. It was the pungent odor of fish and farts again, but this odor was even meatier than the minke's breath. Mixed with an ammonia-like scent, it made his sinuses burn. "Whew!"

Lani was shaking her head. "Stinky minkes and now smelly Adélies! I had no idea Antarctica reeked like this."

"That's the smell of *fully* digested krill," announced Emmett above the barking penguins. He looked at the rocks. "And *that* is the sight of it."

The entire shoreline was coated in pink-and-red goo. On the hillside leading to the beach, patches of snow and ice, along with many of the penguins' white bellies, were also tinted pink. Of course! Krill was the main diet of penguins, and these small shrimplike crustaceans were pink and red.

Cruz glanced at Emmett. "So what we saw on the satellite photo was—"

"Penguin poop!" Dugan called above the babbling birds.

"The term is guano," corrected Monsieur Legrand, heading toward them. He'd expertly angled his boat in the shallow water so that he could easily step out and pull it up onto the rocks.

Lani tipped her head back. "You can see penguin guano from space. Who knew?"

"Somebody did, that's for sure," said Emmett.

"That's why we're here, isn't it, Monsieur Legrand?" asked Sailor. "A scientist must have spotted what looked like guano on the satellite images but needed firsthand observation to verify it."

Every head turned to their survival instructor, who'd pulled down his face covering. Monsieur Legrand didn't respond, but his smirk told them Sailor was right.

"This could be a major discovery," said Dugan.

"This could be really important," said Sailor.

Dugan lifted his sunglasses. "I just said that."

"You did?" She pushed back her hood. "Sorry. With all this chatter, I can barely hear myself think!"

A group of penguins was waddling toward them like a welcoming committee.

"*Arr-rar-rar-rar-rah! Ku-gu-gu-gu-gaaaa!*"

"While we were researching the island," continued Sailor, raising her voice, "we learned that the Adélie colonies on the west side of the Antarctic Peninsula are declining."

"That's why finding so many penguins here could be a big deal," finished Dugan.

Cruz felt a tap on his leg. A black head with two dark eyes ringed in white feathers was staring up at him. The penguin seemed fascinated by the sun's reflection off the gold zipper pull on Cruz's pocket. Cruz dropped to his knee so the inquisitive bird could take a closer look. A rusty-orange bill pecked at the shiny zipper tab.

"We should collect as much data as possible," said Emmett.

Bryndis looked across at the vast icescape of birds. "Do you mean…?"

"Count them," he said. "We need to count the penguins."

"It's a quarter to one," said Sailor. "It took us an hour to get here, so we've got about one hour before we have to start back."

"One hour?" Dugan put a glove to his forehead. "There's got to be fifty thousand penguins here. And that's only what we can see. Who knows how many of them are on the rest of the island? We'll never be able to do it in an hour."

"Maybe *we* can't…" said Lani, bumping Cruz's shoulder with her knee.

That was his cue. Cruz tore himself away from his new penguin pal to glance up at his teammates. "But Mell can."

7

▶ **DARKNESS** was closing in.

A ribbon of orange light on the western horizon was all that separated a steely sky from a sapphire sea. The air was getting colder. Thinner. It scraped Cruz's throat. His arms felt like lead. Cruz could see the white lights of the arch above *Orion*'s launch deck. Lani and Bryndis in the lead kayak were almost to the ship. Chest heaving and arms aching, Cruz forced himself to keep paddling. He had to keep going. They *had* to make it back on time.

"Faster. Must. Go. Faster."

"I'm rowing...as fast as I can, Cruz," huffed Emmett.

Cruz had been coaching himself. He hadn't realized he'd said that out loud. "I...know," he panted. "You're...doing...great."

Everyone *was* giving it their best effort. To complete their mission on Heroína in one hour, they'd once again divided duties. Lani and Emmett tackled programming and deploying the SHOT-bots. They decided to have the morphing camera bots resemble the stones the penguins used to build their nests. Sailor and Dugan volunteered to hike around the island, recording video, taking photos, and collecting information for the team's field report. Meantime, Bryndis and Cruz coordinated Mell's penguin count. Using the MAV's remote, Cruz directed the drone's flight path over the island. Meanwhile, Bryndis used Cruz's tablet to monitor Mell's progress.

If everything had gone according to plan, they would have finished on time. But it didn't, so they didn't. Sailor and Dugan ventured too far out onto a rocky peninsula and nearly got caught on a reef when the tide went out. Emmett and Lani ran into problems, too. The cold temperatures interfered with the morphing process of the SHOT-bots. It took several attempts to get the clear waffle-like robotic cams to look like the angular stones they were supposed to simulate. Cruz and Bryndis also had to overcome weather-related trouble. Within minutes of Mell's takeoff, the drone's eyes began to ice over. Cruz had to keep bringing her back so they could defrost her lenses. To warm her, they used their hands, breath, pockets—even the steam from Emmett's hot chocolate. The repetitive de-icing significantly slowed the counting process.

"It's five after two," said Dugan when they all came together again. "T-minus forty-nine minutes until sundown. We *might* be able make up the time if we leave *now*."

"Mell's almost done." Bryndis's eyes were riveted on Cruz's tablet. "She's counting the last section. Cruz, can you ask her how long it'll take?"

Cruz tapped the honeycomb on his lapel. "Mell, give an estimated time of return to base."

A moment later, her answer appeared on the tablet screen. "Five minutes forty-seven seconds," read Bryndis.

Nobody reacted to the news, though Cruz knew they were as concerned as he was. Every minute was critical. Five minutes might not seem long, but it gave them only 45 minutes to get back, and it had taken them 60 minutes to get here. Normally, Cruz would go on ahead, leaving Mell to finish and fly back to *Orion* on her own. He couldn't do that here. If the bee's eyes iced over again, she wouldn't be able to return to the ship. Cruz wasn't about to abandon her, and his teammates knew it.

Monsieur Legrand stood several feet away from the group. His back to them, he gazed at the deck of low seal gray clouds in the distance. The layer was edging closer, covering the blue sky like a chunky fleece blanket. Thanks to the comm link, their teacher could hear every word that passed between the explorers, no doubt, but they knew he would remain quiet, per mission instructions. That might have been what gave Cruz the courage to say what he said next. "Why don't you guys leave? I'll wait for Mell and take the last kayak."

"Alone?" asked Bryndis.

"I'll be okay." He couldn't keep his voice from cracking with worry.

"No," said Dugan simply.

Lani was shaking her head.

"I'll stay with Cruz," offered Sailor.

"They might go easier on us if only one of us is late," said Cruz. "Besides, I'll only be a few minutes behind the rest of you—"

"*No,*" repeated Dugan so forcefully that even the penguins hovering nearby stopped to look. "We came as a team and we're leaving as a team. How about if we load up now? The second Mell gets back, we're out of here."

Everyone got to work. The drone returned as they were finishing. Shoving off, the race was on for the kayak convoy to make it back to the ship before the sun went down.

Cruz glanced up from paddling, a cramp piercing his neck. *Yes!* Lani and Bryndis had made it to *Orion*'s launch deck. Sailor and Dugan were next. Cruz plunged his paddle into the water for what felt like the millionth time. His hands were being rubbed raw inside his gloves. He could feel a blister forming where his fingers met his palm on his right hand. But he wasn't about to give up now. They were only a few hundred yards away from the ship.

Left, scoop. Right, scoop. Left, scoop. Right, scoop.

Cruz's quick breaths echoed in his own ears. So much exertion mixed with the cold, thin air was starting to make him light-headed. Monsieur Legrand's kayak pulled up alongside Cruz and Emmett's. "Keep it up!" he cheered. "You're almost there!"

Cruz hunkered down. Left, scoop. Right, scoop. Left, scoop. Right, scoop.

He could only see Emmett's back. They had to be close. They were going to—

"Uggggggh!" It was Emmett.

Cruz lifted his head in time to watch the last sliver of light disappear. His throbbing arms went limp. Emmett's shoulders rose and fell as he tried to catch his breath. They'd missed the deadline. Approaching *Orion*, Cruz swept starboard with the edge of his paddle. He leaned left to turn the kayak and place it parallel to the dock. Looking up at the side of the ship, Cruz spotted a figure standing at the rail of the third deck. It was Professor Luben. One foot rested on the lowest rung of the rail as he watched the chain of kayaks glide in.

Squinting against the bright arc of lights over the launch deck, Cruz managed a weak grin. He was exhausted but lifted a hand to acknowledge his teacher.

Professor Luben did not return the wave. Or the smile.

CRUZ STUCK HIS HEAD through the half-open door of his aunt's office. "Hey, Tía."

Poised over her tablet, Aunt Marisol's head came up so fast she bumped it on the red metal shade of her desk lamp. Cruz saw relief in her eyes as she reached to rub her temple. "You're back! Your team is the talk of the ship, you know."

He laughed. He knew. The moment Team Cousteau hit the explorers' passage, the other students poured out of their cabins. The questions came fast and furious. Was the team in trouble with Jaz in aquatics for taking the kayaks? Was it scary coming so close to icebergs out in the open? Did Team Cousteau discover penguin colonies the way the other teams had?

No. No. And definitely yes!

Cruz gently pushed away his aunt's floating trio of connected heart clocks to plant his hands on the edge of her desk. "We found a huge colony of penguins on Heroína."

"Really?"

"We weren't the only ones. *Every* team that was assigned an island to explore discov—" Cruz stopped when he saw his aunt sit back in her chair. She had cocked one eyebrow. It was the same expression his dad had when he knew something that Cruz didn't. Something was up. "You already knew about the penguins, didn't you?"

"We did," she admitted, "but there was plenty we didn't know—like the types of penguins you'd come across or the size of the populations." It was her turn to lean toward him. "So?"

"They were Adélies," replied Cruz. "Some chinstrap penguins on the east side of the island, but mostly Adélies. Mell counted them ..." He took a dramatic pause. "The total was three hundred twenty-seven thousand one hundred and sixty-six."

Her jaw fell. "Three hundred twenty-seven *thousand*?"

"And one hundred and sixty-six." He liked surprising her. It didn't happen often.

She put a hand to her lips. "That's far more than the research team anticipated. I can't wait to see your field reports and photos, and I'm sure Arch—Professor Luben—will be anxious to read them, too." Her cheeks were turning pink. "Uh ... that was ... uh ... some quick thinking, taking the kayaks."

"It was Sailor's idea."

"You have a strong team. One of the best I've ever seen."

"That's why we *have* to keep it," blurted Cruz.

His aunt was studying him. "You mean for next year?"

"Yes ... right. Next year." That was close! He'd have to be more careful, or he'd accidentally let Emmett's secret slip.

"I'm sure you don't have anything to worry about," she soothed. "I can't see any reason why Dr. Hightower wouldn't invite each one of you back."

If only that were true!

"Teams usually remain the same, unless someone requests a change," said his aunt.

"Not me," he was quick to say. "I want everything to stay the way it is."

The floating heart clock was drifting past. Uh-oh! The time on the heart labeled *Orion* read 7:43. Emmett would be placing his call to Prescott at eight, and Cruz had promised to be there for it. He backed out of his aunt's tiny office. "I gotta go. See ya, Tía."

"Good work. Get some rest. Love you."

"Love you, too."

Emmett was pacing in front of the door to the veranda when Cruz came in. The emoto-glasses looked like a broken traffic light, going from red to yellow to green to red again.

"You're gonna do great," said Cruz, kicking off his shoes. "The main thing is to—"

Ting-ting-tong. Tong-tong-ting.

It was the bamboo wind chimes ringtone on Emmett's tablet.

Ting-ting-tong. Tong-tong-ting.

Emmett scrambled to his desk. "It's him! It's Prescott!"

"I thought *you* were supposed to call *him*."

"I was!"

"You'd better answer," urged Cruz.

"You're standing where he can see you."

Cruz scrambled for a hiding place. He started for the closet. Bad idea. He'd never be able to cram himself inside *and* shut the doors. Whirling, he took a few steps toward the bathroom. Even worse idea. In there, he wouldn't be able to hear the conversation at all.

Ting-ting-tong. Tong-tong-ting.

"Cruz!" hissed Emmett. "Get down!"

Cruz dropped to his knees next to his roommate's bed.

He felt the mattress shift. Emmett was sitting on the bed. As long as he didn't hold his tablet high, Cruz would remain out of the camera range.

Emmett cleared his throat. "Hello?"

"Are you alone?"

Hearing the voice of the Nebula assassin sent a shudder through Cruz.

"I am," lied Emmett. "I...uh...thought the plan was for me to call you."

"Plans change, Jaguar. I'm sure you know that. The longer we talk, the riskier it is. I'll make this quick. Zebra was stubborn and greedy. I don't want what happened to her to be your fate, too."

"Thanks for your concern." Emmett's voice was tight. Guarded. Uncertain.

"I know you're close to Cruz," said Prescott. "It's understandable, even admirable. But you can't let it cloud your vision. You must keep your end of the bargain. Lion will stop at nothing to ensure that you do. Everything depends on you, Jaguar. Your *family* depends on you."

Cruz's pulse quickened. He'd been right to be worried about Jaguar's safety. Prescott was going to harm Emmett's parents if he didn't...

What?

What was Jaguar supposed to do?

"Is there something else you want?" asked Prescott. "Something more that will convince you to cooperate?"

"More?"

"If there is, you'd be wise to tell me before you share it with Lion."

"No, there's nothing," said Emmett, his tone as sharp as Cruz had ever heard. "I don't want anything from you."

"I'm happy to see you've learned from Zebra's mistake. So you'll follow the plan, as agreed?"

Cruz inched upward. He crept up until his eyes were peeking above the edge of the bed. His roommate was on his knees, facing Cruz, the tablet propped up between them.

"I'll think about it," answered Emmett. Seeing Cruz appear behind his tablet, he arched his brows as if to say, *I have no idea what I'm supposed to be thinking about!*

"I admire your courage," said Prescott. "I don't know many adults willing to take on Lion, but this game you're playing ... Why would you do it? Guilt? Friendship? Some sort of explorers' code?"

Cruz saw his friend stiffen before he answered. "Maybe all three."

"I have no antidote for a guilty conscience," said Prescott. "However, I can promise that Cruz will never hear from us that you were our spy."

Emmett gave an unimpressed grunt.

"I'm sorry you got mixed up in this," said the Nebula agent, his tone sincere. "But I'm not in charge. If you don't cooperate, things will get... difficult. It's time to fall in line, Emmett. You have to keep your word. You have to give us the stone."

Cruz and Emmett locked eyes above the tablet.

Jaguar had the seventh cipher!

Now all they had to do was find it.

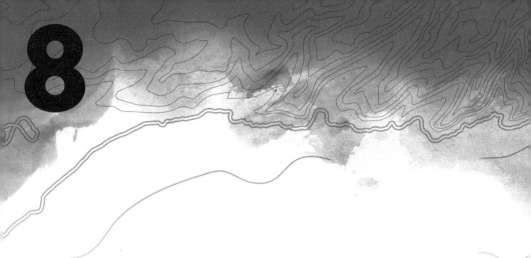

8

▶ **"YOU DIDN'T!"** Lani was rapidly twisting her silver lock of hair around one finger.

"I did," countered Emmett. "I promised Prescott I'd hand over the cipher. What else could I do? He threatened my family."

Lani dropped her hand. Her hair uncoiled, spinning like a miniature gray tornado.

"Your *f-family*?" coughed Bryndis.

"Crikey!" Sailor reached for the handrail as the ship rode up another wave.

Cruz and his friends were slowly making their way down the explorers' passage on their way to breakfast. Sailing through the Drake Passage, *Orion* was being battered by high winds and rough seas. It wasn't too bad once you got used to the rolling motion. Now and then, the ship hit a big swell, and Cruz felt certain that his stomach and throat, and all the organs between them, were going to smoosh together.

"I don't like this one bit," said Sailor.

The brass lantern sconce above her chose that moment to ominously flicker.

"Emmett," whispered Bryndis. "How long before Nebula finds out that you aren't really Jackal?"

"Jaguar," he corrected. "And good question."

"Here's another one," interjected Lani. "How are you going to give

Nebula a stone you don't have?"

"That's easy," said Emmett. "We're going to give them the cipher piece we made."

"They'll compare it to the photo they stole from me," continued Cruz, "think they have the real thing, destroy it, and figure they've won." Cruz had said nothing to Emmett last night as they were formulating their plan, but he doubted it would be enough to end things. Nebula had made it clear from the beginning they wanted Cruz out of the way, too, and Hezekiah Brume was not likely to be satisfied until that happened.

"That could work," said Sailor.

"It could," said Lani. "But it doesn't solve our biggest problem: We're still missing the original stone."

"Yeah, but we know it's on *Orion*," said Emmett.

Sailor made a face. "Do we? Mell's searched most of the ship, and if *she* couldn't—"

"It's on the explorers' deck," announced Cruz.

"It is?" asked Sailor, Lani, and Bryndis in unison.

"It has to be. Think about it." Cruz certainly had. He'd spent most of last night discussing it with Emmett. "Instead of coming up with where you *would* hide it, ask yourself where you *wouldn't* hide it."

"Well, I definitely wouldn't put it in a place where a lot of people go," said Sailor, "like the dining hall or a classroom ..."

"Or a lounge or the observatory." Lani picked up her train of thought. "I'd want to check on it now and then to be sure it was safe, so I wouldn't put it more than a deck away."

"That rules out the library, tech lab, and aquatics," concluded Bryndis. "And there are some places I wouldn't have good access to, like the CAVE, sick bay, laundry, the galley—"

"And the faculty and crew cabins," said Sailor. "So what's left?"

The girls looked at one another. The answer was obvious: the explorers' deck.

"Okay, so you've narrowed it down." Lani turned to the boys. "Now what?"

"This Saturday—" Cruz paused when he heard a door shut. Behind them, Ali, Matteo, and Zane were slowly making their way down the corridor. Having reached the empty elevator, Cruz motioned for everyone to get in. He waited to continue until the door was shut. "On Saturday morning, everyone is going to be hurrying to clean their cabins for Nyomie's inspection, right? It's the perfect chance to search for the cipher."

"Going through other people's stuff?" Bryndis grimaced. "I don't know..."

"It's not like we'd be breaking into cabins or anything," assured Emmett. "We're going to help the other explorers clean and, while we're at it, do a little snooping around."

"A *little* snooping?" Sailor's scowl was deeper than her roommate's. "The cipher isn't going to be in plain sight. We're going to have to unzip duffels, turn socks inside out, go through drawers—you know, really dig through things. It's a recipe for disaster."

Cruz understood what she was getting at. Explorer Academy had a strict honor code. If an explorer thought one of them was trying to steal something...

"Excluding our three, there are ten cabins to search," said Emmett.

Sailor crooked her finger at Bryndis and Lani. They put their heads together.

Cruz and Emmett knew they couldn't search all the cabins themselves. For their plan to work, they needed the girls' help.

Stepping back, Sailor sighed. "It's a big risk. If we're caught, we could get in serious trouble—"

A violent jolt nearly cut Cruz's feet out from under him. The elevator was going up. And fast! This, however, was not the smooth lift of an elevator. This was a wave—a big one! Like a bug being shaken from a jar, Cruz felt himself falling backward.

"Hang on!" yelled Emmett a second before Cruz crashed into him. The emoto-glasses went flying.

Hitting the wave's crest, *Orion* teetered for a moment, then plunged downward, flinging the explorers forward. They tumbled over one another again. Cruz's shoulder slammed into the wall. He felt the air rush from his lungs. It took several more seconds for the ship to stabilize, and when it did, Cruz was on his side, pinned under Emmett and shoved against the door. Something sharp sticking up from the floor was poking him in the side of his rib cage. His neck bent and his head tucked, Cruz's face was less than a foot from Lani's. Her eyes were closed. "Lani? Are you okay?"

Her eyelids fluttered. "Still in one piece. I think."

The pretzel of bodies began to untangle themselves. Cruz felt Emmett's weight lift off him. He sat up to find that the thing digging into his ribs was Emmett's glasses! The lenses weren't broken, but one stem on the frames was bent. Cruz did his best to straighten it before handing them back to their owner. Emmett put them on. They sat crooked on his nose, the left side a good inch lower than the right.

There didn't appear to be any injuries.

Sailor was on her knees. Her ponytail hung loose, stray hairs orbiting her head. The bottom of her unzipped jacket was twisted around her waist. "Anyway, as I was saying before the colossal wave hit, the three of us agreed we could get in mega trouble if we're caught—"

"I know." Cruz's heart sank. She was right, of course. "It's too much to ask, especially after all you've already done—"

"If you'd let me finish," admonished Sailor. She straightened her jacket. "Which is why we *also* agreed that we'd better not get caught."

Cruz's eyes widened. "You mean...?"

She gave him a smirk. "We're in."

AT BREAKFAST, DUGAN WAS LOOKING a bit green around the edges as he ate cereal. Or tried to. He'd put too much milk in the bowl, and the seesawing motion of the ship on the waves kept sending white liquid and granola sloshing onto his tray. Cruz pushed bacon around his plate. His stomach was in a knot, though it had nothing to do with the storm. He was worried about Professor Luben. Cruz hadn't told anyone on his team about their teacher's chilly reception at the rail yesterday, not even Emmett. Everyone felt bad enough for missing their deadline. He didn't want to make it worse. Unless . . .

Professor Luben mentioned it in class today. *That* would make it worse.

Maybe Cruz should tell his teammates. Would it make it any easier, though, to know what was coming?

"Cruz?" Bryndis was standing beside his chair. "You finished?"

He was alone at the table. Cruz had been so deep in thought he hadn't noticed that everyone else had gotten up. The rest of his team was over at the recycle station, emptying their trays. He pushed back his chair. By the time Cruz took his seat in Manatee classroom, he'd made up his mind. If Professor Luben said anything in front of the class about Team Cousteau's late arrival, Cruz would take the blame. What was it Monsieur Legrand always said? *Everyone makes mistakes. The weak make excuses. The strong take responsibility.*

"Prescott just messaged me," whispered Emmett, and Cruz leaned toward him. "He gave me the address where to send the cipher by overnight drone. It's Nebula headquarters in London."

Naturally.

From Cruz's right, Lani was crooking her finger at him. He leaned her way. "There's something I don't get," she said softly into his right ear. "Double-crossing Nebula is dangerous; even Jaguar has to know that by now. So why do it? Why not simply turn over the stone?"

"Maybe Jaguar is having doubts about this spy stuff," said Cruz. "I mean, he or she *is* one of us. Prescott seems to think Jaguar wants something in return for the cipher, like money."

"Money?" She tapped her stylus against her chin. "Jaguar's turning out to be either a very good friend or a very bad enemy."

Cruz agreed. He wished he knew which it was.

"What scares me most about all of this is—" started Lani.

"Good morning, explorers!" Professor Luben bounded into class.

"Good morning!" came the response.

"Well done yesterday," he applauded them as he jogged to take his place at the front of the room. "The faculty has been talking nonstop about you—all of it good, I promise. You met and exceeded our expectations for this mission. I'm looking forward to reading your field reports, which are due tomorrow, by the way. And if they are anything close to what I've been hearing from your guides, you'll be able to take credit for being part of an important discovery."

"*Ark, ark, ark!*" barked Dugan, doing his best penguin impression.

It got a big laugh.

The knot in Cruz's stomach began to loosen. Professor Luben seemed to be in his usual jovial mood. Maybe he'd gotten over being upset. Or maybe Cruz had misinterpreted what he'd seen. It had been a long day for everyone. And it *was* dark.

A holo-map appeared next to the professor, revealing *Orion*'s current position in the middle of the Drake Passage. The ship was on a northwest heading. "I know you're anxious to hear about your final mission, but we're not ready to share those details quite yet," said Professor Luben. He put up his hands to calm the chorus of disappointment. "I *can* tell you we'll be sailing up the east coast of Argentina, so let's begin our study of South America there. Argentina is the world's eighth largest country, bigger than the U.S. state of Texas and the nation of Mexico combined. It's home to some diverse habitats, from the multicolored mountains and gorges in the north to the rolling desert plateaus of Patagonia in the south..."

Cruz had to wait until Professor Luben strolled to the opposite side of the room to resume his conversation with Lani. "So?" He nudged her. "What scares you most?"

Lani turned, a tiny pink hibiscus flower at the end of her earring swinging. "That Jaguar will decide to give the real cipher to Nebula *before* we find it."

The knot in Cruz's stomach was back. This time, to stay.

HEARING HIS **TABLET** ping, Cruz hopped off his bed. Hubbard, taking his usual Saturday morning snooze on Cruz's pillow, lifted his head. *"Arrr?"*

"Sorry, Hub, but this could be it!" Cruz grabbed the computer on his nightstand. It was a message from Sailor! His pulse quickening, he tapped the icon. *Taking longer than expected. Two cabins down. One to go. Nothing yet.* ☹

Cruz hoped Lani, Emmett, and Bryndis were having better luck. The searchers had left almost two hours ago. Cruz had planned on going, too, until Emmett pointed out that the explorer spy might get spooked if Cruz showed up at his or her cabin door. "It's better if you lie low on this one," he'd said.

"He's right," said Sailor as Lani nodded. "We can handle it."

Cruz had reluctantly complied. Emmett and Sailor had volunteered to take three cabins each, while Lani and Bryndis took two apiece. Their instructions: Message the group via tablet *immediately* if the seventh piece was located. When the mission was complete, they were to meet back in cabin 202. While his friends were gone, Cruz spent the first hour cleaning the cabin from top to bottom to be ready for Nyomie's inspection at two. After that, he found other ways to keep busy. He'd given Hubbard a bath. He'd also read ahead in Aunt Marisol's dinosaur unit, learning that dinosaurs are divided into two distinct groups based on the shape of their hips: Saurischia (lizard-hipped) and Ornithischia (bird-hipped).

Cruz spun up at the sound of the cabin door opening. It was Emmett. He stopped halfway in. "Bryndis is coming. Lani, too …"

If they were returning without messaging first, it could only mean one thing: failure.

Bryndis scurried into the room. "Hi … Sorry … Didn't find it. I gave it my best … Practically ransacked Weatherly and Blessica's closet. Yulia and Tao's room was awfully messy, so I got a decent look there, too."

Emmett was still in the doorway. He'd been assigned to the cabins belonging to Zane and Matteo, Kwento and Felipe, and Hitoshi, who didn't have a roommate. Cruz didn't have to ask how Emmett's search had gone. A pair of somber brown emoto-glasses with tangerine corners told Cruz everything he needed to know. Emmett hadn't found the cipher, either.

Lani zipped in. She'd taken Kat and Cory's cabin, along with Dugan and Ali's. She flopped into a chair. "What a pigsty! So gross."

Cruz grimaced. "I figured Dugan's room might be a challenge—"

"Dugan's was fine. I'm talking about Cory and Kat! I nearly passed out from the smell. Pick up your dirty clothes, people! Now I totally get why Nyomie does inspections."

Sailor showed up 20 minutes later. She'd covered the cabins of Femi and Pashelle, Shristine and Kendall, and Seth and Misha. Sailor dropped to her knees beside the bed to pet Hubbard. "Femi collects rocks. *Lots* of rocks. They're cool and all, but it took a while to go through them. Sorry, no cipher."

"Thanks anyway, everyone." Cruz tried to hide his disappointment.

"Sailor and I … uh … should probably get moving," said Bryndis. "We still have to straighten our own cabin."

"Need some help?" offered Cruz. It was the least he could do.

Sailor patted his arm. "We'll be fine."

There was no need to ask Lani if she needed a hand. Like her bedroom back home, her cabin was always tidy and well organized. Lani loved bins. She had them for everything—books, shoes, school supplies, the electronics for her inventions. Big bins. Small bins. Round bins. Skinny bins. She even had bins for the bins. Some of the little bins nested inside larger bins.

"Lunch?" suggested Emmett after the girls left.

"You go ahead," said Cruz. "I think I'll walk Hubbard."

Alone in the cabin, Cruz traded the crew shirt that went with his uniform for his favorite long-sleeved tee. On weekends, the explorers were allowed to wear something different, if they wanted. On the front of the white shirt was a print of a blue wave cresting over stacked words: *Wake. Surf. Repeat.* On the back it read: *Goofy Foot Surf Shop, Hanalei, Kauai.* It was the most popular tee they sold at their store. When he wore it, Cruz felt a little closer to home.

Hubbard was sleeping so peacefully Cruz didn't want to wake him. Instead, Cruz sat on the bed, watching the easy rise and fall of the dog's breathing. Cruz curled himself around the Westie and rested his cheek against the softest fur in the world. So soon after his bath, Hubbard *really* smelled like fresh strawberries. Cruz closed his eyes, more to shut out his thoughts than anything, but it didn't work. Time was ticking away. He needed to find the real cipher piece before Nebula figured out they had been tricked. Where could it be?

Ting! Cruz stirred at the chime of an incoming message on his tablet. He'd fallen asleep, though he didn't know for how long. He carefully stretched across a still-dozing Hubbard for his tablet. There was no name in the FROM column. The subject line was blank, too. Opening it, Cruz's eyes swept down the page past the message to the signature.

Jaguar!

9

▶ DEAR CRUZ,

I took your carved stone. I could explain why, but the reasons don't matter. The important thing is I shouldn't have done it. I'm sorry. I want to give it back. It's too dangerous for us to meet. I've hidden the stone on board the ship for you to find. Decipher the message below to discover its location.

A sport you love will unlock the decoder.

1. EET   2. ENSLNR   3. RHUEOE   4. GOME

Be *safe,*

Jaguar

"A sport you love," said Lani. "That's easy: surfing."

It was Saturday night, and the four explorers were gathered around the short, circular table in cabin 202. Emmett and Lani sat in the two navy chairs with Cruz and Sailor at their feet. In the center of the table lay Cruz's tablet with Jaguar's message. The room was lit only by Emmett's mad scientist lamp. The round bulb inside the clear glass of an upside-down lab beaker cast spooky shadows on the walls. They could hear Felipe practicing his violin next door, though most everyone else had gone up to the third-floor lounge to watch a movie. Nyomie had extended their curfew to eleven o'clock. Emmett's clock read 9:39.

Emmett peered at the tablet. "Could be a substitution code."

"A jumbled one, you mean," said Sailor.

Cruz saw their logic. How many words in the English language could there be that started with double letters? It was a good bet this series of letters had to be rearranged into words. Meantime, the numbers had to be a clue, too. Were they columns? Rows? A hint on how to unscramble the letters or decode the message?

"Let's get to work," said Lani.

Cruz began writing out possible combinations on a pad of paper.

1. EET   2. ENSLNR   3. RHUEOE   4. GOME

1	2	3	4	
E	E	R	G	EERG
E	N	H	O	EHNO
T	S	U	M	TSUM
	L	E	E	LEE
	N	O		NO
	R	E		RE

4	3	2	1	
G	R	E	E	GREE
O	H	N	E	OHNE
M	U	S	T	MUST
E	E	L		EEL
	O	N		ON
	E	R		ER

"Anything?" asked Lani after a while.

"See for yourself." Cruz handed her the pad.

As Lani read, the vertical crease between her eyebrows deepened. "LEE NO? MUST EEL ON?"

Cruz let out a sigh. "We need the decoder."

"We sure do. How about all the postcards your aunt used to send you to decode? Does Jaguar's message remind you of any of those?"

Cruz studied it again. He put both palms against the sides of his head and pressed as if he could push the answer out of his brain. It didn't work. Nothing looked familiar.

Sailor sat up. "I've got something!" Holding up her tablet, she gazed at the circle of eager faces. "Does 'GNOMES TURN HERE' mean anything to anybody?"

Emmett snickered. "Only if I was giving directions to a troll."

That made everyone, including Sailor, crack up.

Hubbard lifted his head, but not because of their laughter. He was looking at the door. His keen hearing had no doubt picked up footsteps. Someone was in the passage. Cruz didn't think much of it until he saw an envelope shoot under the door. A new message from Roewyn!

Cruz jumped up, bolted across the room, and flung the door open. "Weatherly?"

"C-Cruz?" Weatherly was about to walk away. "I didn't know you were ... I mean, I thought you ... you ... were at the movie."

"Nope. Staying home tonight. This must be for me, huh?" He reached down to pluck the pink envelope from under his toe.

"Not here," hissed Weatherly. She pushed him back into the cabin and shut the door. Seeing Emmett, Sailor, and Lani, she froze. "Oh no!"

"It's all right," Cruz said. "They know about Roewyn. But how do you?"

"We're old friends. We know each other from school back in London. When she called me and said it was important that she stay in contact with you, I agreed to deliver a few messages." She frowned. "Cruz, I'm not totally sure what's going on, but I do know that whatever it is, you're probably in over your head. Don't you think you should tell Nyomie?"

"She knows."

"She does? Okay. G-good." Weatherly looked like she wanted to ask him more but thought better of it.

Cruz opened the envelope and took out the pink note.

> *Dear Cruz,*
> *I wish I had better news. Nebula is closing in. You MUST leave* Orion. *I've tried to talk to my father, but he refuses to listen. Someday I will make right every-thing my father has done wrong. Please be careful. Trouble is coming. Don't be there when it arrives.*
> *Your friend,*
> *Roewyn*

Crumpling the page, Cruz looked at Weatherly. "You've been relaying her messages to me all this time?"

"Guilty. Roewyn said it was a matter of life and death." Green eyes probed his. "You're both my friends; if there's any way I can help—"

"You already have, more than you know. Thanks, Weatherly."

"You're welcome. Cruz, please listen to Roewyn. She's right. I mean, she loves her father and all, but the guy *is* off the rails. His company is the only thing that matters to him, and if you get in his way..."

"I know." Boy, did he!

"Uh...I'd better get back up to the movie." She turned away. "I told Blessica I was coming down to grab a sweater."

"Thanks again," said Cruz.

Weatherly gave a quick wave, eased open the door, and slipped out.

"You know I haven't always trusted Roewyn Brume," said Emmett. "But maybe this time you should take her advice. Maybe you should get off the ship."

"Leave *Orion*?" squeaked Sailor. "Cruz would miss our last mission and finals and—"

"Better to miss them and live than be a sitting duck for Nebula."

"Okay, you may have a point, but still…"

"Guys, quick, write down the date and time Sailor said I had a point," joked Emmett.

"That's it!" exclaimed Cruz. "Fence rail!"

His revelation was met with bewildered stares. Cruz rushed to explain. "When Weatherly said Roewyn's dad was off the rails, it reminded me of one of Aunt Marisol's postcards. She sent it to me from a dig in Saskatchewan, Canada, a few years ago. You know how the photo on the front of each card is always a clue, right? This one had a picture of a prairie and a split-rail fence, which, at the time, I realized meant I had to use a rail fence cipher to decode her message—"

"I get it," jumped in Lani. "A sport you love! The sides of a surfboard are called rails."

"Exactly!" Stuffing Roewyn's note into his pocket, Cruz grabbed his pad. He ripped off the top sheet and turned the long pad on its side. "If I'm right, Jaguar used a rail fence cipher." Cruz drew in a new grid, this time, filling in the letters across the page.

Once he was finished, he held out the pad, instructing, "Read it again, but this time, start with the G in the bottom left corner and read *diagonally.*"

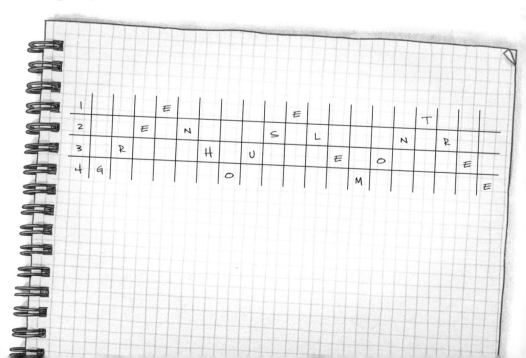

It took her mere seconds to get it.

"Greenhouse lemon tree!" called Lani. "You did it, Cruz. You solved the puzzle."

"Yeah, but..." Sailor gulped hard. "Is that *our* greenhouse?"

It was against the rules for the explorers to go inside the enclosed plant nursery in the observation roost without permission from Chef Kristos, Nyomie, or a teacher.

"Taryn let us off with a warning when we stayed the night there to try to fix the holo-journal," said Emmett, "but a second offense..." He let out a whistle.

"I have no choice. I *have* to go," said Cruz. "But I don't want any of you getting in trouble on my account. I'd better go alone."

"You could take one of us as a lookout, you know, to stay in the observatory and alert you if anyone shows up," suggested Sailor.

"Good idea." Lani lifted her chin. "You should take along someone with experience in surveillance."

"Someone who knows all about security gear in case there are new cams up." Emmett's emoto-glasses were two eager yellow pinwheels.

"Real subtle, you two," grunted Sailor. "So, Cruz, who do you want to go with you?"

"Um..." Cruz looked from one hopeful face to the next. His lips were dry, his head hot. No matter whom he selected, two people were going to be disappointed. Maybe even mad. He looked from Emmett to Sailor to Lani and back to Emmett again. How was he supposed to choose? Glancing helplessly between them, the answer came to him.

"Hubbard," announced Cruz.

Hearing his name, the drowsy Westie opened one eye and yawned.

"Hubbard?" Sailor put her hands on her hips. "Your lookout is going to be a dog?"

"Why not?" Cruz quickly wiped away the beads of sweat that had formed at the top of his forehead. "We walk together all over the ship, so anyone who sees me going or coming from the observatory won't think twice about it. Plus, he is the best person... uh, I mean, pup...

for the job. Nobody has better hearing than Hub."

They couldn't argue with that, and before anyone tried, Cruz slapped his thigh. "Come on, Hub. Let's go for a walk." Hearing the w-word, Hubbard sprang off the bed. Cruz snapped the leash on the dog's collar before grabbing his jacket off its hook. Cruz opened the door and glanced back at three dejected faces. "I'll contact you as soon as I have it."

Lani gave him the grin he was looking for. "Be careful."

"Aren't I always?" He shut the door on Sailor's snort.

Cruz and Hubbard took the elevator up to the bridge deck. The door opened, and Cruz leaned out. He peered left, toward the bridge, then right to his destination at the end of the passage. The corridor was empty. The pair got off, turned right, and walked briskly past the darkened library. In the oval observation roost, Cruz's gaze swept past shelves of antique sailing instruments and cherrywood walls papered with old nautical charts to the clusters of brown leather chairs and sofas. They were empty, too. No one was at the telescopes, either. Everyone was probably at the movie, including Jaguar. Cruz checked the little nook on the far side of the fireplace to be certain they were alone.

"All clear, Hub," he whispered.

With one last check over his shoulder, Cruz opened the glass door to the greenhouse. The air inside was warm, heavy with the mingling scents of flowers and herbs. Six months at sea had turned hundreds of seedlings into a lush jungle. Thick stalks of golden sunflowers, clusters of white daisies, and spikes of lavender crowded the flagstone pathway. Tendrils of potato and bean vines curled around wood lattices. Nasturtiums, geraniums, and strawberries spilled over the rims of their hanging baskets. The solar lights were off. Cruz would have to find his way using only the strings of tiny star lights that spiraled up the poles and dripped from the ceiling. He did have Mell if he really needed her. Cruz and Hubbard made their way through the plants to the center of the greenhouse, where rows of tables overflowed with trays of peppers, tomatoes, lettuce, and cucumbers. Next to the veggies grew basil, oregano, sage, and mint. Moving between the packed tables, Cruz's elbow hit a rosemary plant in a round bamboo planter that had been placed too close to the corner. He caught it as it fell off the counter, and put it back.

Reaching the roses, the pair turned off the main path toward the back of the solarium, where the potted trees were kept. Moving swiftly, Cruz scanned one side, then the other, for any sign of yellow. They passed kumquats, figs, oranges, and limes, each one in a blue-and-white ceramic floral planter with a matching dish of rocks beneath for drainage. At the end of the row was a bushy lemon tree in a pot. The tree

was in full bloom, its limbs sagging under the weight of a few dozen of the tangy fruit.

"Sit. Stay," he directed Hubbard. The dog settled down on the flagstone.

Sliding the loop of the leash up past his elbow, Cruz knelt in front of the planter. He began sifting through the dark, rich potting soil. He pushed the dirt toward the curved sides of the pot as he worked his way around the front part of the tree. Finding nothing, Cruz pushed the mound of soil back into place and moved around to the other side of the planter to repeat his efforts. Again, he came up empty. He inspected the trunk, branches, and waxy green leaves. He even checked the fruit in case Jaguar had gotten creative and decided to hide the stone inside a lemon. Nope. Every last lemon was whole. Where could the stone be?

Maybe he hadn't dug deep enough. Cruz was about to plunge his hands into the dirt again when Hubbard snapped to attention. Looking back the way they'd come, the dog tipped his head.

Bang!

Cruz jumped at the sound of a pot hitting the floor. There was no wind in the greenhouse. Planters did not fall on their own. Someone else was here.

What if Cruz had been wrong about Jaguar? What if the explorer spy wasn't sorry? What if he never had any intention of returning Cruz's stone?

What if all this...

His heart skipped.

...was a trap?

10

JAGUAR'S EITHER *a very good friend or a very bad enemy.*

Lani's words haunted Cruz.

On hands and knees, he inched backward between the planters until his foot hit the glass wall. He pulled Hubbard in with him. There was barely enough room for the pair, but Cruz had little choice.

I'm at a dead end, thought Cruz.

"Lie down," he whispered to the dog. "Stay quiet."

Hubbard obeyed, resting his chin on his front paws.

A voice! Whoever it was, was getting louder...

And closer...

"Ow!"

The cry startled Cruz.

"Watch those thorns," said a man. "I suggested we grow something a bit more inspiring than roses—say, titan arum. Kristos shot me down."

Professor Luben!

"Isn't that the corpse flower?"

Aunt Marisol?

"It is," answered the professor. "It's also one of Earth's largest and rarest flowers—"

"And smelliest," interjected Cruz's aunt.

Cruz let out a grateful breath. He was in here without permission,

86

so it would be smart to keep out of sight until they left. But at least it wasn't Nebula! He was safe.

"That's why we need one," said Professor Luben. "What better way to teach how scent works in tandem with color and temperature to attract pollinators than a three-foot blossom that smells like garlic, rotting fish, and Limburger cheese all rolled into one? The explorers would love it."

Aunt Marisol laughed. "My nephew certainly would."

She was right about that.

"Besides, titan arum only blooms for a couple of days every *five* years," said Professor Luben. "Think of it as a short inconvenience for the memory of a lifetime."

"You've got my vote, but I doubt you'll convince Kristos to give up that much space in his beloved garden," said Aunt Marisol. "Ah, Algerian tangerines!"

Cruz could hear his aunt's sandals clicking against the flagstone. A dark head appeared above the trees. Uh-oh! They were heading down his row. Cruz hunkered down as low as he could go. Straight ahead were two black loafers and a pair of red sandals, gold toenails peeking through the thin straps. Aunt Marisol and Professor Luben were less than 10 feet from Cruz and Hubbard's hiding place!

Beside him, the Westie bared his teeth. If he growled, they'd be discovered.

"Quiet, Hub," hissed Cruz.

Professor Luben cleared his throat. "Marisol, I've been meaning to talk to you about … Cruz. Is he doing well in your class?"

"He's one of my best students. Why? Is he having a problem in yours?" asked his aunt.

"No, no, nothing like that. His grades are fine. It's just … I don't know … He seems different from when I was here last fall. Nothing's *really* wrong," continued the professor, "and yet, I can't help feeling something isn't right."

"I think I may be able to enlighten you," said his aunt.

Cruz's chin smacked stone. He knew his aunt liked Professor Luben—maybe even more than liked—but that didn't mean she should tell him about Cruz's hunt for the cipher. He was so close to completing the formula. This was no time to start trusting someone new.

Don't do it, Aunt Marisol. Don't say anything that would—

"This has to stay between us," said Aunt Marisol. "The explorers can't know anything of what I'm about to tell you."

She was going to do it! She was going to spill his secret!

"You have my word," said Professor Luben.

Noooooooooo!

"It sounds like recruititis to me," said Aunt Marisol.

"Sorry," replied the professor. "Re-what?"

Yeah. Re-what?

"Recruit-itis," enunciated Aunt Marisol. "It usually hits first-year students about this time each year. The missions are getting tougher. Final exams are coming up. They're wondering if they'll get an invitation to return next year. And then, of course, there's the North Star award."

"It *is* a lot of pressure," agreed Professor Luben.

"Our extra encouragement will see them through this final push," said Aunt Marisol.

"I'll do what I can, Marisol."

Cruz's right hand was starting to tingle. Slowly, he lifted his elbow, balancing it on the outer edge of the dish under the lemon tree to get the blood flowing again to his fingers.

"Remember, this is confidential stuff," said Aunt Marisol. "We *never* use the term 'recruititis' when an explorer is within earshot. No sense throwing fuel on the fire."

"Got it," said Professor Luben. "About Cruz, I didn't mean to alarm you—"

"It's all right. I'm glad you spoke up. It's important to keep an eye on the explorers' emotional and physical health. Serious problems are rare, though they happen. I'd like to think I'd know if Cruz was having difficulties, but I could certainly talk to him or reach out to Nyomie—"

"That's not necessary," said Professor Luben. "I wouldn't have brought it up; it's just that I know how close you are to Cruz. You're like a mother to him, aren't you?"

"The nearest he has to one, anyway. He's so much like his mom. Petra was an explorer, too, you know; she won the North Star, graduated at the top of her class, became a world-renowned geneticist—"

"It's quite a legacy for a young man to live up to."

"And I don't want him to try." Aunt Marisol's tone was firm. "Cruz needs to follow his *own* heart. I think he knows that. I hope he does, anyway."

I do, Aunt Marisol.

He heard her soft laugh. "I sure love that kid."

I know that, too, Aunt Marisol.

"Oh my, I didn't realize how late it was," said Cruz's aunt. "Thanks for the walk through the park, Archer."

"Any time."

Cruz saw the heels of the red sandals lift off the ground. Was Aunt Marisol kissing Professor Luben? The heels came down before Cruz had too much time to think about it, and the two of them went back the way they'd come.

Once everything was quiet, Cruz waited a few more minutes. He tapped his comm pin. "Cruz Coronado to Emmett Lu," he said softly.

"Emmett here. Did you find—"

"What's going on?" broke in Sailor. "Are you okay? We were about to come up there."

"I'm fine." Cruz sat up. He wiggled his fingers. "A little squished but otherwise all right." Cruz stretched his neck, turning left, then right. His bones crackled. "I'm going to stay a little longer. I haven't found the stone yet. Jaguar must have buried it deep—"

Cruz stopped.

Tucked into the ring of smooth gray drainage rocks in the dish beneath the lemon tree was a little wedge of black marble.

BEAMED FROM A TIP in the floating orb, the holo-image flickered. "Hi, Cruzer."

"Hi, Mom."

"Cruz, do you have the seventh piece of the cipher?"

"I ... d-do." He'd meant to sound more confident.

Cruz watched her sweep her long blond hair over her shoulder, as she always did at this moment in the program. "Here we go," he muttered to his friends, who'd gathered around the table—Emmett in a chair and Lani and Sailor standing behind it. Well, Lani was standing. Sailor was bouncing. Cruz stretched out his arm, uncurling his fingers to reveal the stone in his palm. He'd been clutching it so tightly the black marble was shiny with sweat.

Cruz tried to hold still while his mom inspected the stone fragment. It wasn't easy. He was nervous. His arm felt heavy. His head, too. It was a quarter to 11. Cruz was exhausted and could tell by the bleary eyes and frequent yawns of his friends that they were as tired as he was. But this had to be done. Nobody was going to be able to sleep a wink until they knew for sure if the stone was the real deal.

His mom glanced up. Cruz's heart began to gallop. The more seconds that passed, the faster it went. Faster and faster . . .

"Well done. This is a genuine piece. You have unlocked a new clue."

"*Yes!*" Closing his fist, Cruz brought his arm in so fast, he punched his own collarbone, lost his balance, and fell backward into Emmett's lap.

Lani and Sailor were dancing.

"Hey!" called a muffled voice from under Cruz. "The program is still going!"

Cruz hopped up. A street scene was materializing behind his mom. First, a tall black iron lamppost with antique lights appeared and, behind it, a large building. The three-story structure was made of old beige stone bricks. Each of the first two stories had a long row of rectangular windows, while individual arched dormers that looked like a row of upside-down U's spanned the top level. Nearly every inch of the building was decorated with carvings and reliefs: flowers, leaves, eagles, scrolls. Angelic statues peered over the roof. Above the gated arched entry was some gold block lettering. The letters were blurry; however, Cruz had no trouble making out the big, raised letter *N* on the building above his mom's head. Beneath a crown and interlaced among several swords, it looked to be an emblem. On each side of the main gate, a pair of columns rested on a pedestal. A small black triangle was attached to each base; an arrow on each side of the triangle pointed up.

Cruz started to reach for his tablet, until he saw that Lani was already recording.

"To find the final cipher, look around me," said Cruz's mother. "Look carefully. Everything you need to know is here." She stepped a few feet to her right, to the closest pedestal.

"Seek that which both fascinates and elevates humanity. For thousands of years it has existed, formed from stone, metal, and glass, even written in the stars. Follow in the footsteps of the curious and courageous who have gone before you. Only then can you unlock the greatest mystery of all. P.S. Don't forget your roots, kiddo. Good luck."

"Freeze program," ordered Cruz. He wanted to get a better look at the inscription over the main door. He squinted to make out the words. "'Musée...du...Louvre.'"

"The Louvre!" exclaimed Emmett. "She's in front of the Louvre."

"Cracker!" cheered Sailor. "All we need to do is figure out *where* the cipher is hidden in the museum."

They moved in to study the holo-scene.

Emmett pointed to the emblem. "The *N* stands for Napoleon."

"There are more *N*'s on the columns," noted Cruz.

Lani reached for one of the black triangles on the pedestal base, her fingers passing through the image. "Looks like the triangles were placed on the building to help tourists know where to go. See the arrows telling people to go inside?"

"That makes sense," said Sailor. "Everybody knows about the museum's big glass—" She swung to face Cruz.

"Pyramid!" they shouted.

"That's it, all right." Emmett began ticking off the clues. "Fascinates and *elevates*. Has existed for thousands of years. Formed from stone, metal, and *glass*. She's talking about the glass pyramid at the main entrance of the Louvre. That's where we'll find the last cipher."

Everyone was nodding.

"Continue program," directed Cruz.

They watched in silence as the holo-image vanished. Within seconds, the orb returned to its flattened state. Cruz removed the lanyard from around his neck and attached the seventh piece to the sixth one. It clicked easily into place.

Lani put a hand on Cruz's shoulder. "Only one to go. This is getting exciting!"

Exciting . . . and scary, too. It was nerve-racking wondering what his mother was going to tell him to do with the stone once it was whole. What if he couldn't complete the final task? What if the person she wanted him to give the formula to was no longer alive? What if . . . ?

The cabin lights dimmed, signaling their bedtime. They all said their good nights.

"We're going to Paris!" crowed Sailor as the girls dashed for the door. "Thank goodness we finally got an easy clue."

Cruz stared at the nearly complete circle of black marble in his palm.

Maybe a little too easy.

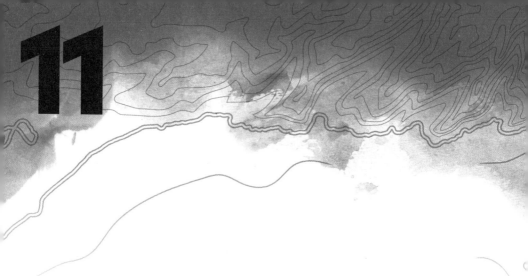

11

▶ **"THE LOUVRE?"** Perched on her black throne of a chair, Dr. Hightower loomed over the camera like a hawk. "That is a surprise! I wouldn't have expected your mother to hide the cipher in such a busy place."

Cruz tilted his tablet away from the morning sun streaming through his cabin porthole. "So you've been there?"

"Many times. Most people go to see the art, of course, but I find the architecture equally fascinating. The museum was built in the twelfth century as a fortress, then rebuilt as a royal palace a few centuries later. The pyramid was added in the late 1980s. It sits like a jewel in the center of the courtyard, a masterful example of geometric lines as well as the meshing of new and old. Looking up through the clear peak as the clouds roll past the palace rooftop—it's spectacular. I. M. Pei, the architect, insisted the glass for the windows be as transparent as possible." She let out a gasp. "Perhaps the cipher is tucked into the frame of a pane. Or hidden in one of the spiral steps leading down to the entry hall, like the secret drawer you found in Petra." Her eyes sparkled, and Cruz had the feeling that if Dr. Hightower could go with them to search for the stone, she would in a heartbeat.

"Anything's possible," he said. Cruz began ticking through all the places where he'd found pieces of the cipher so far: his silver holo-dome, the Svalbard seed vault, the ancient city of Petra, the cheetah conservation center in Namibia, India's Taj Mahal, the monastery in Nepal, and the dragon's blood warrior in China.

What concerned Cruz most was the thing that always worried him when he began looking for a fragment of engraved marble: Would it still be where his mom left it? Seven years—almost eight now—was a long time. By now, the stone could be long lost. Or long found. The sooner he got to the museum, the better. "Could we go this weekend?" begged Cruz.

The Academy president swiveled her chair, perhaps to look at another computer. Cruz saw a dangling fan-shaped diamond earring swing; however, the stiff peaks of her white whipped-cream hair did not move. He could hear tapping on a keyboard. "*Condor* will be back in Washington in a couple of days, and there is nothing on the schedule until later next week," reported Dr. Hightower. "Let's see . . . Your present location is . . ."

"In the Argentine Sea," assisted Cruz.

"Right. I see that you're southeast of Puerto Santa Cruz. By Sunday, you should be weighing anchor for your mission—"

"Yes?" A word he regretted the instant he spoke it. Waaaaay too enthusiastic.

She gave him a side glance. "Have you been given the details?"

He shook his head.

The corners of her mouth went up slightly. "You'll like this one, I think. A full briefing will be coming soon. All right, if we have *Orion*'s helicopter fly you to a mainland airport in Argentina, *Condor* can take you on to France. The flight from the mainland is fifteen hours. Factoring in the stop in South America and the time difference, if you left Friday, right after school, you'd be in Paris . . . about twelve thirty on Saturday afternoon."

"Saturday . . . afternoon?"

"It's not much time, I know."

They had less than 24 hours to find the cipher!

"I'll make the travel arrangements," said Dr. Hightower, "and I'll assign someone to accompany you."

Cruz put up a hand. "That's all right, Dr. Hightower. We don't need—"

"Yes, you do. Now more than ever." She faced him, her jaw set. "If all goes well, you'll be coming home with a complete cipher. It's the perfect opportunity for Nebula to strike. So, you will take Nyomie or an *Orion* security officer or you will not go—"

"Nyomie," he clipped. Ever since Officer Wardicorn had turned on them in Iceland, Cruz was wary of the security team. "We want Nyomie."

"I'll check on her availability." More typing. "Speaking of Nebula, they seem to be rather silent of late."

"Uh-huh."

"So, you've heard nothing from them?"

Cruz didn't want to lie, but if the Academy president knew about recent developments— Prescott's threat, Roewyn's warning, Jaguar's confession—she might insist they take a security officer to Paris, instead of Nyomie. She might even say it was too dangerous to go at all.

"Cruz?"

"No." He said it quickly, yet the word still tasted sour on his tongue.

After a tense moment, Dr. Hightower leaned back into her enormous black chair. Her shoulders went down. She believed him, which only made him feel worse.

Cruz tried to shake off the guilt. There was another important matter he needed to discuss. "Dr. Hightower, is it true about Emmett? That once I finish my mission, he'll be leaving the Academy?"

"That is the plan."

He could tell by her curt tone that she didn't want to talk about it, yet Cruz knew this might be his only chance. He pressed on. "Emmett is one of the best students here. Ask anybody. Look, I know he didn't start off an explorer, but he is one now. We'd be lost without him on Team Cousteau. Emmett belongs at Explorer Academy, Dr. Hightower. Please, you can't send him home."

"Your loyalty is admirable."

"But—"

"I appreciate your concern, Cruz, I truly do. I will take it under advisement. Nyomie will be in touch regarding your travel. Be careful, Cruz. This last leg of your journey is likely to be the most dangerous of all. You cannot let your guard down for even a second."

"I won't," he vowed.

"Good luck in Paris."

The screen went dark.

That could have gone better.

Cruz's comm pin was trembling. "Fanchon Quills to Cruz Coronado. Do you have a moment?"

"Yes. I'm in my cabin."

"I'll be right there."

A minute later, Cruz was opening his door for the tech lab chief. A green head scarf with a turtle print held back her curls. Over her jeans and tee, she wore a black apron with a diagram of an atom on the front pocket. Below the graphic of orange electrons circling a nucleus of red protons and blue neutrons it read: *You Matter!*

Fanchon's eyes darted around. "Is Emmett—"

"Helping Lani with her tree experiments. They're probably in the bio lab or library—"

"Good. I wanted to speak to you alone. Remember the other morning when you brought Mell in for a diagnostic? The program detected an irregularity and asked if I wanted to restore the MAV to normal function. I responded affirmatively, of course, but you were in a hurry and I was swamped, too, helping the teams prepare for their missions. I didn't get a chance to review the full bug report until this morning ..."

"Is something wrong with Mell?"

"No, no, she's fine." Fanchon put a hand to her head. "I'm just glad you brought her in when you did, Cruz, because if you hadn't—"

"What?"

"The next time you'd have used your remote to contact Mell, you would have activated her self-destruct mode."

"You mean—"

"Thirty seconds after you'd have said 'Mell, on'—"

"She'd have exploded in a big ball of fire?"

"More like a small ball of fire, but the result would have been the same. Her electronics would have been toast, and unlike certain other robotics, I wouldn't have been able to save her."

Stunned, Cruz lowered himself onto the corner of his bed. "I didn't even know Mell *had* a self-destruct mode."

"It's a last-resort measure. In case the drone goes haywire and you're unable to control it or shut it down, you can destroy it in flight. It's in the Apis 774-A's owner's manual." Fanchon sat beside him. "Does anyone besides you have Mell's password?"

"Uh ... no." Cruz was still in shock. The last time Cruz had used the drone's remote had been on Heroína Island. Someone on his team could have been injured. Or worse.

"I got some interesting results when I ran the data logs through my Hacker Tracker program," Fanchon was explaining. "It indicated there was no security breach but could not pinpoint an ISP address where the self-destruct order originated. A hacker may have found a way to fool my program. It's always a challenge to stay one step ahead of the bad guys."

"Tell me about it." Cruz didn't need to ask Fanchon why anyone would sabotage his MAV. Mell had saved the day, and Cruz's life, plenty of times. Somebody—probably Nebula—wanted to make sure the drone never did it again.

The tech lab chief glanced at the miniature honeycomb attached to Cruz's jacket. "Didn't you tell me Lani designed the MAV's remote?"

Cruz stiffened. "Yeah, but that was last summer. I ... uh ... I've changed my password since then. Even if she did know it, Lani would never do anything to hurt Mell."

"I'm not implying she would," said Fanchon, "but she might have included a pathway bypassing the authentication protocol to allow for emergency entry."

"A back door?" Cruz knew it wasn't uncommon to include a secret portal when designing a program, in case you ever wanted to get back into the program in the future. He'd done it a few times himself.

"Maybe she shared the password when she was designing the remote with someone in tech support, or a teacher," suggested Fanchon.

"Or someone could have stolen it," said Cruz. "You know, swiped it off her tablet or something."

"Maybe."

"Lani would never hurt Mell," Cruz said again. "Or me. I'm glad it all worked out. Nobody got hurt and Mell's okay. Everything's fine now, right?"

"Right." She was fidgeting. Fanchon was not a fidgeter.

"What's the matter?"

"I ... uh ... have some more bad news."

"M-more?"

"Now, don't get upset. I have to confiscate Mell."

"*What?*"

"I'm sorry. I have no choice. Chapter Four, section C, paragraph five of the student handbook makes it very clear that no explorer is to be in possession of a flammable decoration, appliance, accessory, or device, even one as tiny, cute, and helpful as Mell." She held out her hand.

Cruz drew back. "But ... but ... you gave me the octopod and that's got *poison* in it."

"Not poison; a temporary *nonflammable* paralytic, which, technically, isn't banned in the manual, but probably should be." Her palm edged closer. "I *am* sorry, Cruz."

Cruz's hand went protectively to his top-right pocket. "What's going to happen to her?"

"School regulations require all incendiary devices be immediately dismantled and properly disposed, however—"

"NO!" He flew off the bed.

Hubbard, who'd been dozing on Cruz's pillow, popped his head up. Fanchon stroked him, and he settled back down.

"School regulations require all incendiary devices be immediately dismantled and properly disposed," she repeated. "*However,* I did have something else in mind."

Cruz eyed her. "Like what?"

"Several things, actually. First, I'd delete the self-destruct option from Mell's menu so it cannot be triggered, either accidentally or intentionally. Next, I'd move Mell to the robotics section of the merry-go-lab—it has reinforced steel walls—and do a bit of micro-surgery to remove the switch, fuse, power source, and any other parts connected to her self-destruct mechanics. I'm fairly certain I can do this without damaging her core processor or harming any internal components. After that, I'd install a biometric security protocol so that only you and I could control the drone, perform diagnostics, and upload new software. Finally, I'd return Mell to you, making no mention in my logs or to anyone what I have done or how I have done it, with the hope that you would do the same so I don't lose my position at Explorer Academy, a job that I love and would very much like to keep." She stopped long enough to take a breath. "If you want, take out the virtugraph and I'll say all that again, if I can remember it. It's okay."

While she'd been speaking, Fanchon had bunched up the lower front of her apron in her hands. It was now a twisted ball of fabric. Several deep squiggle lines had also etched their way across her forehead. A pair of wide, unblinking brown eyes now stared at him. Cruz didn't need the truth compass to interpret what he could plainly see. Fanchon was telling the truth.

"I believe you," he whispered.

Fanchon released her apron, smoothing out the wrinkles over her knees.

Without a word, Cruz removed the honeycomb from his lapel. He opened his upper-right front pocket of his jacket and carefully took out Mell. She was lighter than a jelly bean. Her yellow-and-black-striped body was curled into a little C shape, two golden eyes dark. Mell looked so fragile.

"You said you were *fairly* sure you could do everything without damaging her," said Cruz, extending his hand to Fanchon's. "How fairly sure?"

"Ninety percent. There is always an element of risk involved in these things."

"I'd let you come, but it's safer if you don't," said the tech lab chief, closing her fingers around the MAV and its remote. "It'll take me a couple of hours."

"Will you call me—"

"The second I finish."

"Thanks, Fanchon," said Cruz. "Sorry I got so upset."

"It's all right. Figuring out who to trust is never easy. Even when you think you truly know someone, they can surprise you ..."

He knew whom she meant. "Dr. Vanderwick."

"You never think the person you're closest to will betray you. I never stopped to think maybe that's *why* she was close to me. Gaining my confidence—little by little, day by day—waiting to strike. Remember that, Cruz." She cupped her free hand around the one containing Mell as if holding a delicate butterfly. "And don't let your guard down."

"I won't," he promised for the second time that day.

Cruz took his mind off Mell's surgery by preparing for the trip to Paris. Settling on his bed with Hubbard and his tablet, he began researching the Louvre. Dr. Hightower was right about the pyramid. It did resemble a big, glittering diamond. Photos revealed that under the pointed glass roof of the pyramid was a large open lobby with a winding staircase. He could find no explorer statues or artwork, as his mother had relayed in her clue. Maybe the pyramid contained another hint that would point them to the stone's hiding place somewhere else in the museum. The place was huge! One story said it would take a person six months to see all 35,000 works of art on display. Cruz would be there for less than a day, and his treasure wasn't anywhere near the size of a painting. Feeling his frustration build, Cruz quickly swiped to the next article. It was all about the Louvre's state-of-the-art security system. The Louvre was the most visited museum in the world and the pyramid the busiest of its three entrances. Cameras, sensors, and guards were everywhere. Cruz pushed his tablet away. He knew he'd have to figure out how they were going to navigate things, but not right now—not with Mell's fate hanging in the balance.

Cruz's hand hovered above his comm pin. He desperately wanted to know how things were going in the tech lab, although he didn't want to bother Fanchon. She said she'd call him when she was done. This was taking forever.

Cruz sat on his hands to keep them from pressing his comm pin.

"Hey, Cruz!" Dugan poked his head around the side of the half-open door. "Wanna head up for lunch?"

"Uh...yeah."

He supposed it would take his mind off things. Even so, Cruz could only manage to down a few bites of his spicy beef empanada. Dugan was more than happy to finish the flaky turnover. After they ate, Dugan headed off to the CAVE to play games, while Cruz took Hubbard for a long walk. They covered the entire ship, ending up in Hubbard's meadow. They had the entire stern deck to themselves. Cruz was tossing the ball for the Westie when...

"Fanchon to Cruz Coronado."

Cruz slapped his comm pin. "I'm here!" Finally! It had been two hours and 24 minutes. "How'd it go? Is she okay? Are you okay? Is everyone okay?"

"Mell came through like a champ. As did I. You may come to get her anytime."

Cruz and Hubbard were already running down the passage. Cruz was so grateful that Mell was all right that he almost forgot to feel guilty about deceiving Fanchon.

Almost.

When the tech lab chief had asked Cruz if Lani knew Mell's password, he'd answered no. It was a lie. Lani *did* have Mell's password. Cruz had not changed it, as he'd claimed. Even so, he *had* been honest when he'd said his best friend would never do anything to hurt Mell or him. Cruz believed that with his whole heart.

He only hoped it was true.

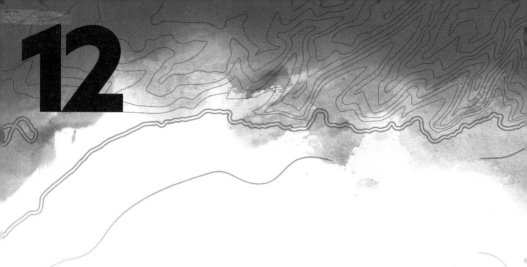

12

▶ **ON THURSDAY** morning, the message Cruz had been waiting for popped up on his tablet near the end of first period. He shot out of class the second Professor Luben let them go, sped one deck down, and through his adviser's open door. "Nyomie?"

"One sec." She stepped out of the bathroom. A blue hair band in her teeth, she was braiding her long gingersnap brown hair. Her hands moved at the speed of a magician's as she deftly wove three small sections of hair together. Nyomie plucked the band from her mouth, and with a few quick spins of her hand, the braid was secure. She tossed the plait over her shoulder. "Shouldn't you be in class?"

"Your note said to stop by when I had a minute. I've got ten." He glanced at the hand-painted half-sun–half-moon clock on her wall. "Well, eight now…"

Nyomie chuckled. "You could have come at lunch."

True, but then he would have risked someone overhearing or interrupting them. With only 10 minutes between classes, the explorers typically stayed up on the third deck during breaks and hung out in the lounge or dining room.

Cruz pushed the door closed. "I know, but…"

"I get it." She crossed to the desk and picked up her tablet. "I've got our travel itinerary. For security reasons, I wanted to tell you in person. Captain Roxas wants us to report to the weather roost by three fifteen for a three thirty departure tomorrow, which doesn't give you much time after school lets out to grab your gear and hightail it topside. I'll have Chef Kristos leave some fruit and snacks in the dining room for you to pick up on your way. Will you let Lani, Emmett, and Sailor know, too? Tell them to pack their stuff tonight so they're not running at the last minute. Oh, and you'll need to make sure Hubbard—"

"Fanchon said she'd look after him."

"Good." Her gaze went to the corner where Hubbard's bed used to be.

Fanchon and Cruz brought the Westie by to visit her as often as they could, but of course it wasn't the same. *It must be hard,* thought Cruz, *to change your whole identity—even for an artificial life-form.* Everyone she'd known and everything she'd done as Taryn had been wiped away everywhere, except in her own mind—or, rather, core processor.

"There's one more thing." Nyomie placed the tablet on the desk. "I want it understood, Cruz Coronado, that on this trip, you and the other explorers are not to leave my side for any reason."

"*Any* reason? What if we have to—"

"Maybe then. We'll see. Do I have your word that you will not ditch me?"

He held up a hand as if to swear. "You do."

"Thank you." Her face relaxed. "Now run."

"Huh?"

She tipped her head toward the clock. "*Run!*"

Cruz had two minutes to get to second period!

"See ya, Nyomie!" Cruz was off, sprinting down the passage, charging up the grand staircase two steps at a time, and vaulting over the scattered footstools in the lounge. Arms pumping, his tablet clutched tightly in his right hand, he raced past the stairwell. Feeling a rush of air, Cruz glanced left. Lani was running next to him. She must have come down the steps, probably from the bio lab. Lately she'd been spending all her free time there. Cruz gave her credit for her stick-to-itiveness, though her experiments in learning to speak

"tree" hadn't been going well. Still, if anyone could do it...

"I did it," she huffed as they ran side by side down the corridor. "I talked to a tree!"

"Nuh-uh!"

"Uh-huh!" She laughed, and when he slowed, she took the opportunity to surge ahead of him.

Lani slid around the corner into Manatee classroom first. The pair collapsed into their seats. His chest heaving, Cruz glanced up to see the digital clock click from 9:10 to 9:11. They were one minute late. At the front of the room, Aunt Marisol was tapping together long fingernails the color of lime sherbet. Her lips were drawn in a straight line.

"Sorry, Professor Coronado," said Lani sheepishly.

"Sorry," echoed Cruz.

Aunt Marisol gave a terse nod, but Cruz knew he wasn't out of the woods. She would find a way to remind him that, as her nephew, he *must* follow the rules. Being even one second late for class was unacceptable.

Cruz saw a holographic rocky cliff with horizontal bands of red, orange, and white rock come into view behind Aunt Marisol. "Explorers, you'll remember that in our fossil unit we discussed the law of superposition, which says what...?"

Several hands shot up, including Lani's and Emmett's. Cruz kept his arm down. He knew what was about to happen. Why invite it? He sat up and waited. Aunt Marisol was scanning the room. As Cruz expected, her eyes found him. "Cruz?"

"That in undisturbed rock the oldest rock is on the bottom and the youngest is on top, with each layer being younger than the one beneath it and older than the one above it," he said smoothly.

"Correct. This principle, along with modern methods of dating rock, has allowed us to create a timeline of Earth's geologic history. If you completed your assigned reading, you will be familiar with this..." She stepped to her left, and the holo-mountain was replaced by a large geologic timescale chart that was identical to the one in their text. "The scale divides Earth's four-point-six-billion-year history into units:

eons, eras, periods, and epochs…"

Cruz leaned toward Lani. "What did the tree say?"

"Shhh."

"The tree shushed you?"

"Cruz!"

He tapped his chin. "Let's see … I'll bet it said, 'Where am I? On a ship? You're kidding! Do me a favor and drop me off at the nearest forest, will you?'"

Lani bit her lip. He knew it was to keep from laughing.

"Our focus for now will be on the Mesozoic era," his aunt was saying. "We'll be taking a closer look at the Cretaceous, Jurassic, and Triassic periods…"

"Come on." Cruz tugged Lani's sleeve. "Tell me how you got the trees to talk to you."

"Okay, okay. Anything to shut you up," she whispered. "I was reading about how trees use their senses to protect themselves. If they're being munched on by predators, acacia trees will send toxins into their leaves to make them taste bad. They'll also release ethylene gas into the air to warn other nearby trees to do the same. I thought if trees are sensitive to touch, taste, and smell, maybe the same goes for sound, too. Professor Ishikawa told me studies have shown that tree roots will grow toward water by sensing its vibrations. I found a study where tree roots made crackling or clicking noises when they heard sound waves at two hundred and twenty hertz. Guess what vibrates at *exactly* that frequency?"

Cruz shook his head.

"An A note just below middle C on the musical scale. So, I recorded Felipe playing A notes in Morse code on his violin. I had him play the complete alphabet in code first, then perform a simple word: *Hello.* I've been playing these to the seedlings in the bio lab twenty-four/seven and nothing—until this morning, when the roots started repeating the musical greeting message back to me in Morse code clicks!"

"Seriously?"

"Yep. Plus, all the trees have turned their roots toward the speaker. They're listening *and* responding!"

Cruz was dumbfounded. "That's ... unbelievable."

"I know! Fanchon is going to help me build a device to see if I can duplicate my lab results with tree roots in a real forest. I'm sure trees have a language to teach us, too, but it'll help if we can find some common ground first. Get it? Common *ground*?"

He did. And groaned.

Applause filled the classroom. Cruz and Lani looked around. Clearly, they'd missed an important announcement. But what? Emmett, whose emoto-glasses had become dandelion yellow wheels, saw their confused expressions. "It's our next mission!" he said above the ovation. "We're going to explore Patagonia for dinosaur fossils!"

Now they understood! Cruz and Lani joined in the celebration.

"Sweet as!" Sailor tapped her knuckles to Cruz's. "The last mission of our first year!"

Cruz's excitement evaporated as quickly as it had appeared. It might be Team Cousteau's last mission for the year, but it was likely Emmett's last mission *forever*. If only Sailor knew the full story. If only they all knew.

"Let's make it our best one yet!" called Emmett.

Cruz didn't know how his friend could be so upbeat. Hadn't Emmett grown to love Explorer Academy as much as the rest of them? Didn't he want to come back? Forcing a smile, Cruz held his fist out toward Emmett, who bumped it with his own. If anyone had been looking closely at Emmett's emoto-glasses, they would have seen a starry trail of clear beads floating in liquid gold. The mist was barely perceptible, yet Cruz saw it. And he knew his roommate well enough to know the transparent crystals were created by feelings so great, so intense, that no color existed to match them. Behind the frames, Emmett's eyes revealed what had overcome his emotion-sensing frames: sadness. Cruz had proof. Emmett Lu *did* want to stay at Explorer Academy. More than anything.

THAT NIGHT, ALL THE HOWS KEPT CRUZ AWAKE: How could he convince Dr. Hightower to let Emmett remain at Explorer Academy? How could he figure out Jaguar's true identity? How could he find a tiny stone in a huge museum with only a vague clue about unlocking the greatest mystery of all? And what *was* the greatest mystery of all, anyway? Okay, that was a "what" question, but still...

Cruz was staring at the ceiling when, precisely at 6 a.m., the sloth cooed from the depths of Emmett's alarm clock. Cruz and Emmett got up, showered, dressed, and packed. They placed their duffels near the door so they could grab them right after school. Cruz drifted through the school day, half listening to the lessons of his teachers until, at last, Professor Benedict said, "Have a good weekend, everyone. You're free to go!"

Cruz, Emmett, Lani, and Sailor bolted out of sixth period. Scurrying down one deck, the explorers peeled off at their respective cabins to grab their gear. While Emmett was in the bathroom, Cruz got his mom's aqua box out from under his bed. Removing the top, he gently pushed aside the photo of himself as a child with the swirl decoder on the back and the birthday letter from his mom. He took out the box of bandages, the mini stapler, the ruler, and the little key. He wasn't sure if he'd need any of these things, but they were the only items in the box, besides a few ordinary pens and pencils, that he hadn't yet used on his quest for the cipher. Cruz dropped the key into his right-front pocket with Mell. He tucked the bandages and stapler into his backpack.

His tablet was ringing. Cruz answered. "Hi, Dad."

"Hi, son." Cruz could see the shelves of the Goofy Foot stockroom behind his father's head. Kauai was seven hours behind *Orion,* so his dad was beginning his day. "Won't keep you long, Cruz, just wanted to wish you a safe trip. Last piece of the puzzle! Pretty thrilling, huh?"

"Um . . . yeah."

"What's the matter?"

How did his dad *do* that?

"I—I can't explain," sputtered Cruz. "We have to leave . . ."

"You've got a minute. What's going on?"

He sighed. "In her clue, Mom said I was supposed to follow some explorers who have gone before me, but she didn't say *which* ones. What if I can't figure it out? Or what if nothing in the pyramid relates to an explorer? Or what if it does, but we can't get past security?" His pulse climbing, Cruz was talking faster and faster as he shared the worries that weighed on his mind. "I read they have this new state-of-the-art security system. Plus, we've got less than a day to find the cipher. Do you know how huge the Louvre is? It's bigger than a football stadium—"

"All right, son," broke in his dad. "Take a breath. Seriously, Cruz. To the count of three."

Cruz filled his lungs, counted to three, then exhaled for three seconds.

"That's better," said his father. "Twenty-four hours isn't long, that's true, but you've done more in less time. You have a long flight ahead. Why not take a virtual tour of the museum starting at the pyramid entrance? It'll give you the chance to go through it slowly. You can poke in all the nooks and crannies and look for the explorers your mom spoke of. Maybe the clue refers to a memorial or a piece of art."

That sounded good. Sailor, Lani, and Emmett would probably want to take the virtual tour, too.

"The more familiar you are with where you're going, the more comfortable you'll be," continued his dad, "and the more comfortable you are, the less likely you are to arouse suspicion. Remember what I used to tell you when you were a beginning surfer? Learning to surf is mostly about learning to . . ."

"Manage your emotions," finished Cruz.

"That's right. Stay calm. Focus on what's in front of you. Trust your instincts. Your mom knew you were up to the task, Cruz. And so do I."

It was exactly what he needed to hear. Cruz nodded and felt his pulse returning to normal.

Emmett came out of the bathroom.

"I've got to go, Dad," said Cruz. "Thanks. Talk to you soon."

"I love you."

"Love you, too." Cruz hung up.

At 3:31 p.m., *Academy One* lifted off *Orion*'s helipad carrying one pilot, one adviser, and four explorers. Twenty-eight minutes later, the helicopter touched down at Almirante Marcos A. Zar International Airport in Trelew, on the eastern coast of Argentina. Gathering their bags, the passengers thanked Captain Roxas and headed into the terminal. The rectangular airport was small but modern, with low ceilings and

polished white tile floors. Along with the usual coffee stands and gift shops, it had something Cruz had never seen at any other airport: dinosaurs! They were everywhere. Fossilized dino teeth, bones, eggs, and coprolites were on display behind glass cases. There was even a full-size diorama of a model *T. rex* in her nest. Tourists were taking selfies in front of the exhibit. Cruz especially liked the big wall behind the conveyor belt at baggage claim that was embedded with 3D dino skeletons (fake, of course). It was part of an ad for Museo Paleontológico Egidio Feruglio, or the Mef, the paleontology research museum based in Trelew.

Nyomie took in the panorama. "Hello, Patagonia."

"You mean goodbye, Patagonia." Sailor sighed. She was looking the other way, out the window to where the Academy's black-and-gold plane was parked on the apron.

"We'll be back in time for your fossil mission," said Nyomie, leading them to the gate.

Condor's flight attendants, Mr. Neering and Ms. Bukhari, greeted them at the door of the plane and helped them stow their gear. Emmett slid into the window seat in the first row. Cruz sat next to him. Sailor and Lani took the seats across the aisle. Nyomie sat several rows behind the girls. Cruz buckled his seat belt, turned off his tablet, and settled in for the flight. Captain Wada and First Officer Ionescu made a brief appearance from the cockpit to welcome them, and 15 minutes later they were in the air. Cruz closed his eyes; just for a few minutes, he told himself, then he'd take the Louvre virtual tour. The hum of the engines and Lani's and Sailor's whispers relaxed him.

"...so the trees actually echoed Felipe's message in Morse code? That's incredible," said Sailor. "This could totally put you in the running for the Franklin award, you know. Maybe the North Star, too."

"I'd love to get a trophy," gushed Lani.

"Sorry, no trophies at Explorer Academy," replied Sailor. "Something to do with not needing shiny objects to prove our self-worth, but I think you get a medal for the Franklin award. And if you win the North Star, you get your name on the crystal pyramid."

"Crystal pyramid?"

"That's right. You haven't been to the Explorer Academy campus. See, since forever ago, the winner of the North Star award gets— Oh no! Oh. *No!*"

At Sailor's outburst, Cruz opened his eyes.

"Mr. Neering? Ms. Bukhari?" Sailor was leaning into the aisle, her head swiveling. "Where they'd go? Captain Wada!" She tried to stand. Her seat belt yanked her back down.

"It's okay, Sailor." Cruz stretched an arm across to her. "It's normal to be scared, especially after last time—"

"I'm not scared ... Arrrgh!" Sailor struggled to free herself. "This stupid thing."

Ms. Bukhari came scurrying from the back of the plane. "Is everything all right?"

Nyomie was out of her seat. "I think she's a bit nervous about flying."

"No, no, no!" Sailor gave the buckle an angry tug. It opened, and she popped up, banging her head on the overhead bin. "Ouch!" She put a hand to her head. "That's not it. We misunderstood the clue. We made a mistake! You guys, we're going the wrong way!"

➤ **HIS ANKLE RESTING** on his knee, Thorne Prescott was in the last chair in the last row at the end of an arched glass concourse. He'd taken a seat behind a post about 20 yards from the gate where Cruz and the others were due to arrive at Charles de Gaulle Airport any minute.

Prescott had cut his hair to within an inch of his head and shaved his chin stubble. He'd traded his cowboy boots for a pair of black loafers, his jeans for black dress pants, and his favorite jacket and cotton tee for a gray blazer, a white button-down shirt, and a teal blue tie. At his feet rested an empty black briefcase. Prescott looked like any other business traveler, which was the point. Cruz and Emmett might recognize him, once he got close enough, but Prescott had the element of surprise.

Having followed instructions and sent the seventh cipher to Nebula headquarters, where it had been promptly destroyed by Swan, Emmett would be assuming that he and his friends were now safe. Wrong. Lion never let anyone walk away. His orders were clear. Emmett, Cruz, and anyone with them could not be allowed to leave France. Scorpion and Komodo were waiting at the Louvre to intercept the explorers should they slip past Prescott. He had no intention of letting that happen.

Prescott scoped out the area. A young woman with long, wavy copper hair wearing a blue-and-black-plaid vest stood behind the desk at the gate. She was talking on her headset. An elderly couple in matching royal blue tracksuits had settled into seats in the corner opposite him. A family with two children, an older boy around five and a girl of about two, had brought their kids down to the end of the concourse to play. The little girl was running in a figure eight, a white ribbon clinging to a wisp of brown hair on the top of her head. Nothing appeared out of the ordinary. Yet Prescott couldn't shake the uneasy feeling he often got when things were about to take an unexpected turn.

The toddler came rushing down the length of the big window, going as fast as two short, chubby legs in a pink jumpsuit and purple galoshes could take her. Her boots were on the wrong feet. Her dad, a few steps behind her, caught Prescott's polite grin. "We can barely get her to take them off let alone put them on correctly."

As the father scooped up his daughter, Prescott began absently scrolling through the photos on his phone. He suddenly lifted his thumb. It was Piper, frozen in time. She was coming down a yellow plastic slide, two little arms outstretched, trusting him to catch her. She had on her teal narwhal coat with the white furry hood and gold horn. Piper loved that coat. Wouldn't take it off—even for bed. Aubrie and he would try to coax her out of it, but most times they ended up having to wait until she fell asleep to put her into her paja-mas. Piper coming down that slide in her favorite coat was a perfect moment on a perfect day in a perfect world. But that world no lon-ger existed. With the swipe of his thumb, his daughter was gone.

Condor was a half hour late.

Prescott waited another 15 minutes, then stood, picked up his briefcase, and walked to the gate. "Excuse me," he said to the woman in the plaid vest, with friendly eyes. "I was supposed to meet a private plane from Explorer Academy. It's forty-five minutes overdue."

"I can check on that for you, sir." She got to work on her computer. "Okay, it looks like the flight left on time from Trelew, Argentina, at 4:32 p.m. yesterday . . ." She knitted her brows. "I don't see any weather delays or diversions. Ah, here it is: a new flight plan."

He frowned. "Are you saying the plane isn't coming to Paris?"

"That's right."

"Where's it going?"

"According to this, Washington, D.C." She gave him a pleasant customer service smile. "And actually, sir, with the East Coast of the U.S. six hours behind Central European Summer Time . . ."

Prescott clenched his jaw. "It's already there."

14

WASHINGTON,
D.C., U.S.A.

W. VA.

MARYLAND

Potomac

Chesapeake Bay

VIRGINIA

Potomac

CRUZ STEPPED out of the SUV, his eyes immediately going up to the steel doors and the words etched in stone above them: TO DISCOVER. TO INNOVATE. TO PROTECT.

It felt good to be back at Explorer Academy headquarters; different, but good. The explorers had left port last October surrounded by the reds and golds of fall and were returning to the budding greens of springtime. The ornamental cherry trees sprinkled pink petals over the city like confetti. Dr. Hightower got out of the driver's side of the vehicle. The Academy president had met the explorers and their adviser at the airport, eager to learn why their plans had suddenly changed.

Cruz and the others had already heard Sailor's explanation on the plane. "The clue ... Watch it ... again," Sailor panted as *Condor* soared out over the Atlantic.

Lani produced her tablet from her backpack and handed it to Sailor. Cruz knelt in the aisle, while Emmett stood in the row behind the girls, peering over Sailor's seat as she started the video. As before, the antique light post and one of the Louvre buildings appeared. "To find the final cipher, look around me," said Cruz's mom. "Look carefully. Everything you need to know is here."

"Clue number one." Sailor paused the video. "She's standing under the big letter *N* on the building." She hit the play icon, and Petra Coronado strolled a few steps to her left, stopping next to one of the stone pedestals that held up twin columns. Sailor pointed to the black triangle that was attached to the stonework. "Clue number two."

"Seek that which both fascinates and elevates humanity," Cruz's mom was saying. "For thousands of years it has existed, formed from stone, metal, and glass, even written in the stars."

Sailor halted the video again. "Clues three and four: formed from glass and written in the stars? She was talking about a pyramid, all right, but not the one at the Louvre."

"You mean the North Star pyramid?" broke in Emmett.

"Uh-huh. Think about it. It sits under the dome in the library that was painted to look like the *night sky* on the exact date the Society was founded in 1888. Plus, there's this . . ." Sailor hit the play arrow.

"Follow in the footsteps of the curious and courageous who have gone before you," continued Cruz's mom. "Only then can you unlock the greatest mystery of all. P.S. Don't forget your roots, kiddo. Good luck."

"Follow *in the footsteps*," repeated Sailor. "Remember how we had to weave through the explorer statues in the library to get to our class-room? They led us directly past the North Star award. Guys, everything we need to know *is* right here." Sailor touched the *N* on the building, then slid her finger down to rest on the black triangle. "Cruz's mom is telling him to go back to the Academy."

Cruz knew instantly that Sailor was right. How could he have missed something so obvious? Lani and Emmett were nodding as well. There was only one course of action to take: to change course. And that's exactly what *Condor* did.

"No time to waste," said Dr. Hightower, interrupting Cruz's thoughts. She glanced up and down the empty street. It was early and the traffic was light, as usual on a Saturday morning, but Cruz knew she was worried. So was he. Nebula agents had a way of appearing when and where you least expected them.

Cruz grabbed his backpack and hurried up the stairs with the others. At the Academy entrance, Dr. Hightower peered into the iris scanner, and a door swept open. They filed into a dark lobby.

It was strange to see the school so empty. And a little creepy, too. Cruz was used to it bustling with activity. It wouldn't be long, though, before all the explorers would be back for end-of-the-year ceremonies. Cruz was surprised not to see any security. He'd expected an officer to be in the grand room and escort them to the library. Something felt wrong.

Passing the front desk, Cruz broke out in a cold sweat. Could they be walking into a trap? He had one piece left to find. One piece! Had the Academy president been pretending to be on his side all this time only to turn him over to Brume now? Anything was possible, and everyone was a threat. There was nothing Cruz could do but play along. He'd have to wait for a chance to break away from the group and call security on his own—if it ever came.

"Overhead corridor lights on," said Dr. Hightower, taking the corner into the wide marble hallway. Two rows of lights flickered to life.

Cruz lagged behind, trying to figure out his next move. It did not go unnoticed. Sailor fell back, too, and gave him a quizzical look.

"Stay alert," he whispered, his eyes boring into Dr. Hightower's back. Sailor swallowed hard.

Dr. Hightower stopped at the biometric scanner outside the library. She looked around. "A security guard should have met us at the front entrance. I was hoping that perhaps the officer misunderstood and would be here instead."

Cruz let himself relax. A little.

Dr. Hightower tapped her comm pin. "Regina Hightower to security."

"Security here," said a woman. "Apologies for being late, Dr. Hightower. We're short-handed today and dealing with some comms issues. Officer Holt is on his way."

"Thank you. Tell the guard to meet us at the library entrance. Hightower, out."

The officer arrived a few minutes later. He was shorter than the Academy president but fit, his biceps and pecs bulging through his uniform. Officer Holt led them through the biometric checkpoint and into the library.

"Lights on, thirty percent, level one," ordered Dr. Hightower.

A few seconds later, about a third of the lights came on.

Lani stared up at the rotunda's five levels of books. "Wow!"

It was exactly how Cruz had felt the first time he'd seen the impressive dome.

There was no time for a tour. The group moved quickly and quietly through the stacks. The Academy president followed Officer Holt. Cruz fell in behind her. He stayed on her heels, never losing sight of the flowing tail of her long white coat. The group passed statues of Galileo, Sir Francis Drake, Ferdinand Magellan, Lewis and Clark, Nellie Bly, Bessie Coleman, and Rachel Carson. Reaching the figure of Charles Darwin, who stood guard over the natural science section, Cruz saw a strip of light between the shelves. He took the corner, and there it was. Lit with white

lights from inside its base, the six-foot-tall Egyptian-style crystal pyramid gleamed like a Christmas tree. All that was missing was a star.

"This place is one surprise after another," breathed Lani, coming to stand beside him.

She had no idea! Someday, once it was safe, Cruz would tell her about the Synthesis and the Archive right under her feet!

Dr. Hightower turned to them. "It's all yours, explorers. Try not to break it."

Cruz tossed his backpack onto the floor. Three more packs landed beside his. On the plane ride, they'd come up with their plan: Each explorer would take a side and search for a lock, button, swirl, emblem, gap—*anything* that might reveal a secret opening or drawer.

Cruz approached the pyramid from the front; Sailor went to his

right, Lani to his left, and Emmett headed to the back. Up close, Cruz couldn't see a single crack, flaw, or bubble—not even a fingerprint—in the crystal. The lights obscured the view of the floor inside the pyramid, but it appeared to be made of crystal, too. A large gold plate with an inscription was attached to Cruz's side, about waist high.

> NORTH STAR HONOR, Est. 7 May 1898
> Centuries before the invention of the compass, explorers found their way due north by following the North Star. This celestial beacon has led the trailblazer to distant lands, the navigator through treacherous seas, and the weary traveler home. The North Star award recognizes one explorer from each recruiting class who stands as a guiding light to others. These "stars" of our universe remind us that the future shines bright and boundless for those who seek to serve.

The engraved names of the winners began below and continued on to the other sides of the pyramid. Cruz felt around the edges of the inscribed plate, looking for a space or latch. It was firmly attached to the crystal. Starting at the bottom left vertex, he slid his hand up the angled edge, stretched for the apex, and came down the other side. The seams were solid.

"I'm not finding anything," called Sailor. "Anybody else?"

Cruz stood back. "Nope."

"Me neither," said Lani.

"Hey, I found my dad," called Emmett. "His name, I mean."

That got everyone to the back of the pyramid. There it was, carved into the glass: ALEXANDER JONATHON LU.

The explorers let out a collective sigh. Cruz knew that his friends were imagining what it would be like to have their names etched into the crystal. He was, too. Cruz began looking for another name likely to be near Dr. Lu's.

Lani found it first. It was in the same row as Emmett's dad. Everyone shifted to see it.

Cruz gently ran his fingertips over the block letters.

Weee-ooo-wee-ooo-wee-ooo!

The siren blared through the library. Four heads swiveled. Cruz didn't see or smell smoke. Within seconds, Dr. Hightower and Nyomie came around the pyramid.

"We may have a security breach," shouted Dr. Hightower. "Or you may have tripped an alarm connected to the award that I wasn't aware of—"

The piercing noise suddenly stopped.

Officer Holt peered around the corner. "Looks like we've got a faulty sensor at one of the entrances to the library, but my comm link went down before I could find out the location."

Dr. Hightower tried to call security, but her link didn't work, either.

"We'd better check them ourselves," said Dr. Hightower. "Maybe it's a false alarm, and maybe it isn't. I'll go with you, Holt. Nyomie, can you stay with the—"

"We'll be fine," said Nyomie. Cruz caught the wink she gave the Academy president.

Dr. Hightower and Officer Holt disappeared into the stacks.

"If Nebula *has* breached building security, they could show up any second." Emmett's emoto-glasses had gone dark. "We've got to find the cipher—and fast."

Lani twisted her silver strand of hair. "We've searched the pyramid top to bottom. What are we missing?"

"We followed in the footsteps of the curious and courageous. That's the entire clue," said Emmett. "Except for the P.S., of course, where she told Cruz not to forget his roots."

"That's got to mean something," said Sailor.

By now, they knew better than to gloss over things that seemed small. Those were the hints that usually ended up meaning the most. "My roots, huh?" Cruz thought out loud. "Okay, there's my dad and Aunt Marisol and my grandparents. I've got a great-uncle in Mexico City and some cousins in California…" Cruz found himself squinting at his friends.

Dr. Hightower must have turned up the lights to deal with the sensor issue. It took him a minute to figure out that the glow wasn't coming from above. It was coming from below. The lights in the base of the pyramid were getting brighter.

And brighter!

AND BRIGHTER!

Sailor shaded her eyes with her hand. "I think the North Star pyramid is about to blast off!"

"Everyone, get back," ordered Nyomie. "Don't look directly into the light."

Cruz heard her order but couldn't tear his eyes away from it, even when they started to water. Just when he thought he couldn't possibly stare at the sunburst another second, it vanished. It took a minute for him to blink away a few hundred spots, and when he did, he saw there was white smoke swirling inside the pyramid. Next to him, his mother's name was glowing blue!

Lani leaned in, still blinking. "Is it me or are some of the letters brighter than the others?"

She was right!

PETRA ALEXANDRIA SEBASTIAN

"P-R-E-S-S," spelled Cruz, putting them together. "Press. But how did it know—"

"You must have activated a biometric fingerprint ID when you touched your mom's name," concluded Emmett.

Sailor was elbowing him. "Don't keep us in suspense."

Cruz placed three icy fingers on his mom's name. "Here goes." He gently pushed on the glass, expecting a drawer to pop out. None did. Instead, a tremor shook his boots. A second later, the entire side of the pyramid began sliding up! The triangular pane of glass moved about four feet toward the apex before stopping. A wispy cloud floated through the space in the glass structure.

"My mind is officially blown," whispered Lani.

Cruz bent in front of the trapezoidal opening. Sailor edged closer, too.

"Careful, Sailor," warned Emmett. "It's meant for Cruz. If the program thinks an intruder is trying to gain access, it could shut down."

Sailor backed off.

Cruz extended his hand, putting it through the entry. He held his wrist there for a few tense seconds before pulling it out. The reading on his OS band reported no toxins. With one final look at Nyomie, Lani, Emmett, and Sailor, Cruz crept into the North Star pyramid.

At first, he couldn't see much through the haze, but the farther in he went, the clearer the air became. The fog was drifting to the walls of the pyramid, making it hard for anyone to see in. Or out. Was this by design? he wondered. Crawling toward the center, Cruz saw the floor was imprinted with a large chessboard. Instead of being black and white, however, the squares alternated between frosted and mirrored. Pausing at the rim of the board, Cruz touched one of the frosted squares. Immediately, a holographic 3D black chip appeared where his finger had been. Black circles began to materialize on every frosted square in the first three horizontal rows. Likewise, a dozen white chips began popping up on all the opaque squares in the last three rows. This left two full rows in the middle of the board without any chips. Ah, a game of checkers! Near Cruz's knees, a sentence appeared, as if written by an invisible hand: *Your move.*

When Cruz was four, his mother had taught him to play checkers. Well, she'd *tried* to. Instead of moving the pieces according to the rules, he'd wanted to build a fort, so that's what they'd done. From then on, their version of checkers involved constructing castles, bridges, and towers, which Cruz got to demolish when they were finished.

What should he do here? Play the right way? Or their way? His gut said fort, but if he was wrong ...

Cruz selected one of his black pieces and carefully placed it on top of one of the white ones in his mom's front row. Nothing happened. The two markers sat there. He was beginning to regret his decision when a white piece floated up to settle on his piece. *Yes!* Cruz placed another black piece on the white one and his mom's program did the same. They'd formed a four-piece tower. They made three more similar towers, positioning them to serve as the corners of the fort. Between these, they built four small towers, each two pieces tall. They were all out of checkers. Normally, they'd break out another box, but there wasn't one here. Instead, a new message was being scrawled near Cruz's knees: *Finish the game.*

Did she mean the way they'd done it when he was little?

Cruz stared at the board, the minutes ticking by. He knew he needed to make a decision, but what if it was the wrong one? Cruz took a deep breath. With one swipe of his hand, he toppled the fortress. The black and white chips scattered across the board.

A new message appeared: *Thanks for playing, Cruzer.*

He'd made the right choice.

"Sure, Mom," said Cruz softly, watching the words and checkers evaporate.

Once the last chip was gone, Cruz heard a whirring. Something was happening to the board. One of the mirrored squares in the center of the grid had begun to rise. It was connected to a cube—a *real* cube. The solid square stopped about six inches above the board. On its front vertical side, Cruz saw a small keyhole. A box!

Cruz fumbled for the gold key in his pocket. His hands were shaking so much it took him a couple of tries to get it into the lock. He turned the key. Cruz heard a click and the top of the box popped up slightly. His heart thumping, he nudged the lid up a little more.

Please let it be here!

He peered in. Looked left. Then right. Leaning against the corner of the box was a wedge of black marble.

The eighth cipher!

Cruz scooped out the stone. The moment he did, the box began descending into the floor. Cruz tapped the hinged lid shut before it did. It came to a stop, once again looking like all the other mirrored squares on the board. Cruz lifted the lanyard from his shirt. His fingers were still trembling when he snapped the new piece into place between the

seventh and first stones. It was a perfect fit.

Cruz let out a long sigh. The cipher was complete! All that was left now was to get instructions from his mom on where to deliver the formula. The most likely candidate was Dr. Fallowfeld, her colleague from the Synthesis. Of course, there was also a chance the recipient would be someone else Cruz knew, like his mom's friend Dr. Jojozi—

"Nice place you got here, but awfully snug even for a sub pilot."

Cruz closed his fist around the cipher. There was no need to turn. He knew who it was.

And why he was here.

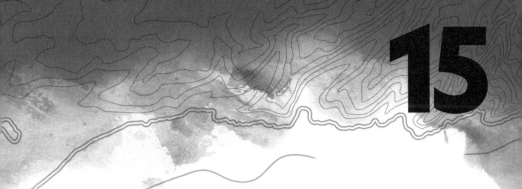

15

▶ **CRUZ HAD BARELY** enough time to open his crewneck and drop the lanyard inside before he was being jerked backward by the collar of his jacket. He heard a seam rip.

"There's one thing I'm dying to know," Tripp Scarlatos hissed into Cruz's ear. "How'd you survive that cave-in? What are you, some kind of magician?"

"Hardly." Cruz felt his temper simmer. "You don't need magic when you have science." Cruz's brain was a tornado. Nyomie would have never let Tripp into the pyramid without trying to stop him or, at the very least, called out a warning. What had happened out there? Where was everybody?

Tripp tightened his grip. "Hand over the piece."

"I...uh...I don't have it," choked Cruz, the front of his uniform cutting into his throat. "Not yet. I'm supposed to play a game to get it. See the checkerboard on the floor?"

Tripp tossed him away, giving Cruz the chance to scamper to the opposite side of the checkerboard. Cruz hadn't seen *Orion*'s sub pilot in almost six months. He looked the same—maybe a little thinner. His clothes were faded and wrinkled. The goatee was new. So was the gleaming hunting knife in his hand.

"Get on with it," barked Tripp. "Play the game."

"I'm...uh...supposed to wait for the program to start." He knew he had to stall until help arrived, if any was coming. "I still can't believe I ever looked up to you."

"Why shouldn't you?" Tripp puffed up. "I taught you how to pilot the sub, didn't I?"

"Only to gain my trust." Cruz inched a hand toward his jacket pocket. If he could reach his octopod . . .

"Uh-uh." Tripp wagged the silver blade. "Hands where I can see 'em."

Reluctantly, Cruz placed both palms on top of his thighs.

Tripp scowled. "What's taking so long?"

"I don't know."

"I think you do. Eh, it's only one piece. Give me the rest of the cipher. I know you wear it. She told us about the bio force field."

"F-force field? I don't know what you're talking—"

Tripp suddenly lunged for Cruz. A hand latched on to the shoulder of Cruz's jacket, twisting the fabric. Cruz felt a point against his throat. "You like science so much, here's some for ya," spit Tripp. "A bio force field relies on the body's electromagnetic impulses. You know what that means, don't you? Once you're gone, so is the force field. Game's over."

A wave of panic rolled through Cruz. Tripp was right. Cruz would bleed to death before his regenerative cells could repair a knife wound. The bio force field would then disintegrate, allowing Tripp to steal the cipher—the *entire* cipher.

Every problem has a solution—isn't that what Monsieur Legrand had said?

The challenge is to keep your emotions in check until you find it.

He heard his father's voice, too. *Manage your emotions, Cruz.*

Stay calm, Cruz told himself. *Breathe. Think.*

Tripp had the knife in his right hand and a chunk of Cruz's jacket in his left. That *was* a lot to hold. Cruz might be able to get away if he could tangle up Tripp. He'd have to be fast. Bold. Decisive. He'd have to act . . . NOW!

Spinning away from the blade, Cruz ducked under Tripp's left arm and came up on the back side of the sub pilot. Swerving to his left, he slammed both fists into the middle of Tripp's upper back. Tripp's legs went out from under him. He hit the floor, the impact knocking the knife from his hand. It skittered across the crystal. As the Nebula assassin struggled to get up, Cruz flew toward the pyramid opening. He was halfway out when he felt Tripp's hands lock on to his ankles. A hard jerk brought Cruz's knees out from under him. He crashed onto his stomach, bumping his chin on the floor. He flung his arms out and grabbed the edges of the pyramid entrance. The sides were sharp and slick. Glass dug into his fingers. Cruz thrashed his legs but couldn't seem to shake Tripp loose. Cruz clung with all his might, but he could feel his grip going. He was getting pulled back into the pyramid!

Just when he thought he could hold on no longer, a hand clamped on to his left wrist. Another hand went around his right wrist. Cruz strained to lift his head.

Lani!

She was crouched in front of him, her knees bent to near 90 degrees. "Grab on to me!"

Cruz let go of the pyramid and latched on to Lani. She started to pull. She pulled *hard*.

"Where is ... everybody?" grunted Cruz, trying to kick Tripp off.

"Locked in ... closet."

"You got away?"

Lani grimaced. "Could we ... discuss this ... later?"

"Sorry."

Cruz heard the bones in his wrists and shoulders popping. The veins in Lani's neck bulged. Her knuckles were bright white. She was fighting for every inch, but she was losing ground. Cruz could feel his strength draining, too. He looked up into fierce brown eyes. "Let me go, Lani," he hollered. "Shut the pyramid ... Get security."

Digging in her heels, Lani sank lower. "You'll be stuck in there ... with him."

"It's the only way."

"No!"

"You've got to do it!"

"NO!"

Cruz was suddenly skidding over the library floor. He was free!

The momentum had flung Lani back several feet. She'd landed on her rear. "Cruz, the door!"

Swiveling, Cruz stretched up to hit his mom's name, but his hand smacked the bottom of the crystal pane. That's right! The door was up. Her name was higher now. Tripp was crawling on his elbows toward the opening. He'd found his knife. There was blood on his mouth and hate in his eyes.

"Hurry!" screamed Lani.

Cruz staggered to his feet. He threw his arm up and hit his mother's name. The triangle of glass began to slide down.

"Arrrrrgh!" shrieked Tripp, launching the knife. It soared through the opening in the pyramid like an arrow searching for a target. Cruz made a C-curve with his stomach, and the blade whizzed past. Lani dropped flat onto her back. The knife flew over her, lodging in the side of a bookcase. The force of the impact whipped the handle back and forth.

"You'll never escape Nebula," bellowed Trip. "Brume is—"

The glass panel sliced off the rest of his sentence.

Cruz staggered over to Lani. He collapsed beside her, rolling onto his back.

"You . . . all right?" he panted.

"Yeah. You?"

"Uh-huh." Cruz rubbed his sore wrists, in turn. "I think my arms . . . are a foot longer."

She let out a weak laugh. "You got it, though, right? Tell me you got it."

He put a hand to his heaving chest. "I got it."

They stayed there for a few minutes, on their backs, gasping for air.

Lani was looking at the pyramid. "There's probably not much oxygen in there. We'd better get security to get him out and arrest him."

Typical. Lani hated to see anyone suffer, even the bad guy.

"I hope Dr. Hightower won't be too mad at us," said Lani. "Technically, we didn't break the pyramid but . . ."

"Lani?"

"Yeah?"

"Thanks for not letting go."

She turned to him. "Never."

"ONCE LANI AND I HAD TRIPP LOCKED** in the pyramid, we got everyone out of the storage room." Cruz sat on a peacock blue ottoman in the Academy president's living room, relating the events of the morning to his dad. He was surrounded by Emmett, Sailor, Lani, Nyomie, and Dr. Hightower—all trying to peer over his shoulder into the camera. "That part turned out to be a lot harder than we figured," he continued. "Tripp had jammed a piece of metal into the scanner. Mell had to fly into the cylinder and remove it so we could open the door."

His father shook his head. "What an ordeal!"

"It's certainly not how I'd intended for things to go," said Dr. Hightower. "I take full responsibility, Mr. Coronado—"

"Nebula is a formidable force," broke in Cruz's dad. "They have eyes and ears everywhere. Putting Tripp Scarlatos behind bars without any of you getting hurt or worse counts as a victory in my book."

Everybody chimed in to agree, and Dr. Hightower gave them an appreciative grin.

"I do have one question, though," said Cruz's dad. "Lani, how *did* you escape the storage room?"

"That's easy." She shrugged. "I never went in. When Tripp showed up, I ducked out of sight as fast as I could. I knew he'd be expecting Sailor and Emmett, but he's never met me. I saw him herd everyone into the back room and tried to call security. Unfortunately, my comm pin wasn't working. Tripp had shut down all comms."

Dr. Hightower's phone was ringing. "I'll need to take this," she said. "It's my security detail. Excuse me." She got up off the sofa to answer the call in a quieter spot.

"We told her we'd spend the night in our old dorm, but she insisted we come and stay with her," said Sailor. "Dr. Hightower says it's not safe at school."

"She's right," interjected Nyomie. "Nebula knows you're in Washington, D.C., and by now they must also know you took down one of their agents."

"The sooner you deliver the formula to its final destination, the better," said Cruz's dad.

Cruz patted the upper-left pocket of his jacket that held the holo-journal. He couldn't wait to open it! Unfortunately, he had to.

When she returned, Dr. Hightower insisted they have lunch. It was nearly two o'clock, and they hadn't eaten since having breakfast on the plane. Once they said goodbye to Cruz's dad, the group headed into the kitchen. Lani and Sailor helped Dr. Hightower get burgers on the grill. Nyomie went to work on a fruit salad. Cruz and Emmett prepped the potatoes for french fries.

At the sink, Cruz peeled a russet potato. Emmett stood beside him, waiting to put it through the slicer. "Tripp said something in the pyramid," Cruz whispered to his friend. "He knew about the cipher's bio force field."

"How did he know?"

"He said *she* told Nebula."

"She?" Emmett frowned. "Zebra?"

"I don't think so." Cruz shaved the last ribbon of skin off the potato and handed it to Emmett. "None of us knew about the force field. Dr. Vanderwick didn't know it was there until she tried to grab the cipher off my neck, and she sure didn't have time to tell anybody before she, you know..."

Emmett placed the potato in the bed of the slicer. "That leaves only one other Nebula agent still on *Orion* that we know of."

Their eyes met.

Jaguar! The explorer spy was a girl.

"Emmett!" squealed Lani. She was standing at the grill with a raw hamburger patty in one hand. "Your glasses!"

The emoto-glasses were a bouquet of flowers blooming in time-lapse—yellow, orange, pink, and white petals spilling over one another.

"What *are* you guys talking about?" wondered Sailor.

"What else?" replied Emmett. "Food!" He pushed down on the handle of the slicer, and a handful of little raw potato bars slid into the outer tray.

After lunch, the explorers gathered in Dr. Hightower's living room to open the holo-journal. Dr. Hightower and Nyomie took a walk in the garden to discuss Academy business, they said. Cruz knew it was really to give them privacy. He was grateful. Dr. Hightower promised all along she would support but not intrude on Cruz's mission. Even now, in her own home, she remained true to her word.

Forming a semicircle around the coffee table with Emmett, Lani, and Sailor, Cruz activated the journal. Lani pointed her tablet camera up to record everything. When prompted, Cruz presented his mother's holo-image the eighth piece of the cipher. It was always nerve-racking, waiting for her to confirm the authenticity of a piece, but this time, the final time, was much worse. After what felt like the longest minute on Earth, his mom said, "Well done. This is a genuine piece."

The explorers sighed.

"Congratulations, Cruz," said his mom. "I know it must have taken courage, perseverance, and sacrifice to come this far. I'm so proud of you. I only wish I could be there to tell you so in person."

Cruz beamed. "Thanks."

"I'm also pleased to report that you have unlocked your final clue," said his mom.

Cruz's smile vanished. "Final c-clue?" he stammered. He hadn't expected he'd have to solve *another* puzzle. By the shocked looks on the faces of his friends, they hadn't, either.

"Although you are nearing your final task," Cruz's mother went on, "this is by far the most difficult part of your journey. You must be willing to go where few have gone. You must expect the unexpected. You must keep an open mind and heart no matter what you find. Can you do this? Will you?"

Although still stunned, Cruz did not hesitate. "Yes, Mom. I can ... I will."

She was studying him. Was the program looking for biological and behavioral "tells" the way Fanchon's virtugraph measured changes in such things as pulse, blood pressure, breathing rate, and body language? If she was, she'd discover he was telling the truth. Cruz was sincere in his pledge. He would do whatever it took to complete the mission. He would not let her down.

"Good." She seemed to relax. "Cruz, once you attach the eighth piece to the other seven you will activate a sequence of . . . a sequence of . . ."

The program was hiccuping, the picture breaking up.

"Mom?" Cruz instinctively reached out, his hand passing through the fractured image.

". . . slow and inefficient in a high-tech world." The holo-video jumped ahead. "Right now, it's the only way I have to . . . no single person has . . . information." The audio was cutting in and out.

"Mom, wait! Pause program!"

The video lurched again. ". . . to reach you. You must decode . . . to unlock . . . destination . . . have any questions?"

"Yes, Mom. Wait! I have questions!"

"Try rewinding it," prompted Emmett.

"Rewind program!" wailed a panicked Cruz.

"Thank you, Cruzer," said his mother, as if she hadn't heard him. "You will forever have my gratitude." She crossed her hands over her heart. "And my love."

"Pause! Rewind! Freeze! *Stop program!*" Cruz was yelling every command he could think of, but his mother's image was already beginning to fade.

"End journal," she said. "Initiate sequence pi, alpha, gamma, one, one, two, nine."

The last pixel vanished. Cruz stood there, transfixed. His mind was as blank as the air in front of him.

"Don't worry," said Lani. "We'll let it power down, then reboot in a few minutes and go through it all again. I'm sure it'll be okay."

"Probably a minor glitch," said Sailor.

"Or dust in the sphere," offered Emmett.

Their words would have comforted Cruz had the hovering orb deconstructed itself and returned to its flat rectangular state, as usual. That was not what happened. Instead, the white ball began to spin. Slowly, at first, then faster and faster. As it rotated, a top point began spewing a fountain of red, white, and blue fireworks! The explorers gasped, watching the colorful sparks illuminate Dr. Hightower's vaulted ceiling. The show lasted less than 10 seconds before the multi-pointed globe belched a giant puff of smoke and *poof!*

The journal was gone—truly, completely, and forever gone.

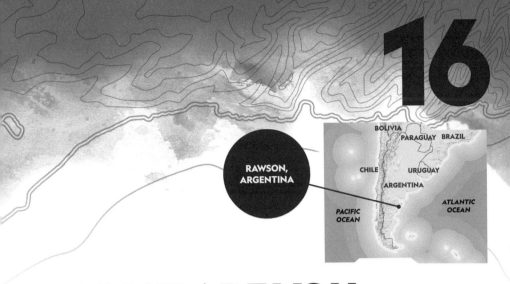

16

"**WHAT ARE YOU** going to do now?"

Looking up at a moonless sky through *Orion*'s bubbled observation deck, Cruz gave Bryndis the only answer he had: "I don't know."

"Couldn't you give the cipher to Dr. Fallowfeld?"

"Yes. I could also give it to Aunt Marisol, Dr. Hightower, Fanchon, Jericho Miles, Dr. Jo, the Synthesis…"

"*Já*, I see your problem. You'll have to pick someone you trust."

She made it sound so easy. But if he picked the wrong person…

"Dr. Jo told me to be careful who I gave the formula to *if* I gave it to anyone at all," said Cruz. "I think she wants me to keep it, maybe even follow in my mom's footsteps."

"That's a pretty big responsibility."

"Tell me about it."

"You don't have to decide right away, do you?"

"No," he answered, but the clock *was* ticking.

Prescott would be coming for the cipher. He would also be coming for Cruz. Emmett was in danger, too. The Nebula assassin still believed Emmett was Jaguar. This is not what Cruz had expected when he'd opened the journal for the final time. Things were supposed to be getting less complicated, not more!

"You look knackered, as Sailor would say," observed Bryndis.

They'd had to get up at three o'clock that Sunday morning to make it back to *Orion* by bedtime. Between the plane and helicopter flights, it was 13 hours of travel time, plus two more hours lost crossing time zones. They'd returned to the ship, now anchored off the port city of Rawson, Argentina, with an hour to spare. Cruz should have been in bed like Sailor and Emmett, but he needed to stretch his legs and he wanted to see Bryndis.

"When did you last eat?" she asked.

"Uh...a couple of hours ago." He shoved his hands in his pockets.

"You did not. I can always tell when you're lying."

"You can? How?"

"Not a chance. If I tell, you'll fix it."

He laughed.

"Come on. It's almost bedtime. We can stop at the snack table on the way down."

"Okay." Bryndis was right. Cruz *had* lied about eating, but he hadn't been hungry for dinner. They'd had a big lunch on the plane.

"Did you see that Professor Luben graded our field report?" asked Bryndis as they strolled out of the observation lounge.

"I did," replied Cruz. "I got his message but didn't open it. Figured I'd had enough bad news for one weekend."

"We got an A."

His neck snapped around. "Really? After we got back late, I thought for sure—"

"Me too. Not only did we get an A, but—" She stopped.

"What?"

"I don't want to spoil it. This is one you have to read for yourself."

Now Cruz *was* intrigued!

Inside the dining room, on the long table near the entrance, they found the usual assortment of fruit, nuts, seeds, chips, and juice. Chef Kristos had also set out small paper cups of his homemade trail mix: a combo of peanuts, cashews, dried cranberries, popcorn, chocolate chips, and white-chocolate-covered pretzels. Cruz took one of the cups. Bryndis chose a paper tube of honey-roasted almonds. They left the dining room, heading down the passage and past the empty third-deck lounge. Cruz had just tossed a handful of trail mix into his mouth when his comm pin blared "Professor Coronado to Cruz Coronado."

He tried to answer. With his mouth full it came out, "Cruth, ear, Am Mahwithall."

Bryndis laughed.

"I guess this means you're safely back on board," said Aunt Marisol.

He chewed and swallowed. "We got back around eight thirty."

"Can you talk?" She snickered. "Or should I say, can you speak freely?"

"Bryndis and I are on our way down to the explorers' deck," he said, which meant no.

"I just got off the phone with your dad," she said, which meant she knew everything. "We'll chat later. See you both in the morning. Professor Coronado, out."

"I'm excited we're going on a fossil hunt but bummed it's our last mission," said Bryndis. She paused at the top of the grand staircase. "I just had a terrible thought. What if they switch up the teams next year?"

"Aunt Marisol says they keep them the same, unless someone wants to change."

"Not me. I don't want to change a thing. I like being on Cousteau." She dropped her head. "With you. Do you? Like it, too, I mean?"

"Uh ... yes." Cruz had a weird feeling they weren't talking about the team anymore. "I like things the way they are ... a lot."

Ugh! Could he not say a simple sentence without screwing it up?

Bryndis had lowered her hand from her face. She was smiling that smile that always made his heart thump faster. It worked this time, too.

With five minutes to curfew, the explorers' passage was deserted, as usual. At Bryndis's door, they said their good nights. Cruz started to walk on when he felt a hand on his arm.

"Don't do it," said Bryndis. "Don't keep the cipher, Cruz. If you do, you'll always be running from Nebula."

He looked into her pale blue eyes. "If I trust the wrong person, I'll always regret it."

Looking left and right down the passage, Bryndis leaned in and gave Cruz a feathery kiss on the lips. Turning, she waved her wrist over the scanner, opened the door, and was gone.

Cruz put his hands in his pockets, spun, and began strolling toward his cabin. He felt lighter than a cloud.

The lights flickered.

Uh-oh! Zipping the rest of the way to the end of the passage, Cruz entered cabin 202 as quietly as he could so he wouldn't wake his roommate. Emmett had dimmed the lights enough so that he could sleep, but not so much that Cruz would crash into things when he came in. Cruz brushed his teeth in record time, put on his pajamas, and got into bed.

Cruz closed his eyes. Five minutes later, he opened them again. This was not working. He flung out an arm, fishing around in the dark for his tablet on the nightstand. Finding it, he slid it onto his pillow, flipped onto his stomach, and opened his teacher's message.

SUB: Team Cousteau Heroína Island Mission Evaluation

FROM: Professor A. Luben

Field Report Comments: Excellent use of resources and equipment to collect data. Supporting research, observations, and photographs were thorough. Monsieur Legrand's evaluation is below.

Faculty Observer Evaluation

Team Cousteau was well prepared. Members

were cooperative. Decisions were made with all opinions valued and considered. Succeed or fail, they were in it together. Magnifique! Due to transportation issues, Team Cousteau's mission was originally canceled. The explorers devised a clever alternative to take the kayaks. We proceeded, but precious time was lost. It is my recommendation that Cousteau not be penalized for returning to Orion past deadline and that they earn bonus points for demonstrating the poise, innovation, and perseverance we encourage. The easy choice would have been to accept the cancellation and take the day off. Cousteau did neither. Row on, brave explorers! M. Legrand

Field Report: 98 points
Mission Performance: 100 points
Bonus points: 50 per team member
Final Grade: A

Well done, Cousteau!
Professor A. Luben

Smiling, Cruz set his tablet on the nightstand. He rolled onto his back. He felt for the stone on his chest under his tee, absently tracing the seams between the pieces. It was Cousteau's most positive evaluation all year, though the mission had been far from smooth. Maybe the best missions weren't the ones where everything went perfectly but where you had to think fast, fight hard, and push past obstacles. As long as you didn't give up, you were always in the game, right?

A completed cipher, a Nebula agent captured, and a good grade. Oh, and a kiss, too. Not a bad weekend, all in all.

Cruz fell asleep still grinning.

HANDS CLASPED BEHIND THE BACK of her kiwi green sweater, Aunt Marisol paced in front of the holo-map. "Searching for dinosaur fossils may sound easy and fun." Dark eyes surveyed the classroom of explorers. "I can assure you prospecting is *not* easy. Finding a fossil is like looking for a needle in the desert. And that's just where you are headed. Over the next four days, you will travel over rough roads, hike up to ten miles per day through rugged terrain, and endure some of the hottest fall daytime temperatures this part of Argentina has seen in more than a century. You will work harder than you've worked on any mission so far, probably harder than you've ever worked in your *life,* but"—her eyes brightened—"it will be worth it. You *will* have fun."

Emmett bent toward Cruz. "Her idea of fun and mine? Totally different."

"Each team will have two adult guides," continued Aunt Marisol. She motioned to the back of the room, where their other professors stood, along with Fanchon Quills and Jericho Miles. "You're guides will have several potential fossil-bearing sites for you to search in Patagonia, based on geologic maps and Fossil Net."

Fossil Net was the Society's predictive computer program. In class, they'd learned about software that could scan satellite photos for geographic clues to pinpoint fossil hot spots, places where the preserved remains of ancient animals or traces of them (like footprints) were more likely to be found. Such programs could help paleontologists narrow their fossil search areas and sometimes discover ones they hadn't even considered.

"Be sure to bring your PANDA units," said Aunt Marisol. "You'll also be provided with all the necessary hand tools—chisels, hammers, brushes, and so forth. Once I release you, please go to your cabins to pack, then report to aquatics at nine a.m. sharp. Jaz and her staff will transport you to the mainland via tender boat, where your Auto Autos will be waiting. We've already preassigned guides for each team through random drawing." Aunt Marisol reached for her tablet. "Team Galileo, your guides will be Professors Benedict and Modi. Team Magellan, you're with Professor Luben and Fanchon. Monsieur Legrand and Professor Ishikawa are assigned to Team Earhart, and Jericho and I will lead Team Cousteau."

At last! It was all Cruz could do to keep from letting out a whoop. He'd been on a dig with his aunt once before, in Turkey, but that was with the rest of the class. Finally, she would lead them on a breakout mission. This was what he'd been waiting for all year!

"Explorers?" Monsieur Legrand marched down the aisle. "There's one more thing."

"Wuh-oh," groaned Emmett. "Here it comes."

"For your last mission," said Monsieur Legrand, "two members of each team will rotate to another team."

Monsieur Legrand's words sinking in, Cruz heard popcorn cries of "No!" and "Why?"

"Why else?" Monsieur Legrand arched an eyebrow. "To stretch your wings."

"Or crash to earth," moaned Dugan.

"It's only for this mission," soothed Aunt Marisol. "No one expects you to have the same connection with your hybrid team that it's taken your regular team months to build. However, it's critical that you learn how to work with others outside your circle. Remember how the teams were shuffled for the robotics Funday activity? That was a practice run, and you all passed with flying colors. I know you will face this twist with your usual enthusiasm and optimism."

Lani leaned toward Cruz. "When she asks for volunteers, I'll raise my hand."

"You don't have to—"

"I don't mind. I'm the newbie. It's only fair."

Feeling a thump on his shoulder, Cruz turned to find Emmett with his head tipped back. He was pointing up at a ceiling that had become a holographic sky! Six miniature hot-air balloons were flowing from the front of the room to the back to the front again, as if caught in a jet stream. A small square rattan basket dangled from fishing line below each black-and-yellow-striped balloon.

"Switching teams is not a punishment," said Monsieur Legrand. "This is not a competition, and there are no winners or losers. You will draw for placement."

The six balloons began to descend—one over each team. Team Cousteau's landed in Sailor's lap. As she reached into the basket, Cruz went up on one knee to see her take out...

A deck of playing cards. *A little boring, considering the balloons and all,* thought Cruz.

Monsieur Legrand directed them to open their packs. Bryndis, Dugan, Emmett, Lani, and Cruz gathered around Sailor's desk. She broke the seal and fanned out the cards. On the back of each card was a different photo of a place or animal. Dugan tapped a picture of a metal rectangle jutting out of a mountainside. "Hey, it's the Svalbard seed vault."

"There's the Horta maze in Barcelona," said Emmett.

Bryndis pointed to a close-up photo of the delicate pink petal-shaped insect. "And the orchid mantis from Borneo."

"These are all places we've explored and animals we've seen this year," said Sailor. She flipped a card. It was blank. She turned over several more. They were blank, too.

"Uh... Monsieur Legrand." Dugan raised a hand. "We got a misprinted deck."

"So did we," chimed in Weatherly.

"Same here," said Zane.

It looked like everyone had bad cards.

"You ought to know by now that we do things differently at Explorer Academy." Monsieur Legrand's words were spliced with impatience. "Please shuffle your deck, then fan out the cards on your desk, photo-side up. Each team member please choose a card. Explorers, once you have your card, hold it flat against your palm, again, photo-side up."

Sailor cut and shuffled the deck a few times, while Dugan griped about how silly it was to shuffle cards with nothing on them. Cruz had to admit, he had a point. They watched Sailor slide the cards out into a semicircle on her desk. She pushed them apart a bit so they could see the pictures. Bryndis went first. She selected a photo of right whales breaching in the Bay of Fundy and placed it on her left palm, picture-side up. Dugan searched until he found the seed vault card and took it. Emmett chose a photo of an Adélie penguin on a pinnacle iceberg. Cruz went for an aerial view of Waterberg Plateau Park in Namibia. His teammates grinned, remembering how they'd foiled the pangolin poachers. Lani slid a picture of *Orion* out of the deck. Sailor chose the thylacine. Naturally!

Monsieur Legrand was checking to make sure everyone was holding a card the way he'd instructed. Once he was satisfied, he said, "You may now turn your cards."

"This is dumb." Dugan snorted. "We already know there's noth— Whoa!" There was a big green 31 on his card where it had been blank before: no suit, like spades or diamonds, only a big green 31.

"An incalescence deck!" said Lani.

Dugan made a face. "An inka-what?"

"Incalescence. The ink is invisible until it's activated by the heat from our hands."

The rest of Team Cousteau quickly turned their cards, too. Emmett had drawn a 19, Lani got a 39, Bryndis had an 8, and Sailor's card was 26. Cruz's card read 47.

Now what? The class fell silent, waiting for Monsieur Legrand's next instructions. Nobody wanted to switch teams. Nobody. Cruz and his teammates exchanged worried looks. Monsieur Legrand was wrong. Two of them were about to lose.

But which two?

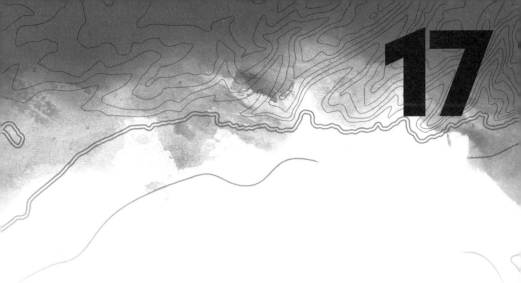

17

EMMETT STOOD in front of the

dresser, flinging socks into his open duffel bag. "Talk about unfair."

"It was luck of the draw." Cruz reached to the top shelf in their closet for his safari hat. "How much fairer could it have been?"

"I meant springing the switch on us at the last minute."

"I think that was the point—you know, to shake us up a little."

"Yeah. Well. It worked."

Cruz could see that. The emoto-glasses were practically shooting flames. "It's only for one mission, Emmett. It'll be okay."

"How will it be okay? You're going to another team, and I'm staying on ours, which gives Nebula the perfect chance to strike. I don't like this."

Cruz didn't like it, either, but they would have to play the cards they were dealt—literally. "Professor Luben and Fanchon will be there, too," he reminded his roommate. "Nebula would hardly come after me with the whole team around."

"Tripp did. And aren't you forgetting something—I mean someone— else?"

He meant Jaguar.

"And then there's Magellan." Emmett gave him a pained grin. "Of all the teams to get stuck on ..."

It was bad enough Cruz wouldn't get to go on a mission with Aunt

Marisol, but to get stuck on their archrival's team, too? Worse, Matteo and Yulia were the two members of Magellan who were being shifted. That meant Cruz would have to work with Ali, who didn't like him. Scratch that. Ali *hated* him.

"Yulia is going to Earhart." grumbled Emmett, still pitching socks into his bag. How many pairs did he have anyway? "But that still leaves Kat and Tao. What if one of them is Jaguar?"

Cruz had no argument for that. All he knew was it was a done deal. He had to go, and he didn't want to leave with Emmett in such a sour mood. "Can't we try to make the best of it?" pleaded Cruz. "You... uh... I don't mean to tell you what to wear, but you might want to take something else besides socks..."

"Huh?" Emmett peered into his duffel, then started yanking out socks and tossing them back into his drawer. "I'm supposed to stay with you. Maybe I should call Dr. High—"

"No!" Cruz didn't want any special treatment.

There was a knock on the open door. "Hi, partner." Bryndis grimaced. "Ready to go?"

"Almost," said Cruz. The only bright spot in his banishment to Team Magellan was that Bryndis would be there, too. She'd drawn the low card. That's how Monsieur Legrand determined who would be swapping teams—lowest and highest cards.

Cruz slid his arms into his jacket. He did a quick inventory to make sure he hadn't forgotten anything. He felt for his shadow badge and GPS pin attached to his left lapel, then his comm pin and Mell's honeycomb remote on the right. Opening his top-right pocket, he peered in. A tiny black-and-yellow body rested in the corner. Mell. Check. Octopod? That was in his bottom-right pocket. Check. Virtugraph? Cruz tugged down the zipper of his bottom-left pocket. A beam of light shot out!

Something must be wrong with the virtugraph. Turning his back on Bryndis and Emmett, Cruz lifted out the truth compass. The device was perfectly fine, yet his pocket was *still* glowing. Cruz dipped his hand in again. This time, he scooped out something he'd nearly forgotten was there: the ankh pin from his mother. Weird. The little looped-cross pin was giving off a solid golden light. Cruz couldn't find a switch. How was he supposed to turn it off? He wasn't even sure how he'd turned it on. *Had* he turned it on? Or was something else happening? Maybe Aunt Marisol could shed some light on his light...

"Cruz?"

Bryndis and Emmett were waiting.

"Uh... right. Coming!" Cruz dropped the ankh pin and virtugraph back into his pocket. He pulled the zipper tight so the light didn't shine through. No time to worry about it now. He'd have to deal with it later.

In the crowded passage, the trio found Dugan, Sailor, and Lani, and they made their way to aquatics. Once they arrived, Cruz and Bryndis said a solemn farewell to their teammates and crossed the compartment to where Professor Luben, Fanchon, and the rest of Team Magellan were gathered. On their way, they passed Felipe and Weatherly, who were moving to Cousteau from Galileo. Everyone was trying hard to look confident and happy. Too hard.

Zane, Tao, Kat, and Ali took up both benches next to the door. Cruz lifted a hand. "Hi."

Tao gave them a friendly smile. "Hey, guys."

"Welcome to Magellan," said Kat. She sounded like she meant it.

Hunched over his tablet, Ali didn't look up.

Zane scooted closer to Tao so Cruz and Bryndis could share his end of the bench. "Professor Luben says our instructions are on our tablets," he told them. "Our base camp is in Los Altares. It's about a three-and-a-half-hour drive from the port of Rawson. We'll stop in Trelew to pick up food, tools, and supplies on our way."

"Okay, thanks." Cruz pulled his tablet out of his pack. He found Los Altares on the satellite map. It was a tiny village in a valley along the Chubut River west of Trelew, about halfway across Argentina. Los Altares was Spanish for "the altars," a name it earned for its tall rock formations that resembled pedestals. From the beautiful photos, it looked like a great place to search for fossils. Maybe this mission wouldn't be so bad after all.

"Magellan, we are ready to transport you to Rawson." Jaz's voice came over the loudspeaker. "Report to *Rigel*, please."

Cruz kept scrolling through images of Los Altares's monolithic outcrops, until Zane nudged him. "That's us."

"Oh yeah." This new team was going to take a little getting used to. Cruz grabbed his gear and followed the others through the door and down the steps to the launch deck. Waiting to board, Cruz glanced up.

Sailor was at the rail. "Be careful," she mouthed.

"You too," he mouthed back.

Cruz felt a bump against his backpack. It sent him staggering forward. He banged his hip on the rail as Ali shoved past him to get on the hovercraft.

"Right, Aunt Marisol." Cruz winced. "So. Much. Fun."

BENEATH A BRILLIANT BLUE SKY feathered with lazy cirrus clouds, Team Magellan trekked across the desert shrublands. They were bound for a 200-foot-tall cathedral of rock, its sandstone strata laid down in horizontal strips of browns, golds, and rusty reds. It was a majestic ancient formation more than a quarter mile in length. However, all heads were down, all eyes scouring the ground. The explorers may have had the latest in modern technology at their fingertips, but little of it applied when it came to finding a fossil.

That part of prospecting hadn't changed much in centuries. The students had learned that the best way to discover a fossil was to look for fragments of one on, or sticking out of, the ground. Today, Cruz had an extra pair of eyes helping out, thanks to Mell circling overhead.

As the explorers hiked, the only sounds were the warm wind fluttering their clothes and the shuffling of boots over hard-packed soil. Aunt Marisol had warned them that discovering a dinosaur fossil would be like finding a needle in a desert, but Cruz hadn't truly believed that. Until now. Tomorrow, Team Magellan would be heading back to *Orion*, and what did they have to show for three days in the Patagonian Desert? A handful of small hunks of rock bearing fossilized leaves, rodent bones, and bird tracks. But not one needle.

Once they reached the slope a few hundred yards from the outcrop, Professor Luben let his pack slide from his shoulders. "Let's break for water and a snack."

"How about some shade?" joked Zane, wiping the sweat from his brow. "I'd give anything for a tree right now."

Tao shook the dust from her hair. "I'm so ready for a shower."

"Funny how little things become big things when we're away from the comforts of home," said Fanchon. "Out here, all that matters is what you need to survive."

It was true. Shade, hats, water, sunglasses—without these basic necessities, they would have been in trouble. They'd discovered for themselves how the temperatures in the Patagonian desert this time of year could swing widely from night to day. In a matter of hours, the explorers had gone from shivering in their sleeping bags to roasting under a midday sun. Although his uniform kept his core cool, Cruz's feet were broiling. The dry, sandy air scraped his cheeks and chapped his lips.

Dropping his pack, Cruz tapped his honeycomb remote. "Mell, return to me, please." The MAV came zipping back, landing on his shoulder.

Fanchon began refilling water bottles, while Professor Luben handed out Chef Kristos's homemade granola bars. Unwrapping his bar, Cruz tipped his head to study the massive skyscraper of rock. There had to be a dinosaur fossil in that thing *somewhere*. If only he had Emmett's emoto-glasses with magnified vision to search the enormous outcrop...

Wait! He might have something even better!

Cruz knelt next to Bryndis. "What if we used our PANDAs?"

"For what?" She munched on her granola. "We haven't found any fossils to identify."

"I meant *our* PANDAs." He gave her a smirk. "Yours and mine."

"I don't see why—Oh! You mean, our upgrades!" She wrinkled her brow. "How exactly will they help?"

"I'm not completely sure," he admitted. "But something called high-definition ultra-sensitive ingression analysis sure sounds like it ought to tell the difference between fossilized rock and regular rock, right?"

"Right." Fanchon's head appeared between them. "Apologies. Listening to other people's conversations is so rude. That aside, not only can your PANDAs detect the tiniest bit of exposed cast, mold, trace, or true form fossil, but they can peer approximately 4.25 inches below the surface of the rock face to locate these specimens."

Cruz and Bryndis stared at her, stunned. Did she say their PANDAs could see through stone?

"Which you would have known had you read the manual," admonished Fanchon. She began refilling their water bottles. "Also, I can connect your PANDAs to Fossil Net, allowing you to screen a larger area of rock and zero in on the places that are most likely to contain fossils. If you want me to, I mean."

Cruz started to tell her to hook their PANDAs up to the software, when Bryndis shook her head. When Fanchon moved on to fill more water bottles, Bryndis tugged Cruz back down. "Are we sure we want to do this?"

"What do you mean?"

"The upgrade was *our* prize. Now we're going to share it...with *them*?"

Cruz understood how she felt. It was Cousteau's reward for winning the geography bee. He thought it over for a minute. "I know it's weird, but things are different now and we have to think differently. It's not us versus them anymore," reasoned Cruz. "We *are* them. It's not betraying Cousteau to use the technology we won. I think everyone on Cousteau would agree." He chuckled. "Well, Dugan might stomp his feet a little, but he'd come around. If things were reversed, if they were in our place, it would be okay with us, wouldn't it?"

"*Já*, I guess."

Cruz could tell she wasn't sold.

He watched Fanchon pour water into Ali's bottle. That's what the tech lab chief had meant by "if you want me to." It had to be Bryndis and Cruz's decision to share their prize.

"We don't have to do it," said Cruz. "We could say nothing, but the way things are going, that's probably what we'll be going home with: nothing."

Bryndis bit her lip. "That would be a disappointment. Okay. Let's do it."

Before she could change her mind, Cruz was on his feet and telling the rest of the team about their upgraded PANDAs. Before he'd finished, the tech lab chief had pulled out her tablet and was connecting them to Fossil Net. "It'll take a bit to complete the interface, so give it, say, about fifteen minutes before using your devices," directed Fanchon.

Reenergized, everyone was suddenly on their feet.

"It's after three o'clock," said Professor Luben. "We can cover more territory faster if we split up. Tao, Zane, and Bryndis, why don't you come with me to the east corner of the rock face? Ali, Kat, and Cruz, you head with Fanchon to the west corner. We'll meet back here in one hour. No climbing. It's too remote here to get help in a timely manner should anyone get injured."

Cruz slid his water bottle back into the netted pocket on the side of his pack. "Mell, lift off for ten seconds, please," he instructed. His drone helicoptered up to let him sling on his pack, then settled back down onto the shoulder strap. Cruz felt Ali's eyes on him but did not meet his gaze. He'd been doing his best to stay out of Ali's way on this mission. So far, so good.

With calls of "Good luck," the teams went their separate ways.

"Fanchon, Professor Coronado told us you used to do dinosaur reconstruction," said Kat, falling into step beside her. Ali and Cruz followed. The four stayed at the bottom of the hill, hiking parallel to the rock.

"I did," replied Fanchon. "While getting my master's degree, I worked for the Society's museum creating 3D computerized models of dinosaurs. We used photogrammetry and bio robotics to simulate how a particular dinosaur might have looked and moved."

"Did you ever see skin and fur fossils?" wondered Kat.

"Oh yes. Skin, fur, feathers, spikes, spines, even stomach contents."

"You mean ...?"

"Yep. Every once in a while, I got to glimpse a dinosaur's last meal."

"Cool!" the explorers cried in unison.

As Fanchon continued sharing her knowledge of dinosaur digestion, which also included their favorite topic, coprolites (aka poo), Cruz noticed Ali kept sneaking glances at Mell. She'd moved off the strap of his pack and was clinging to her honeycomb remote.

"She won't fall," assured Cruz, the next time Ali glanced at the drone. "She has tarsal claws like a real bee. They give her a firm grip."

Ali gave a nod minus his usual scowl.

"Cruz and Ali!" Fanchon was walking backward, gesturing to the outcrop. "How about if you guys start here and work east? Kat and I will continue on to the corner."

The boys turned and headed up the slope, stopping about 30 feet from the mammoth wall of rock. Cruz shrugged off his pack, opened it, and took out his PANDA. Switching the unit on, he held it out to his teammate.

Ali hesitated. "But ... I thought ... Don't *you* want to use it?"

"Nah." Cruz zipped open the outer pocket of his pack, where he'd stored his safety goggles, chisel, hammer, trowel, brush, and small knife. "Excavation is my favorite part. I'll uncover anything you find."

"O-okay." Ali took the PANDA. "Thanks."

It was the first nice word Ali had said to him in, well, he couldn't remember how long.

Ali looked down at the pear-shaped unit. "We're linked to Fossil Net. You ready, Cruz?"

Gazing up at the fortress of sandstone, Cruz felt a surge of excitement. He sure hoped this worked. He put on his safety goggles. "Ready."

Ali aimed the PANDA at the rock. "Since we can't climb, how about if I do a slow sweep from the bottom to about five feet up in sections?"

"Sounds good," said Cruz. "I'll be right behind you."

It was hot and getting hotter by the minute. Cruz felt the crunch of sand between his teeth. And his toes. He took off his hat to wipe the sweat from his brow.

Fifteen minutes later, Ali was still scanning. Cruz was beginning to think it was hopeless—then his PANDA unit started to emit a low hum.

"I think I've got something!" Ali called over his shoulder. He walked faster and faster toward the cliff until he was jogging, then running! Ali dropped to his knees at the base of the wall. "Here! Here!"

Cruz, who was quick to catch up, didn't see anything. "Are you sure...?"

Ali placed his index finger on a small bulge. "It's a dinosaur bone!"

Cruz scrambled to pull the thick round brush from his pack. "What kind?"

"Uh...let's see...The analysis says it's sedimentary sandstone dating back to the Cretaceous period." Ali hopped to his feet. Hunched, he began moving along the outcrop, pointing the PANDA to where stone met dirt. "It's ninety-seven million years old."

Cruz was frantically brushing dirt from the fossil. Seeing the rounded bulb of a bone appear, he reached for his chisel. The idea was to carefully remove the soil and rock around the fossil without damaging it or any other bones that might be around it.

"We'd better call Fanchon," yelled Ali, now 20 feet from Cruz. "There's a dinosaur skeleton under the surface, and it looks like it's nearly complete."

Cruz sat up. "But what *kind* of dinosaur?"

"I... I don't know."

The sun was in their eyes.

"Can't you read the screen?" asked Cruz.

"No... Yes... I meant *it* doesn't know. The unit says it's a saurischian skeleton, a sauropod likely in the Dicraeosauridae family, but it's unable to identify it."

The boys looked at each other.

A PANDA could name all the *known* dinosaurs that had ever existed on planet Earth. If the device couldn't pinpoint this one, it could mean only one of two things: Either the unit was broken, or...

"Did we do it?" Ali's face lit up. "Did we find a *new* dinosaur?"

18

▶ "CONGRATULATIONS!"

shouted Team Cousteau the second Cruz threw open the door of the SUV.

"Thanks, guys." Cruz wasn't surprised that the news had traveled faster than six exhausted explorers and their guides returning to Trelew after four days in the desert.

After finding the fossil, Cruz and Ali had uploaded the data from their PANDAs to the Society's museum for analysis. While making their way back to Trelew, Magellan had received word from the museum's paleontologists that their discovery was related to *Amargasaurus cazaui* from the Dicraeosauridae family; however, this skeleton was smaller, and the two rows of neural spines running down the back of its neck were shorter. In other words, they *had* uncovered a new type of dinosaur!

Dugan pressed his nose against the back side window of the car, cupping his hand around his face to try to see through the tinted glass. "So, where's the dino?"

Sitting on the other side of Cruz, Ali snorted. "You think we have it? Do you know how long it takes to dig out a *single* dinosaur bone?"

"Two hours!" yelled Cruz, Bryndis, Kat, Zane, and Tao. The dinosaur may have been small for a sauropod, but it was still nearly 20 feet long.

"The tibia was all we were able to remove from the rock matrix," explained Cruz. "That and a few pieces of spine. We did uncover part of the skull. It's shaped like a horse's head."

"Can we see what you brought back?" asked Lani.

"Afraid not." Professor Luben turned from where he sat beside Fanchon in the front seat. "Everything is carefully packed in a cast of toilet paper and plaster, and there it will stay until we can safely deliver it to the Mef. We're on our way there now."

"The museum is less than a mile away," said Fanchon. "Team, you go ahead and eat. We'll be back as soon as we can."

Swinging his legs out of the car, Cruz saw the blue neon sign: MI CIELO. A real restaurant! He could smell meat on the grill. Ahhh!

"Have you thought about what you're going to name the dinosaur?" asked Emmett as they all headed toward the one-story brick building.

"Ali came up with one we all like," said Cruz.

"*Altaresspinosis,*" said Ali proudly. "*Altares* for where we found it and *spinosis* for its spiny neck."

Emmett nodded his approval.

Nearing the front door, Cruz noticed that Lani kept looking over her shoulder, toward the street. "Everything all right?" he asked.

"Yeah ... yeah," she said, uncertainty in her voice.

Cruz scanned the road but didn't see anything suspicious.

They joined the rest of the explorers and faculty on the outdoor deck, where a dozen or so powder-blue-and-white-striped umbrellas shaded circular wood tables. Clear round bulbs strung through the spokes of the umbrellas swayed in the cool evening breeze. On the center of each table was a tubelike pewter vase holding two or three small white roses. Cruz quickly spotted Aunt Marisol. She was sitting at one of the tables on the other side of the deck with Felipe, Weatherly, and Jericho. She'd taken a white rose from its vase and was twirling it in her fingers. Seeing Cruz, she stopped spinning the flower and smiled at him. He smiled back. They would catch up later.

A server swept past, balancing a tray on his shoulder. Cruz caught a whiff of bubbling cheese and his stomach gurgled. *Pizza!* Taking a seat between Ali and Bryndis, Cruz learned it was a type of traditional Argentine pizza called *fugazza*: mounds of Parmesan and mozzarella cheese mingling with ribbons of caramelized red and sweet onions on a thick sourdough crust. Cruz wasn't sure about the onions, but once he tried it he was hooked. Cruz had four slices! For dessert there were plates of *alfajores,* round shortbread sandwich cookies filled with *dulce de leche,* caramelized milk and sugar. Some of the cookies were dipped in chocolate, while others were plain, their wheeled sides rolled in shredded coconut. Everything was delicious!

"Let's take the rest of the pizza and cookies with us," suggested Lani when they were ready to go. "I'll bet Fanchon and Professor Luben didn't get a chance to eat."

Standing on the sidewalk in front of the restaurant, Cruz looked up and down the street. He didn't see their SUV among the Auto Autos parked at the curb or in the small parking lot next to the building. Everyone was heading for their assigned vehicle. Emmett, Lani, Sailor, and Dugan peeled off to ride with the rest of hybrid Team Cousteau: Felipe, Weatherly, Aunt Marisol, and Jericho. One by one, the cars drove away. With only one car remaining, there was still no sign of Fanchon or Professor Luben.

A front window lowered. Aunt Marisol leaned out. "Do you want us to wait with you?"

"No," called Cruz. "I'm sure they'll be here soon."

Even so, waiting on a dark corner with Zane, Bryndis, Kat, Tao, and Ali as the minutes ticked by, Cruz began to wonder. Ten minutes passed. Fanchon or Professor Luben would have called or messaged if they were going to be *this* late. Where could they be? Cruz felt a wave of panic swell within him. What if they *couldn't* contact them? What if Nebula had—

"There!" Bryndis pointed. A block down, a black SUV was rounding the corner. It cruised toward them. Cruz held his breath as it pulled up to the curb and didn't exhale until he could see that Fanchon and Professor Luben were safe.

"Sorry we're late," said Professor Luben as everyone piled in. "The museum is planning to send out a team to excavate the rest of the skeleton, so we wanted to give them as much information as possible."

Tao held up the pizza box. "We brought you fugazza!"

"And alfajores," said Kat, who held the smaller box with the cookies.

"*Gracias!*" Fanchon turned, two eager arms reaching back. "We're starving!"

"You all get A's on this mission!" declared Professor Luben, making them laugh.

By the time they arrived back at *Orion*, it was 8:30. They were the last team to return. Slogging up the steps from the launch deck, Cruz's bag and pack felt a hundred times heavier than they had when he'd gone down these stairs at the beginning of the week.

"Home ship home," sang Kat.

Cruz had missed *Orion*, but he'd missed a certain white pup much more. He'd left Hubbard with Nyomie, who'd been only too happy to look after him while both Cruz and Fanchon were away. Tomorrow was Friday. Cruz couldn't wait to pick up the dog after school. He'd get him for the whole weekend.

"In case you forget to check your tablets before bed, field reports are due Tuesday and all classes are canceled tomorrow," said Professor Luben.

It was welcome news, even if they were too tired to cheer.

Cruz and the rest of the team were filing off the elevator on the explorers' deck when Sailor's voice came over Cruz's comm link. "Are you *here* here?" she asked when he responded.

"Yep, I'm headed—"

"Report to your cabin *immediately*. Sailor, out."

Cruz glanced at Bryndis, who lifted a shoulder to signal she had no idea what could be so urgent. They picked up the pace, hurrying side by side down the passage. When Bryndis stopped in front of her cabin, he motioned for her to come along. She opened the door and tossed her gear inside. The pair hurried down the passage. Heading into cabin 202, Cruz smelled citrus. His friends must have grabbed some oranges from the snack table upstairs or, more likely, somebody had accidentally activated a shadow badge. It happened. Tossing his pack and duffel on his bed, Cruz saw that Sailor, Lani, and Emmett were huddled around his desk.

"You got some snail mail while we were away," announced Emmett. "Have a look."

There were four postcards laid out on the starry granite tabletop. They were end to end, the back sides facing up.

The swirl cipher!

Cruz rubbed his bleary eyes to make sure he wasn't imagining things. He wasn't! Each card contained several lines written in the code Cruz's mother had created to communicate with him. Cruz flipped the first postcard to see a photo of his gold ankh pin, or one like it.

"They all have that picture on the front," noted Emmett.

His ankh pin! Cruz had nearly forgotten about it. It was still in his pocket.

"We're pretty certain the codes were written by the same person," said Sailor. "See how the writing style is the same? The black ink, too?"

"However, the handwriting addressing them to you at Explorer Academy is different on every card," interjected Lani. "We noticed they were all mailed on the same day by *express mail* from different places." She tapped the canceled stamp on the first card. "This one came from Washington, D.C. That one was mailed from Otjiwarongo, Namibia. The third one is from Paro, Bhutan, and that last card came from—"

"Hanalei," noted Bryndis, who now stood beside Cruz.

"We figured the postcard from Namibia has to be from Dr. Jo," said Sailor. "And the one from Bhutan from the monks at the Tiger's Nest."

"We're not sure who sent the card from Washington, D.C." Emmett shook his head. "Dr. Fallowfeld is the most likely candidate, but it could have someone from the Academy or the Society or"—he raised an eyebrow at Cruz—"somewhere else..."

He meant the Synthesis or the Archive.

"The one from Kauai is probably from your dad," added Lani.

Cruz's mind was racing. "So, you're saying—"

"Your mom wrote a coded message, divided it between four postcards, and gave it to the people she most trusted to mail them to you once you'd found the final cipher," concluded Emmett.

Lani twisted her silver lock of hair. "What we can't figure out is how they all knew *when* to send the cards to you."

"I think I know." Cruz unzipped his lower-right pocket and took out the ankh pin. It was still glowing as brightly as ever. He set it on the desk. "It's been lit up like this ever since we got back from the Academy."

"The journal!" cried Emmett. "I bet that's what your mom was trying to tell you before the video started hiccuping. She was trying to say that once you attached the eighth piece to the cipher, you'd activate a series of ankh beacons just like yours that would signal to her friends that it was time to send you their cards."

Of course! That had to be it!

"Let's decrypt them," said Cruz, scurrying to get his mom's box out from under his bed. He fished out his photo with the swirl cipher key written on the back. Emmett rounded up pens and paper, and they all moved to the small circular table between the two navy chairs. While the others got on their knees, Bryndis took a seat in the chair behind Cruz. It wasn't easy, craning their necks and straining their eyes to match the swirls on the cards to those on the decoder. Plus, the swirl variations were subtle with a single dot or the ever-so-slight curl of a tail making the difference between a match and a miss.

Cruz's postcard had the shortest code, so he was the first one finished. Cruz stared at what he'd written: *Wedge 4, front, 11th letter. Wedge 2, front, 3rd letter.* He glanced up at Bryndis, who was hovering over his shoulder. "Did I do this right?"

"*Já.*"

Once everyone was done, they began to compare messages.

"Mine says 'wedge two, front, third letter,'" said Emmett. "'Wedge six, back, tenth letter. Wedge four, front, second digit.'"

Sailor and Lani had similar phrases.

"Wedge?" Cruz put a hand to his chest. "Could she mean...?"

Lani's jaw fell. "The stones."

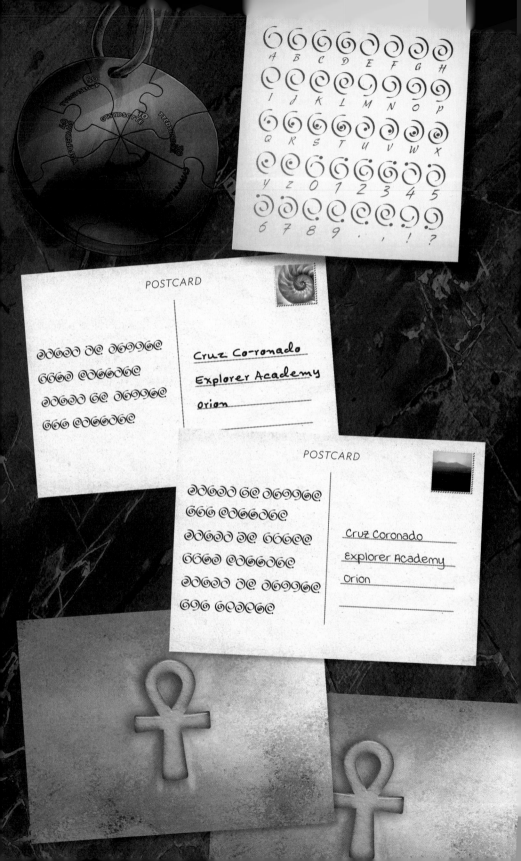

"A double code!" exclaimed Emmett. "Brilliant!"

Cruz took off his lanyard and handed the cipher to Emmett. They all knew the emoto-glasses had the necessary magnification required for reading such tiny engravings.

"I'll read the cards out to you, if you want," Lani said to Emmett as he bent over the cipher. She started with Cruz's card. "'Wedge four, front, eleventh letter.'"

Emmett tracked to the fourth wedge on the front of the cipher. "That's an *N*."

She recorded it on the bottom of the postcard. "'Wedge two, front, third letter.'"

"Uh ... a *T*," declared Emmett

She wrote it down next to the *N*, then moved on to the next card.

Once they'd decoded all the cards, everyone squished in to read the results. Cruz's card had an *N* and a *T*; Emmett's an *E*, *H*, and *O*; Sailor's read *P*, *O*, and *I*; and Lani's was *P*, *O*, and *L*.

N-T-E-H-O-P-O-I-P-O-L

"It's a word scramble," said Emmett.

Everyone got to work.

Emmett was the first to glance up. "How about Thine Loop?"

"You have a leftover *P*," said Sailor. "Pipton Hole?"

"Leftover *O*," noted Emmett.

"Hotel Nippoi or Popoin?" suggested Lani.

"Those are both good," said Bryndis; however, after a search on Cruz's tablet she could locate no such places.

"'Pool,' 'hoop,' 'thin'—I can make a lot of words," said Sailor, "but nothing that makes sense."

"I'm going to call my dad," said Cruz. "If he sent the postcard from Hawaii, he might be able to tell us—"

"Achoo!"

They froze. No one at the table had sneezed.

Putting a finger to his lips, Emmett tipped his head toward the closet door. It was the most likely hiding place. Slowly, silently, the explorers got to their feet. Lani, who was nearest to the closet, reached out. She placed her hand on the knob, then flung open the door. "Aha!"

Empty.

Bryndis and Sailor scurried to peer under the beds. Emmett took a quick peek in the bathroom. Nobody was there either.

Out of the corner of his eye, Cruz saw the blinds shift in front of the porthole. Soft ripples became a roll of waves. A dark, tousled head was emerging! Cruz knew it. He *had* smelled the passion fruit scent of a shadow badge! One shoulder appeared, then another. It was like watching a butterfly struggle free from its chrysalis, except this was no pretty winged insect.

Cruz stiffened. "Thorne Prescott."

"You stole a shadow badge," accused Emmett.

"Uh … Emmett, I think that's the least of our problems," muttered Sailor.

"She's right," said Prescott, shaking off a jacket that blended in with the blinds. They watched it hit the floor. He was wearing a black nylon vest and, under it, a black turtleneck. "You kept me waiting in Paris, Cruz. That was very rude. And I was so looking forward to showing you around the Louvre." Prescott unzipped a pocket on the front of his vest. He took out a glass vial containing an emerald green liquid. He held it up for them to see. "It's such a fine line between life and death. If I should, say, drop this, we'd all be gone within seconds, which is why I suggest you do exactly as I tell you. Back up against the closet doors, hands folded in front of you. Anybody so much as looks at a comm pin or goes for a weapon, and I *will* drop this." He glared at Cruz. "Trust me when I say I have nothing to lose. Now move."

They moved.

"Leave it!" commanded Prescott when Sailor would have grabbed the cipher.

The explorers lined up, side by side; Bryndis nearest Emmett's bed, then Sailor, Emmett, Cruz, and Lani.

The lights flickered. Prescott looked up.

"Curfew," explained Lani. "Two minutes until lights out."

Prescott narrowed his eyes at her. "I've seen you somewhere before." He snapped his fingers. "Hawaii. The observatory."

Lani lifted her chin. "I've seen you, too."

Prescott picked up the cipher off the table with his free hand. He stared at it in his palm, turning the conjoined marble pieces over with his thumb.

Cruz felt a spasm rip through his stomach. He had to get his friends out of here. "You've got the cipher and me. Let everyone else go."

"You're forgetting the other player in our game." Prescott glared at Emmett.

Cruz's blood began to simmer. "He has nothing to do with this."

"Other than being a spy, you mean—"

"He's not," shot Cruz. "Emmett's not Jaguar. He only pretended to be so we could try to learn more information about Nebula."

Prescott moved toward Emmett like a cat stalking prey. "You told me *you* were Jaguar."

"N-no." Gray streams gushed through the emoto-glasses. "You assumed I was, and I never ... corrected you."

Prescott twisted his neck. It cracked. "How do I know you're telling the truth now?"

Emmett gave Cruz a sideways glance. "Um ..."

They were in trouble. How do you prove you're *not* a spy? Cruz realized he had the one, probably the only, device that could do that very thing: the virtugraph. Except he'd promised Fanchon to keep her invention a secret. If he used it to save Emmett, not only would he break his vow, but the virtugraph would fall into enemy hands.

Sorry, Fanchon.

"I can prove—" started Cruz.

"Leave Emmett alone." The words rang out. "I'm the one you're looking for, Cobra. I'm Jaguar."

The cabin went dark.

19

▶**WITH A FLICK** of his thumb, Prescott switched on the tiny yet bright light attached to the chest of his vest. It blinded the explorers, as he intended it to. He didn't want any last-minute heroics spoiling his plans. Prescott angled the beam slightly upward to hit the ceiling above the so-called explorer spy. Even in the shadows, he could see her eyes. She was determined. Defiant. Done. She was tired of the secrets, games, lies, threats—all of it. Prescott knew this look. He'd seen it in his own mirror. Yet the question remained: Was it a lie? Or was she really Jaguar?

The girl erased his doubts with a single sentence. "Swan told me you'd be coming."

"B-Bryndis?" stammered Cruz.

"Crikey!" burst Sailor. "I don't believe it. Bryndis, you can't be—"

"I am." Bryndis's voice quivered. "I'm the spy. I'm so sorry, everyone. I didn't mean for things to go this far, and I sure never meant to hurt anyone."

Cruz raked his hair. "Why? H-how?"

"It's a long story." Jaguar looked Prescott's way.

"Make it a short one," said Prescott. He'd give her a minute.

"Uh . . . okay . . . After we first set sail on Orion, Dr. Vanderwick came to me," said Bryndis. "She said your mother's formula was dangerous, Cruz, but you refused to accept it. She told me you were on a mission to find the pieces, despite objections from scientists within the Society, including Fanchon and herself. She said you were reckless and that it was going to put us all in danger. I

171

trusted her. I didn't know you well back then, and Dr. Vanderwick did work for the Academy. I had no idea she was involved with Nebula, or even what Nebula was, until Tripp and Officer Wardicorn trapped us in the ice cave at Langjökull. When we almost died there, I thought it was proof that Dr. Vanderwick was right. Cruz, you had put us in danger. I tried to talk to you about it, but you avoided my questions and told me it was some kind of game, remember? That only made me doubt you more." She wrung her hands. "I agreed to help Dr. Vanderwick, and I discovered pretty quickly I didn't like being a spy. Planting recording devices, hacking into your tablets, reporting everything I heard and saw—I hated it. I hated betraying you. I'd had enough. In fact, I was going to tell Dr. Vanderwick I was quitting, but then . . . we went to Africa."

Silence.

Prescott couldn't help his curiosity. "What happened in Africa?"

"Bryndis borrowed my duffel bag for a mission," said Cruz. "She was exposed to a poison Dr. Vanderwick put in it that was meant for me. She'd have died if Fanchon and her team hadn't developed an antidote."

Prescott did recall Zebra telling him about a plan that had failed, something about the right poison but the wrong explorer. Zebra had neglected to mention she'd nearly killed one of their own agents.

"When I got back to Orion, I told Dr. Vanderwick I was finished spying," continued Bryndis. "She confessed to poisoning the bag. She told me we were working for Nebula and that if I walked away she could not protect me. Or my family. It was pretty clear what she meant. I was stuck. After she died, I was contacted by another Nebula agent online—Lion. I didn't know who Lion was but figured if he or she wasn't on the ship that gave me an advantage. I did my best to be as uncooperative as possible. I lied and said Lani and Emmett had blocked my security hacks. I pretended I'd had a fight with Cruz and we weren't speaking. I even gave back the cipher I stole from you."

"That's when you left it beneath the lemon tree," croaked Cruz.

"Já. I couldn't turn the piece over to Nebula . . . I just couldn't. Leaving it somewhere on the ship and giving you a clue to find it seemed the safest way to give it back."

"Okay, you returned the stone, but . . ." Cruz's eyebrows dipped.

"You also sabotaged Mell. She would have exploded, and some-one could have been hurt or killed."

"Mell? Exploded? What are you talking about? I never—"

"It had to be you," growled Cruz. "You were the only Nebula spy on board Orion. You said so yourself."

"I didn't do anything to Mell . . . I swear." Her voice broke. A tear rolled down her cheek. "Look, I'm not proud of what I did. As soon as things started to get out of hand, I should have told my parents and Dr. Hightower, but instead I tried to fix it myself. I told more lies and kept getting in deeper and deeper. I wish I could go back and change it . . . I wish I could make you all understand. All I can say is I'm sorry . . . so very sorry." Her head fell.

Was she through? wondered Prescott. He glanced at the cipher in his hand. He had what he'd come for. There was no sense pro-longing this.

"Do you even know what you've got there?" Emmett's question pierced Prescott's thoughts. "Do you know what that represents?"

Prescott kept his voice cool. "Don't know. Don't care. Don't ask questions."

"Maybe you should!" The emoto-glasses flashed red. "It's a cell-regeneration formula that could be the key to curing incurable diseases. It could heal injuries, save lives—"

"It's the reason Brume killed my mother," said Cruz. "And why he wants it and everyone who knows about it destroyed."

"It's of no consequence to me," said Prescott.

Bryndis's head shot up. "How can you say that? You of all peo-ple! If Nebula had let Cruz's mom live, Piper might still be alive, too."

Her words sent a chill through Prescott. How did she know about his daughter?

Of course. Swan.

Prescott stared at his palm. Eight little pieces of rock with some scratchings hardly seemed like a medical miracle. Still, he knew Hezekiah Brume. The man didn't waste his time on worthless pur-suits. This could be everything the explorers said it was. And if it was . . .

Prescott would have done anything to save Piper. Anything.

But it was too late.

His head throbbed. His chest was tight. He needed to be fin-ished with this whole mess. Prescott backed toward the veranda door. He would step through it, toss the nerve agent back into the cabin, then go over the side of the rail to where his hovercraft waited below. Simple. Quick. Done.

"Cobra!" called Bryndis. "I have something for you . . . from Swan."

He narrowed his eyes at her, suspicious. How dumb did she think he was?

"I promised her I would give it to you," she said. "It's in my pocket. Please, can I . . . ?"

"Fine. But slowly. Nobody else moves a muscle."

Bryndis slipped her hand into a jacket opening and brought out a picture. Prescott motioned for her to step forward and show it to him.

It was a photograph of an oil painting. On the canvas, a large bouquet of poppies spilled out of a dark brown pear-shaped vase. The flowers were bright yellow but for one stem in the front with three red blossoms. The bouquet was drooping, and some of the petals had fallen onto the light brown table. Each petal was a yellow stroke of paint. The artwork was mounted in an antique gold-leaf frame.

It looked familiar.

"I know that painting," said Emmett. "It's a Van Gogh. Wasn't it stolen from a museum?"

"Yes," said Cruz. "The curators at the Arc—I mean, some art experts my aunt knows have been trying to find it for years. It's worth millions."

"There's a note on the back here," said Bryndis. She flipped the picture so Prescott could read the neat handwriting: Brume has this.

Prescott's breath caught. Now he remembered! Brume, who never showed his face on camera, had pointed his phone at it during one of their video calls. "If this is true," said Prescott, "if Swan is right . . ."

"You could put Brume in jail and collect a big reward for recovering the stolen painting," said Lani.

Prescott's mind was racing. Could he outwit Brume? Did he dare try?

Bryndis was right about the spy game. It swallowed you. You never realized you were digging your own grave. At first, the lies were harmless, the hole small. But over time, the lies got bigger,

174

the crater deeper. Pretty soon you were so far down you couldn't see daylight and you sure couldn't climb out. Now he was being given a rare chance to escape. Could he trust Swan? It was a big gamble, but Prescott knew that if he didn't risk it, he'd be stuck in the dark forever.

He hoped he didn't regret what he was about to do.

Prescott tossed the cipher to Cruz. "Take it."

Cruz fumbled, nearly dropping the stones. He quickly put the lanyard around his neck.

Prescott took the photo Bryndis held out. "I'll go to the authorities with this, but it'll take time for them to find Brume. He's a master at going underground, and I'm sure this painting is hidden even better than he is." He carefully placed the vial back in his vest pocket. "For what it's worth, you should know that Lion is Hezekiah Brume. Also, he won't be pleased that I didn't handle things here. Make no mistake, he will come after you."

"I know." Cruz tried to rub the goose bumps from his arms.

Opening the veranda door, Prescott stepped out onto the small balcony. He pulled the thin self-retracting rope from its pocket, attached the end to the rail, and climbed over. He lowered himself into the open hull of the hovercraft, then released the rope from his end. Untying the boat, he shoved it away from the ramp. Prescott tapped the console, and the engine roared to life. He pushed the throttle icon on the touch screen. The boat moved slowly forward, grazing the water. Prescott made his turn, cutting a tight semicircle around the stern of the anchored ship.

He felt his phone buzz over his heart. And ignored it. Prescott knew Brume would send his goons to deal with him, but he'd be ready with money or weapons, if need be. He was finally seeing things clearly. Prescott had clamped the chains on himself. Only he could remove them.

Leaving Orion in the spray of his rooster tail, Prescott aimed the hovercraft toward the harbor lights. The wind felt good on his face. He wasn't sure where he'd go after he contacted the police. Maybe Paris. Maybe Geneva. Maybe back to London to see Aubrie. Maybe all these places. And more.

Prescott could go anywhere. Do anything.

Now that he was free.

20

FOR A LONG TIME, no one spoke. The only sound was the wind flapping the blinds on the open veranda door.

In the darkness, Emmett's emoto-glasses were a swirling galaxy of reds, purples, and browns: anger, frustration, and sadness. Cruz knew how he felt. He knew he should be grateful. Prescott was gone. They had the cipher. And they were still alive. Three wins! Yet, the shock of learning Jaguar's true identity hung over them like a thick fog.

Bryndis had not moved. Her right side was in shadow, her left lit by the soft glow of the outside deck lights. Her cheek was wet.

Teary blue eyes met his. "Cruz...I...I..." She glanced from one face to the next, a plea for help. When no one did, Bryndis turned and bolted from the cabin.

Part of Cruz ached to run after her. Another part of him was glad she'd left. Bryndis had ruined everything: his trust, their friendship, Team Cousteau.

Cruz felt a hand on his arm. "You okay?" Lani's face came around his shoulder.

He shook his head. He was a long way from okay.

"I never suspected her." Emmett said it as if he'd failed a test in class.

"Me neither, and I'm her roommate," groaned Sailor. She went to close the veranda door and lock it. "I should have picked up on *something*."

"She was awfully good at lying," said Lani.

It was exactly like Fanchon had told him. You never think it's going to be someone close to you, but it always is. It has to be. How else can they discover your secrets? Cruz's gaze went to the little painting of Hubbard on his nightstand that Bryndis had made for him. He liked her. Believed she liked him back. Was that part of the lie, too?

Emmett turned on his mad-scientist light and sat down at his computers. "We'd better tell Nyomie and Dr. Hightower about Bryndis. I also need to talk to Fanchon about upgrading our security system."

"Don't mention to anyone that Prescott was here," said Cruz. "If my aunt finds out Nebula cornered us in our own cabin ..."

"I won't." Emmett began to type. "Let's put Mell on guard duty tonight."

"Okay." Cruz rubbed his eyes. His adrenaline no longer pumping, he felt drained.

"We'd better go." Sailor nudged Lani. "We're past curfew. Guys, we'll be back to work on the postcards first thing tomorrow."

Cruz walked them to the door. He poked his head out to be sure the hall was clear, and when he saw that it was, he moved aside. With a quick hang-in-there grin, Sailor scampered away.

Lani started to follow, then stopped. She turned. "You know—"

"Don't say it."

"What?"

"'It'll be all right,' 'We'll figure it out,' or whatever positive thing you were going to say to cheer me up," said Cruz.

"But—"

"Lani, this is one you can't fix."

She gave him a sorrowful nod, then followed Sailor.

Cruz activated Mell, instructing her to monitor the doors and portholes and to wake him and contact security if anyone tried to enter. How had Prescott gotten in undetected? A lapse in security? Or had Bryndis helped? Prescott had said the line between life and death was a thin one. And tonight, they had walked as close to the edge of death as Cruz ever wanted to get. Brume was out there. Cruz had to be ready.

Cruz laid out the four postcards out on his bed, along with his pad where he'd written the letters they'd decoded: *N-T-E-H-O-P-O-I-P-O-L.* He hoped his dad could shed some light on things. Picking up his tablet, he tapped his dad's photo in his contact list. Kauai was seven hours behind *Orion,* so it was 10 minutes after three o'clock in the afternoon back home.

After two chimes, his dad's face appeared. "Cruz!"

"Hey, Dad, can you talk?"

"Yep. Tiko's in the back. What's up?"

"I need to ask about your postcard." Cruz held the card from Kauai close to the camera lens. "We've been trying to decipher Mom's swirl cipher and ended up with some letters we can't unscramble. I thought maybe you could help."

"I wish I could, son, except I didn't send that."

"But it's postmarked Hanalei. We thought—"

"It wasn't me," insisted his father.

Emmett turned from his desk to give Cruz a concerned look.

If not Cruz's dad, then who?

Cruz related to his father the full story of the glowing ankh pin, the arrival of the postcards, and their efforts at decoding them. He left out the part where Prescott had interrupted their work. As he talked, Cruz moved the cards around. It occurred to him that maybe there was some special order they were supposed to be in, perhaps, based on his travels. It was worth a try. Since his journey had started at home, he slid the postcard from Kauai to his far left. "Dad, does anybody else know about Mom's cipher?"

"Your aunt does, of course, but she could hardly send you a postcard from here."

Cruz had gone to the Academy next, so he moved the postcard from Washington, D.C., to the second position.

"Dr. Fallowfeld, possibly," continued his dad. "He's a mystery. I know he helped your mom with the serum, but I can't say if he's aware of the cipher."

"I wondered about him." Cruz shifted the postcard from Namibia to the third spot. "I think he might be the person I'm supposed to find."

"You could be right. Is everything else going okay?" questioned his dad. "You sound dead tired."

Cruz let out a weak laugh. "Close."

Let's see, where was he? Oh yes, the Tiger's Nest had come after Namibia, so Cruz moved the postcard from Bhutan to his far right. Taking his hand away, he leaned back and read the letters across the cards: *P-O-L E-H-O P-O-I N-T.*

Could it be?

His pulse quickening, Cruz brought up a new window on his screen. He typed *Poleho Point* into the satellite map locator, then hit the search icon. The map began to track west over the Pacific Ocean. Cruz's heart was thumping at double speed by the time the red pinpoint popped up on the western-most island in the Hawaiian chain, Niʻihau. Less than 18 miles southwest of Kauai, it was the perfect place. Dr. Fallowfeld had been hiding under Cruz's nose the whole time!

"Son? Are you there? I think I lost you."

"I'm here, Dad. You didn't lose me."

Far from it.

Cruz knew his destination now. He was going home.

"NI'IHAU?" LANI BEGAN TWISTING her silver lock. "The Forbidden Island? Are you sure?"

"Positive," said Cruz. He'd gathered his friends in Lani's cabin before breakfast to share the news.

"The Forbidden Island!" Sailor scooted in beside Emmett to study the map on Cruz's tablet. "Sounds dangerous—like a haunted town from a novel."

"Nah," said Cruz. "It's privately owned, that's all. My dad said it was nicknamed that during a polio epidemic in the 1950s. You couldn't visit unless you had a doctor's note and agreed to quarantine for two weeks. It worked. Nobody on the island got sick. And since access is restricted, the name sort of stuck."

"Only a few hundred people live there now," explained Lani. "It lacks some of the comforts we're used to. There are no restaurants, shops, or hotels; no paved roads or internet—"

"No internet?" Emmett's emoto-glasses flashed a horrified white.

"We've sailed around it and snorkeled off the coast," said Lani, "but you can't step onto the island unless you have permission from the owners."

"We'll get it," said Cruz. "I sent Dr. Hightower an urgent message last night."

If anyone could help them, it was the president of the Academy. He was, however, worried about time. To be back by class on Monday morning, they'd have to leave *Orion* this afternoon, and he was still waiting for Dr. Hightower's response.

"Dr. Fallowfeld has to be *here*." Emmett tapped the map. Poleho Point was on the northeastern shore of the side facing Kauai. Like much of the rest of the Forbidden Island, the area was covered in greenery with only the occasional dirt road or trail fracturing the landscape. They could see the triangles of white waves crashing against rock and a wide sandy beach. A small square building sat where the ivory sands of the shore met the scraggly line of brush. A winding dirt road led to the building. Emmett toggled up and down, then side to side. "This is the only structure on the whole northern part of the island. Fallowfeld is here all right."

Cruz had come to the same conclusion.

"Good. Can we eat now?" Emmett put a hand to his stomach. "I'm starving."

Leaving Lani's cabin, Cruz glanced at Sailor and Bryndis's cabin across the passage.

"She went to see Nyomie first thing to confess," said Sailor.

As they passed their adviser's closed door, every head turned.

"I wonder what will happen to her," said Lani.

"Either suspension or expulsion," replied Emmett. "She broke the honor code."

"And your heart," Sailor added quietly, making Cruz blush. "Bryndis and I stayed up most of the night talking. She thinks you hate her now. You don't, do you?"

"No," said Cruz. In fact, quite the opposite. Feelings don't suddenly disappear, no matter how much you want them to.

In the dining room, Cruz drowned his sorrows with two waffles smothered in boysenberry syrup. He grabbed a glass of orange juice and followed his friends to their usual table. Through the rain-spattered windows, the chunky, dark clouds looked like hunched-over ogres trying to capture the midnight blue waves with thick iron gray fingers. *Orion* had weighed anchor sometime during the night. They were now sailing north up the east coast of South America on their way back to the U.S. Cruz cut into his waffles, and the gooey syrup flowed into the gap like purple lava.

Cruz wondered if Dr. Hightower would expel Bryndis with only two and a half weeks remaining in the term. They would be turning in their last mission field reports next week, then reviewing and studying for final exams, which would be given the following week. After that, the ship would dock at National Harbor Marina on the Potomac. All the Academy's ships were due to return at the same time. The explorers from every grade level would gather back at Explorer Academy headquarters for a busy day that included the closing ceremony and graduation.

"Nyomie Byron to Cruz Coronado."

In his rush to activate his comm pin, Cruz flung a piece of syrup-soaked waffle across the table. It missed Emmett but hit Lani, splattering syrup onto her sleeve. Cruz gave her an apologetic look—and his napkin. "Cruz, here," he said to his adviser.

"I need to see you right away. Can you—"

"Be right there. Cruz, out." He flung back his chair. "Sorry, Lani. I'll get some more napkins—"

"It's okay." She was dabbing at her jacket. "I've got it."

"We'll get your tray," said Sailor. "Just go!"

Flying down to the explorers' deck, Cruz found Nyomie's door slightly open. Bryndis was not around. Cruz went in, quietly shutting the door behind him. The second he turned, a white blur came flying at him. Cruz caught the dog, ruffling the soft cloud of fur on his neck. "Hi, boy."

Nyomie was there, seated in her favorite light blue chair. It reminded him of the time Team Cousteau had burst in to end their Funday scavenger hunt. For their win, Taryn had awarded each member a time capsule. She'd used Cruz to demonstrate how the device worked. Loading a memory of when she'd first met him at the Academy onto her time capsule, she'd placed it in his hand so he could describe the experience to the others. Cruz had never returned the capsule to her, and she'd not asked for it. Cruz hoped she never would.

"Welcome back." Nyomie motioned for him to sit in the chair across from hers.

Cruz held his breath. He was anxious for the verdict. He knew he was pushing his luck, asking to go home even though school ended soon. Dr. Hightower might tell him he'd have to wait. If he did, the delay would give Nebula time to learn about the postcards and reach Dr. Fallowfeld first. He had to make Nyomie see that he had to go— and he had to go *now*.

She didn't keep him in suspense. "Dr. Hightower has consented to let you go to Hawaii."

Yes!

"She was considering having you wait until the end of the term," she continued, "but given the situation with Bryndis, we realize time is critical."

"Thanks," he said. "So, Bryndis... she told you about Nebula?"

"She did." Her response was short, but there was no mistaking her disappointment.

"What's Dr. Hightower going to do?"

"I don't know."

"It wasn't all bad." Cruz picked at his thumb nail. "She returned a piece of the cipher she'd taken from me. If she hadn't, Nebula would have it by now and that would have ended everything. I—I thought you should know."

"I'll pass that along." She leaned forward. "I know Bryndis means a lot to *your team*." The way Nyomie enunciated the last two words, it was obvious she was really saying that she knew Bryndis meant a lot to *him*. "And any time you want to talk, I'm a good listener."

"Okay," he said, his voice husky. Cruz knew he would forgive Bryndis. In time. But trust her? Not likely. And if you can't trust a person you like, maybe even love, what then?

"Anyway..." Nyomie went back to her tablet. "I'll accompany you on the trip. Dr. Hightower is working to secure permission for us to visit the island, though we may have to... uh... break a few rules if she can't. We'll follow our usual routine. Captain Roxas will fly us via *Academy One* to Almirante Marcos A. Zar airport in Trelew, which is still the closest international airport, where we'll connect with *Condor* and—What's wrong?"

She'd caught his downturned mouth.

It was something Prescott had said. The Nebula agent had mentioned he'd been waiting for them in Paris. He'd known they were headed to the Louvre. Bryndis may have told him, or maybe it was Swan or Lion. The point was, he knew.

"Nebula is always one step ahead of us," said Cruz. "The few times we've managed to outwit them is when we've done the opposite of what they expected. And all of *this* is ... well, it's ..."

"Exactly what they expect." Nyomie pursed her lips. She stared at her screen. "Time to throw out the old playbook, huh?" She wove her fingers together, stretched her arms out in front of her, and popped her knuckles. "Okay, I'm game for something new, but prepare yourself. And you'd better tell Lani, Sailor, and Emmett to be ready early. We're going to need all the time we can— What's wrong *now*?"

"I was thinking ... the five of us ... won't Nebula be expecting that, too?"

"Probably—"

"What if only you and I go?"

"Just us? Not the others?"

"Two people have a better chance at slipping past Nebula, don't you think?"

"Yes, but your friends—"

"They'll understand. I'll talk to them. I'll explain."

"It's your decision, of course," said Nyomie in that way adults do when they think you're making the wrong choice but are going to let you deal with the consequences.

Cruz knew what he was doing. And why. He'd been up last night thinking about it.

"There is one other thing that Nebula will anticipate," said Nyomie.

Cruz knew that, too. "My dad."

"You can't tell him you're coming or see him until it's all over."

"I won't," he vowed.

Hubbard was trotting toward Nyomie, his leash in his mouth. He needed to go to his meadow.

She groaned. "Oh, Hub, now?"

"I'll take him," volunteered Cruz.

"Thanks. Can you drop him with Fanchon when he's done? I'll tell her you're on your way and that we're leaving for the weekend. Once you've broken the news to Emmett, Sailor, and Lani, pack and get back here as soon as you can. We're going to need every spare second."

Cruz clipped the leash to Hubbard's collar, and the pair headed for the door.

"Cruz?"

He glanced back.

"You're sure about this?"

"I am."

He wasn't.

Cruz *did* want to take his friends with him. Very much. They were a team—a great clue-solving, cipher-cracking, mystery-unraveling team. Yet the close call with Prescott had hit him hard. Every step closer he came to delivering the formula was more dangerous than the one before. Prescott had called it a game. That was true. There would be a winner and a loser, but the stakes in this game were life and death. Cruz was not afraid to face Lion. To fight. Even die. Okay, maybe he was afraid, but if anything happened to Emmett, Sailor, Lani, Aunt Marisol, or his dad, it would be far, far worse. Cruz knew he would not be able to endure that.

He would shatter into so many pieces that nothing, not even Tardinia Serum, would be able to save him.

21

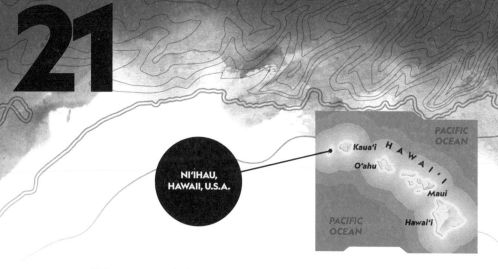

NI'IHAU, HAWAII, U.S.A.

Kaua'i
O'ahu
HAWAI'I
Maui
Hawai'i
PACIFIC OCEAN
PACIFIC OCEAN

TO: *Lani Kealoha, Emmett Lu, Sailor York*
SUBJECT: *C.C.*

Dear Lani, Emmett, and Sailor,

Please don't be mad, but I'm on my way to you know where with you know what with you know who. We're going under the radar. Trust me, it's the best thing for everyone.

> *Cruz*

P.S. Lani, can you play with Hubbard while I'm gone?

P.P.S. Emmett, I heard we're having cupcakes tonight. Can you snag me a chocolate one? Thanks! Sailor, if you're yelling at your screen right now, I am SUPER sorry.

P.P.P.S. Emmett, on second thought, better give Sailor my cupcake.

HIS FOREHEAD PRESSED AGAINST THE WINDOW, Cruz watched the rosy eye of sunrise peek over the curve of the horizon. Below, the ripples of the deep blue Pacific edged closer to the belly of the plane. Cruz could hear the snapping of tray tables being returned to their upright positions.

It had been a long trip—more than 24 hours. Plus seven hours lost in the time change. They'd had more than a few bumps (literally) along the way, but Nyomie had turned their *usual routine* completely upside down. She'd arranged for a local fisherman to transport them from *Orion* to Rawson. Once on land, they rented an electronic motorbike with a side-car, and Nyomie had driven them to Trelew (Cruz was *still* picking bugs out of his teeth). Instead of flying out of the main airport, Nyomie had chosen a smaller private airfield at the edge of town. She'd chartered a single-engine plane to take them to San Carlos de Bariloche on Lake Nahuel Huapi in western Argentina. There, in the foothills of the Andes, they hopped another private aircraft, which flew them north to Arturo Merino Benítez Airport in Santiago, Chile, where they boarded a non-stop commercial flight to Kauai. They'd hit some turbulence on the leg from Bariloche to Santiago, and their slower route had added several hours to the journey, but if they'd lost Nebula, all the time and effort would be worth it.

Nyomie flipped her tray table up. "When we land, we'll grab an Auto Auto and head to Kukui'ula Harbor. Dr. Hightower has a vacation house here, and she's lending us her boat."

Cruz popped back so fast he banged his elbow. "Dr. Hightower has a house on Kauai?"

His adviser put a finger to her lips. "In Poipu."

Poipu was on the south shore of the island, almost directly opposite Hanalei in the north.

Feeling the bump of wheels against asphalt, Cruz turned back to the window.

Home!

Once off the plane, Cruz and Nyomie headed for the closest Auto Auto rental kiosk. Nyomie was careful to pay in cash and not use her real name. Once they reached Kukui'ula Harbor, Nyomie and Cruz grabbed their gear and made their way down the long pier. Cruz kept an eye out for Nebula agents but didn't see anyone that looked suspicious. It was a quiet Saturday morning. So far.

"This is us." Nyomie had stopped next to a small white hovercraft with the name *Polaris* painted on the back in cursive gold writing.

Cruz got it. Polaris was the North Star.

Nyomie unlocked the shell, and they hopped in. She plugged the GPS coordinates of Poleho Point into the computer, punched the throttle, and they were off. Nyomie wasn't saying if they'd gotten permission to be on the island, so Cruz figured the less he knew the better. Skimming west over the calm waves, they left the coastline of Kauai behind to cross the Kaulakahi Channel. Cruz could see the long, craggy silhouette of Niʻihau in the distance. Closing in on the island, Nyomie veered north. The route took them past a long range of flat-topped cliffs.

Cruz's GPS sunglasses identified the plateau as Mount Pānī'au, the extinct shield volcano that had formed the island. At 1,290 feet high, it was the tallest point on Ni'ihau.

Nyomie was pulling back on the throttle. Peering over the side, Cruz saw a shiver of gray reef sharks darting through the teal waters. He counted 23 sharks! His adviser expertly navigated the reef to bring the craft up onto the smoothest section of Poleho Point beach. A half dozen monk seals were sunning themselves nearby. Other than rolling over, they took little interest in their human visitors. Heading up the slope to the house, the wind was biting. Cruz kept his sunglasses on, but grains of sand still blew sideways into his eyes.

When he started up the overgrown path to the back door of the house, Nyomie caught his arm. "Careful. There's no telling what we'll find."

Cruz activated Mell, directing her to perch on the honeycomb remote. The single-story powder gray house leaned slightly away from the

sea, as if wary of being battered by the ocean winds. Nyomie and Cruz went up the two stairs onto a sagging back porch where, from each corner of the overhang, a camera spied on them. They were met by a metal door with no knob. A sand-covered biometric scanner was attached to the right side of the frame. Cleaning the device with his sleeve and a few gentle puffs of air, Cruz put his eye to the recognition lens. His pulse quickened. Dr. Fallowfeld *should* have tapped into the Explorer Academy database for Cruz's iris identification pattern, but if he hadn't...

They heard the latch click. The metal panel slid away.

"Mell, defense mode." Cruz slipped a hand into the pocket carrying his octopod.

Nyomie and Cruz stepped over the threshold. They took in the ivory walls stenciled with green ivy, a yellowing white laminate floor, faded koa wood cabinets, and white tiled counters. It was an ordinary if out-dated kitchen. For Cruz, who had been hoping for a futuristic lab with bubbling beakers and state-of-the art robotics, a cow teapot and a leaky fridge were a bit of a letdown.

"Wow." Nyomie had her head tipped back. "Check this out!"

A hand-painted map of Ni'ihau stretched the entire length of the kitchen ceiling; the colors were bright, the topography detailed. Mount Pāni'au, Pu'uwai village, and other points of interest were labeled in white cursive letters. The artist had included animals, too: whales frol-icking off the coast, monk seals sunbathing on the beach, and antelope grazing in a meadow.

Cruz pointed to the little gray home on the north end of the island. "It should say 'You are here.'"

"It's a gorgeous mural." Nyomie was still studying it. "Must have taken a long time to paint."

Cruz leaned into the narrow hallway. "Dr. Fallowfeld?"

No response.

He started to step into the passage, but Nyomie moved in front of him. "I'll have a look around. You stay here."

"But—"

"Stay."

"I'm not Hubbard, you know."

"If only," she quipped. "Dogs are easier to train than explorers. I won't be long."

Cruz relaxed his grip on his octopod. He took off his pack. Peering into cabinets and drawers, he found the usual: utensils, dishes, and glasses. He opened the fridge door. *Whew!* The odor of rotting food overpowered him. And Mell, too.

Bzzzzzzzz! she said loudly, shaking her head. Like a real honeybee, she had an excellent sense of smell.

Cruz shut the fridge door.

Nyomie was back before Cruz's eyes had stopped watering. "Nobody's here," she said. "And from the look of things, they haven't been for some time."

Did Dr. Fallowfeld leave on his own? Or was it something more sinister? Why was it that every time Cruz answered one question, 10 new ones popped up?

Cruz rubbed the back of his neck. "What do we do now?"

Argh! Another question.

"I'm not sure. Maybe the scientists at the Society can help us—"

"No! I can't afford to trust anyone else right now." Cruz felt panicked. "I made a huge mistake with Bryndis, and if I do it again... Besides, I promised... Nobody seems to understand... I promised my mom I would follow *her* directions. I promised her I'd give the formula to the person *she* chose—"

"No, Cruz, you didn't."

He stopped rambling to stare at her. Cruz was confused.

"You promised *a program*," said Nyomie. "You couldn't know what you'd be up against when you started this journey. And neither could your mom seven—almost eight—years ago. Think of all the challenges Emmett, Sailor, Lani, and you have overcome—the puzzles you decoded, the clues you solved, the assassins you escaped."

Cruz leaned wearily against the fridge. "But what good is it all if I fail now?"

Nyomie started to answer, but her words were drowned out by an engine. It was coming from above. A helicopter.

Nebula!

"Should we make a run for it?" yelled Cruz.

"Too late. They've probably seen our boat." Nyomie started pulling him across the kitchen toward the hallway. "The first door on the left is a hurricane shelter. Go down and bolt yourself inside—"

"No."

"Cruz, this is no time to for heroics. Do as I—"

"*No.* I'm not going. If I hadn't left you at the Tiger's Nest . . . maybe Rook wouldn't have . . ." Cruz grabbed her arm. "Don't make me leave. Please, Taryn—"

"Okay, okay." She patted his hand. "We'll stick together. I could use your help anyway."

The noise from the helicopter was growing fainter.

Nyomie tossed her backpack on the floor and knelt to open the top zipper. Removing two small gray cylinders, she stuffed one in the side pocket of her jacket. "Flash-bangs," she explained. "Big sound. Blinding light. No serious harm. Here's the plan: The minute the door opens, you spray your octopod and I'll deploy one of these. The commotion should disorient them long enough for the toxin to take effect and for us to escape. Do you have a bandanna to cover your nose and mouth?"

"Yes." Cruz dug it out of his pack and tied it on.

Nyomie backed up against the wall on the left side of the door. Cruz did the same on the right. Lifting the octopod from his pocket, he placed his thumb and index finger just outside of the blue trigger circles, extended his arm, and took aim. "Mell, stand by," he whispered.

The drone flashed her eyes.

Voices!

Nebula's henchmen were on the porch. Was Lion with them? Cruz's heart hammered against his ribs. His breath came shallow and fast.

He was clutching the octopod so tightly he was sure it would crumble in his fingers. Cruz heard the latch release. The door was moving! A second from squeezing the octopod trigger, Cruz spotted a burst of lime and bright yellow. Only one thing could create that combination. "Emmett?"

"Cruz!" shouted Emmett. "Are you all right? Is it safe for us?"

Us. Lani and Sailor were with him.

Cruz yanked down his bandanna. "Yes and yes."

Emmett, Lani, and Sailor scurried into the kitchen. Cruz didn't have to ask Emmett how he'd opened the security door. He'd have accessed the Academy files for Cruz's iris pattern and anything else he thought might come in handy to bypass security.

"We heard the helicopter and thought you were Nebula," said Cruz.

"That *was* Nebula," panted Emmett. "We came by boat. A Nebula helicopter just flew over. We saw the logo."

"And they saw us," said Lani. "I don't know how they tracked us. We tried not to leave any footprints. We didn't take the Academy's helicopter or *Condor.* Professor Luben has a friend who has a jet—"

Cruz put a hand to his head. "Professor Luben . . . is here?"

"Uh-huh." Emmett's emoto-glasses were in full fireworks mode. "Your aunt, too. They took off in the boat we rented to draw Nebula to the other side of the island."

"A-Aunt Marisol?" Cruz's throat tightened. "This is exactly what I *didn't* want."

"We didn't have much choice," said Lani. "It was either come with them or not at all. They caught us trying to sneak off *Orion*—"

"Which we wouldn't have had to do if you'd have brought us along like you should have," snapped Sailor. "Sorry, we didn't stick around for the cupcakes. I thought we were a team." The sharpness of her tone was like broken glass against his brain.

"We *are* a team," insisted Cruz.

"Let's go. We can talk about this later." Nyomie was trying to get them to move toward the door.

"Really?" scoffed Sailor. "'Cause a team sticks together. One member doesn't run off and send his friends some crummy note."

Nyomie stopped herding to frown at Cruz. "I thought you were going to *talk* to them."

"Uh...yeah...about that." He shriveled. "I...I...I..."

Glaring at him, Sailor folded her arms. "I think the word you're searching for is 'didn't.'"

"After last night," said Cruz, "I didn't want to put you in any more danger."

"We know what we signed up for," said Emmett

"Wait, what happened last night?" Nyomie's head was bouncing.

"We worked as hard as you did on the clues," spit Sailor. "We deserve to be here. We *want* to be here."

"Okay, we *will* talk about this later," said Nyomie firmly. "Explorers, we need to go now."

Lani looked around the kitchen. "What about Dr. Fallowfeld?"

"He's not here." Cruz reached for his backpack. "Never was. It's another dead end."

"So those ankhs don't mean anything?" Emmett was staring at the ceiling.

Everyone looked up. The mural had changed! A holographic projection was superimposed over the painting. Two gold ankh symbols were now on the map: one on top of this house and the other at Mount Pāniʻau. A dotted white line connected the two places.

Cruz swallowed hard. "Dr. Fallowfeld!"

Sailor was on her toes. "I don't see any GPS coordinates."

"We need them to pinpoint a specific spot," reminded Emmett.

"Maybe Mell could compare this painting to a satellite photo and get us close," said Lani.

She could and did. Mell's analysis of the data provided a location on the summit of the mountain with 99.4 percent accuracy, give or take one-tenth of a mile. "It's only about two miles from here as the bee flies," said Cruz, studying the route the MAV had provided on his screen.

"But the cliffs are in *our* way. We'll have to go around. It'll add another mile and a half to our hike."

Sailor pressed the button to open the door.

"Mell, we'll follow you," said Cruz. "Remember, you're the only one with wings."

The bee blinked twice, then zipped off with the rest of them on her stinger. They hiked swiftly, watching and listening for any sign of Nebula. The giant wall of rock looming in the distance, the drone led the group through a sandy thicket of underbrush on a southwest course. As they went, the brush become thicker, the trees taller. The canopy, they knew, would make it harder for Nebula to spot them from the air. Skirting along the cliff boundary, Mell found a trail winding up the side of the stone tower. The steep path tested their strength and stamina, but the climb was worth it. Mell's recalculation indicated that their shortcut had shaved three-quarters of a mile off their trek.

At the top of the ridge, they cut back, hiking southeast over the low dome of the plateau. From this height, they could see Lehua Island rising from the waters off the northern coast of Niʻihau. Cruz knew the bare, crescent-shaped tuff cone was created from the same volcano that had formed this island. Lehua was now a state seabird sanctuary.

Mell was hovering. She tilted her head to Cruz as if to say, *We're here.* They'd reached the summit.

"Mell, nice work. Thanks for leading us. Mell, rest here." Cruz patted her honeycomb remote pinned to his jacket, and she landed on it.

Low grasses, scrubby underbrush, and kiawe trees sprouted from the rich red volcanic soil. There were no buildings. Not that Cruz had expected to find any. If Dr. Fallowfeld was smart, he'd be hiding underground somewhere in the maze of lava tubes that had once fueled the volcano—deep underground.

"Everybody, spread out and look for *puka*, a lava cave entrance," directed Cruz.

"Don't go far," added Nyomie. "Keep me in your line of sight."

Lani dropped to one knee and opened her pack. Cruz thought she was getting a snack until he saw her take out a small bundle of purple metal pipes. Each pipe looked to be a few inches wide in diameter and a foot long. They were connected. Lani snapped the hinges into place to form one long pipe. Fully extended, the thing came up past Lani's waist. The top end was flat, the bottom pointed and coated with what Cruz figured was rubber.

She saw Cruz's eyebrows rise. "It's my invention to talk with trees, remember?"

A prototype already? Impressive!

Cruz touched the pipe. "This is how you connect to the mycorrhizal network?"

"Right. From my tablet, I transmit a Morse code alphabet at two hundred and twenty hertz through the pipe into the root system. After several repetitions to allow the trees to catch on to the code, I then send a simple message. Just a few words, really. The pipe listens for a reply and relays it to back my tablet, where the software translates the trees' Morse code crackles into English. I call it the Botanical Amplified Root Communicator."

Putting the acronym together, Cruz laughed. "BARC!"

Lani stood. Dusting her hands on the sides of her jacket, she looked around. "These kiawes should do."

"Good roots," agreed Cruz.

Living in Kauai, both explorers knew that kiawes were a type of mesquite tree. In places like Ni'ihau, which didn't get a lot of rain, kiawes had deep taproots with shallower roots that branched out in search of water.

"It's a long shot, I know," said Lani, "but the trees might be able to give us a clue about Dr. Fallowfeld's whereabouts." Pulling a small mallet from her pack, Lani headed toward a large tree. "The biggest and oldest trees are known as hub trees. One study found that one hub tree can connect to more than forty other trees. This oughta do." Pounding the BARC into the dirt, Lani caught Cruz's look of skepticism. "You don't think it will work, do you?"

Squirming, Cruz stared up at the straggly twist of branches with their lacy fernlike leaves and clumps of large dangling seed pods. "It just seems so ... I don't know ..."

"Crazy? Wild? Impossible?"

"Well, yeah ... a little."

"You mean, like Emmett's emoto-glasses? Or Fanchon's octopod? Or my acousticks?"

She was right. "If anyone can make the impossible possible, Lani, it's you."

With a satisfied nod, she turned to her tablet. Cruz left Lani to her work and began scouring the brush. He was debating whether to tackle some thornbushes when he heard Emmett calling him from the other side of Lani.

Cruz arrived to find Emmett standing over a red plastic handle. It was sticking up out of the ground at a 45-degree angle. It looked like the grip of a child's shovel, though it was hard to be sure because the handle was all that was visible. "I tripped over it," said Emmett. "It blends in so well with the dirt. Seems weird to find a toy here, don't you think?"

Cruz was about to say he did when he saw a flicker of brown out of the corner of his eye. Something was moving in the trees! At first he thought it was an antelope but soon realized his mistake. Not horns—hair.

Aunt Marisol!

Arms out, head down, she was almost leaping through the brush. Chunks of hair had fallen loose from her bun. The front of her tan jacket was streaked with red dirt.

Cruz began to jog toward her. "Aunt Marisol!"

Her head shot up. "Cruz!" she shrieked. "*Run!*"

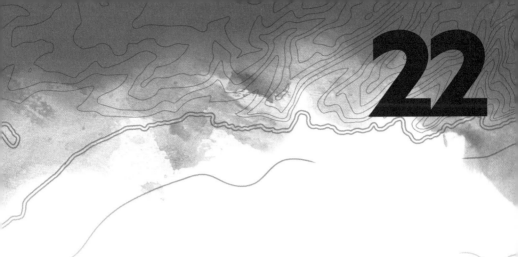

22

▶ **THE TERROR** in Aunt Marisol's voice electrified Cruz's spine, but instead of running, he froze.

Two men swooped in on his aunt from behind: a short muscular guy whose jaw was covered in a woolly beard, and his partner, a gangly man with long, shaggy hair. Cruz recognized them. They were the Nebula agents who'd attacked Cruz and his friends in the Terra-Cotta Army museum. He knew the taller one was code-named Scorpion. Both wore camouflage jackets and carried laser rifles. The shorter one grabbed Aunt Marisol's elbow. Frantic, Cruz looked around. Where was Professor Luben?

Nyomie and Sailor had heard the commotion and were quickly coming back through the brush. Lani was rushing toward them, too.

"Stop!" ordered Scorpion when he saw them all converging. "STOP!" He shot his rifle into the air. The pulse hit a kiawe branch, setting it ablaze.

They obeyed.

Cruz took stock of everyone's positions. Aunt Marisol and her captors were roughly 30 feet dead ahead. Nyomie and Sailor were to his right about 20 feet. Lani was about the same distance to his left. Cruz didn't see Emmett and figured he was still behind him.

"Cruz Coronado!" hollered Scorpion through the haze of the burning mesquite limb. "Our boss wants you and that cipher of yours. We'll let her go if you come with us. You've got ten seconds. Ten...nine...eight..."

"I'll come!" yelled Cruz. He didn't need even one second. "I'm coming!"

"Stay where you are, Coronado," came the next order. "The rest of you, leave the summit. Take the east trail. Don't look back or you'll regret it. *Go now!*"

The agent holding Aunt Marisol flung her away. Nyomie and Sailor ran to meet her. The trio moved off to Cruz's left. Out of the corner of his eye, he could see Lani and Emmett jogging to catch up to them. Watching his friends, Nyomie, and Aunt Marisol disappear into the brush, Cruz swallowed hard.

He was alone.

Cruz knew his fate, and it sent a shudder through him. The Nebula assassins were coming his way. They passed under the kiawe Scorpion had hit. The limb was still smoldering.

Cruz felt another tremor. However, this one didn't come from within. It reminded him of being on *Orion*. Like the slow

roll of a wave being born, the earth began to shift. The sunbaked red ground was cracking.

Earthquake!

Cruz watched, astonished, as a zigzag fracture split the soil right between the Nebula agents. A gap was opening, gulping dirt, rocks, and grass like a greedy mouth. Cruz figured he'd better not wait for the hole to swallow him, too, and made a dash for the trail. He'd taken only a few steps when his toe hit a rock. Cruz crashed down. He tried to get up, but everything was giving way under him. He kept slipping. Dirt in his eyes and up his nose, Cruz lashed out with his arms and legs, trying to find a toehold or *something* to grab on to. It was all disintegrating. He could feel himself sliding, yet there was nothing he could do to stop it. Cruz was going to tumble into the crater of the volcano!

He felt a crack on his shoulder.

"Hold on!"

Cruz clawed at the dirt with one hand while blindly swiping the air with the other. Suddenly, his hand hit something hard. Metal? Lani's BARC! Cruz latched on. He clung tightly to the pipe as he was being hauled out of the crevice. Back on solid ground, he looked up into the faces of Sailor and Lani. "Thanks!"

"Let's get out of here!" Nyomie picked up Cruz as if he were a stuffed toy. She set him on his feet, and they ran to where his aunt and Emmett waited at the edge of the hillside. The six of them huddled together until the shaking subsided. It felt like forever but was probably only a minute or two.

When everything was still again, they lifted their heads. The dust was settling. The mesquite tree was no longer on fire, though the smell of charred wood lingered.

"Everyone all right?" asked Nyomie.

Other than a few cuts and bumps, they were fine.

Cruz scanned the plateau. "Be careful. The Nebula agents—"

"I think they're gone, hon," said his aunt solemnly. She looked at the sinkhole.

The group untangled themselves and inched toward the pit. It was huge, at least 60 feet in diameter. And deep—100 feet, maybe more. Peering over the edge, Cruz could see shards of black lava rock poking up between the roots, bushes, and other debris. It didn't seem likely anyone could have survived such a fall. Still, he had to be sure.

"Mell, fly into the crater and search for signs of life," Cruz instructed his drone.

They watched her swoop down into the hole.

Cruz turned to Aunt Marisol. "What about Professor Luben? Did they—"

"He's okay. The agents disabled our boat and left him on the beach on the east side of the island. I'm the one they wanted. To get to you."

Mell was coming back. She'd sent a report to Cruz's tablet indicating that she'd found both agents but no life signs.

"Guys?" Lani was staring at her own tablet. "The BARC...I don't... Can this be right?"

"What's the matter?" asked Cruz.

"It translated a message." She turned her screen to show them.

Cruz saw four words:

Pain. Danger. Move. Away.

Sailor glanced at the scorched kiawe tree. "Could it have...?"

"It warned the other trees of the fire," said Lani.

"So they shifted their roots away from the one that Scorpion injured," added Emmett.

"Which caused the ground to cave in," finished Cruz. "It did it! It talked to the other trees."

It seemed too crazy to be true. Wild. Impossible.

And yet...

Sailor stared at the kiawe. "I had no idea trees could *feel* things."

"And yet, why wouldn't they?" asked Aunt Marisol. "They're living organisms. Life is extraordinary."

Nyomie softly whistled. "It sure is."

They stared at the forest in amazement, as if they were seeing trunks, branches, and leaves for the first time. And maybe they were.

Lani broke the spell. "I think my invention still needs work, though," she said. "I've got another message from the BARC here, but this one doesn't make any sense."

"What is it?" asked Aunt Marisol.

"'Human. Below. Red. Handle'?"

Cruz and Emmett exchanged looks.

"It makes perfect sense, Lani," proclaimed Cruz.

Soon, 12 hands were digging like mad around the little red handle sticking out of the dirt. Clearing away a foot of soil, they discovered the grip was, indeed, attached to a small plastic shovel. The scoop part of the toy was glued to a six-by-six-foot metal plate. Cruz, Lani, Emmett, and Sailor each took a corner and lifted. They moved the metal sheet aside to reveal a large black computer screen. Embedded in the side of the screen was an oval cradle with the label: *Place finger here.*

Nobody needed to ask what it was for. Or whom.

Cruz blew away a film of red dust before placing his index finger in the indentation. They waited for the print verification to come up on the screen.

"Ouch!" Cruz jerked his hand away to find he had three little puncture marks in his fingertip. "It pricked me."

"Hematological biometrics," said Lani. "Nice touch."

"Good pun," laughed Emmett.

Cruz sucked on his finger to stop the bleeding.

"Hey!" Sailor was poised over the screen. "Something's happening!"

A row of four red padlock icons had appeared. Below each lock were two blank spaces to type in the number that would presumably unlock it. Above the locks, the computer was typing out a message:

Elements of earth and sea,

you study periodically.

Last letter of each postcard's town,

will share all secrets underground.

"I get it," said Sailor. "It wants the last letter of each place where Cruz's four postcards came from. Let's see . . . The first one came from Kauai, so that's an *i.*"

"The riddle says *town*," caught Emmett. "You know, as in a city."

"Oh, right . . . Hanalei." Sailor rolled her eyes. "Which is still an *i.*"

"The second postcard was from Washington, D.C.," said Cruz. "So, *n.*"

"The third one was from Otjiwarongo, Namibia, so that's an *o*," said Lani. "And the last one was from Paro, Bhutan. Also an *o.*"

"*I* is . . . the ninth letter of the alphabet." Sailor was counting out the alphabet using her fingers. "*N* is the fourteenth. *O* is the fifteenth."

On the touch screen, Cruz typed *09* beneath the first lock, *14* under the second, and *15* below both the third and fourth locks.

The padlock icons remained red. And locked.

Sailor grunted. "So much for that idea."

"Wait, we're forgetting the first half of the clue," said Emmett.

"*Elements* of earth and sea? *Periodically?*"

Lani slapped her thigh. "The periodic table!"

"I'm on it." Sailor went for her tablet.

"I'll bet it wants the atomic number for I, which symbolizes the element iodine in the periodic table," reasoned Emmett. "Sailor, what's the atomic number for I?"

"Uh . . . hold on."

"C would be for carbon," said Lani.

"O for oxygen," said Cruz.

All eyes turned to Sailor, whose hands were flying over her screen. "Okay, Cruz, type this in: 53, 6, 8, 8. Those are the atomic numbers for iodine, carbon, and oxygen."

Cruz did as she instructed, inserting a zero before the single digits. One by one, the locks turned green. The curved shanks of the padlocks popped out of the sockets of their square mechanisms.

"It's dissolving!" called Cruz.

"You mean the words?" asked Aunt Marisol.

"The entire screen!"

The screen and scanner were evaporating to reveal a hole. Everyone gathered around and peered into the cavern. It was only about four feet wide. Metal handles had been affixed to one side of the bumpy black lava rock in a vertical row. A ladder!

"You'd better go first," Emmett said to Cruz. "Might be more checkpoints."

"I've already given blood." Cruz rubbed his thumb against his pierced fingertip. "What more could Dr. Fallowfeld want?"

"Saliva," teased Emmett.

"Hair," said Lani.

"Pee." Sailor shrugged. "Maybe a whole kidney."

That got them giggling.

"Explorers, pay attention, please," said Aunt Marisol firmly, and they quickly settled down. "If we were on an Academy mission, I would not let you do this, but since it seems this is the path our host has quite carefully planned, I'll allow it. However, you must follow my instructions precisely. Is that clear?"

It was.

"Cover your arms and put on your gloves," she said. "The rough texture of lava rock can shred skin, so be careful not to touch it. Also, it's very brittle. Pieces can easily break off from above. We don't have helmets and we'll have very little light, so you'll need to stay alert. Look, listen, and watch where you're going. Finally, once we're down there, stay together. There are miles of lava caves in this volcano, and if you get lost... Well, *don't* get lost."

They got the message.

Cruz swung his legs over the gap. Lani held on to him, and he put his feet on the first handle. With Mell lighting the way, Cruz climbed down into the void. Once, he leaned back without thinking, to stretch his elbows, and the coarse rock grabbed his pack and wouldn't let go. It took him several tries to break free of the Velcro-like stone. He continued down, rung by rung, this time hugging the ladder. Cruz counted 174 rungs before his feet at last touched ground.

Cruz moved at a sloth's pace into the cave. Hardened lava bubbled up from the floor in cracked blobs like burned marshmallows. Overhead, wiggly earthworms of rock dangled from the low roof. Cruz now understood his aunt's warning. If even a single twisted spire fell, it could skewer a person. One by one, Lani, Emmett, Sailor, Nyomie, and Aunt Marisol joined him beneath the stringy ceiling.

"Those are lavacicles," explained his aunt. "They form while the cave is cooling. Under pressure, the gases get squeezed out and the lava cools mid-drip."

"It's like another world down here," whispered Lani.

"A weird, weird world," said Sailor.

Mell lit the way as they followed the grooved cave down, down, down in a spiral. Every 100 feet or so, a smaller lava tube branched off the main tunnel, but seeing no signs to indicate they should veer into one, they stayed on the main course. Leveling off, the shaft opened to a

large chamber. It was easily twice the size of the dining hall at Explorer Academy headquarters. Globs of copper-colored rock dripped down the walls like gooey, delicious fudge frozen in time. It looked so real, Cruz's stomach gurgled. Several other tubes also emptied into the chamber.

"Have a look around," directed Aunt Marisol. "But don't leave this room."

They split up.

With Mell resting on her honeycomb remote, Cruz began a visual inspection of the brown globs of rock. He was working his way to the next tube when a space in the rock caught his eye. He poked his head into the nook and saw something he never expected to see deep inside a volcano: his own reflection!

It was a full-length mirror.

"Aunt Marisol! Nyomie! Team Cousteau!" called Cruz quietly, so as not to bring down any lavacicles.

A message was being typed on the mirror's surface in glowing blue letters: *Remain still for identification.*

Cruz didn't move. Neither did Mell. He could see her in his reflection, still clinging to his jacket. Everyone clustered behind him.

"Mirror, mirror on the wall," hummed Sailor. "Please say Cruz is the fairest of them all."

Ten seconds later, it passed judgement: *Cruz S. Coronado Identity: CONFIRMED.*

"Facial-recognition software, likely combined with the blood sample," said Emmett.

The paragraph disappeared. It was replaced by a new message: *Have you completed Petra Coronado's mission? Respond vocally, please.*

"Yes. I have the complete cipher." Cruz felt a little dizzy, which might have had something to do with his rapidly increasing heartbeat.

Congratulations!

Cruz had done it! In a moment, the door would slide open, Dr. Fallowfeld would greet him, collect the cipher, and continue developing the formula, just as Cruz's mother had intended. He had made it to the finish line ahead of Nebula. He had won! Cruz bounced, awaiting the *swish* of the door. Or maybe it would evaporate, too, like the screen. He stopped bouncing. Nothing was happening.

Another message came across the screen: *Is Nebula still a threat?*

He hesitated. If Cruz answered yes, Dr. Fallowfeld might worry that Nebula had followed him into the cave. The scientist might not let him in. On the other hand, Cruz couldn't lie. Brume *was* still out there...

The words repeated, this time in all caps: *IS NEBULA STILL A THREAT?*

Cruz winced. "Uh...uh..."

"What does it say?" asked Sailor.

"It wants to know if Nebula is still a threat," said Cruz.

"Yes!" A familiar voice boomed through the chamber. "I would say Nebula is most definitely still a threat."

In the mirror, Cruz saw a laser pistol pointed at their backs.

And the man with his finger on the trigger?

Professor Luben.

23

▶ **"ARCHER?"** questioned Aunt Marisol.

"Hezekiah," he corrected. "Hezekiah Brume." He shot Emmett a glare. "Code name Lion, for anyone pretending to be one of my agents."

Cruz was dumbstruck. "You're saying ... You mean ... *You're* Nebula?"

"And you call yourself an explorer," scoffed the professor. "I did give you one major clue to my identity. I can't do everything for you."

So it *was* true. The teacher Cruz had learned from, the mentor he'd trusted, the man he'd admired was, in reality, his worst enemy!

Brume surveyed the chamber. "Where's my team? Scorpion?" he called, turning. "Komodo?"

"There was a cave-in near the surface," said Nyomie crisply. "They didn't survive. And you're going to cause another collapse if you keep waving that weapon around."

Brume looked up, scanning the lavacicles, as if he rather liked the idea of bringing the whole thing crashing down upon them. His gaze settled on Cruz. "You'll have to come with me. I need you as well as the cipher so we can study the effects of the serum. You won't be harmed," he said, earning a snort from Sailor. "In return, I'll let everyone else go. I think that's a fair trade, don't you, Cruz? Your life, your very *long* life, for theirs?"

"Absolutely not!" broke in Aunt Marisol. "Listen here, Archer— Hezekiah—whoever you are—this is unacceptable. You are a member of the Explorer Academy faculty—"

"Not anymore," he broke in. "I did enjoy teaching, but it served its purpose. I'm a businessman, Marisol, first and foremost. What's it going to be, Cruz? Do you accept my terms?" Brume glanced up. "Or shall I leave you *all* here?"

Cruz was out of moves. And Brume knew it.

Cruz spit the words. "I accept."

"Decisiveness." Brume's lips curled into a fiendish grin. "I like that."

His response struck a chord. Cruz had heard that somewhere before. It took him a minute to remember where. "In class ... when we were choosing icebergs."

"What are you mumbling about?" demanded Brume.

"On the day of our mission to the Danger Islands, you were kind of uptight in class before we left, and you were definitely mad when we got back," recalled Cruz. "I thought it was because we'd returned to *Orion* after our deadline, but that wasn't it at all, was it? You were angry at Bryndis. She messed up your plan. Bryndis was supposed to choose the wedge iceberg. You'd told her to do it so you'd be our faculty guide on the mission. She didn't. She chose the pinnacle instead, which meant you couldn't get to me." Cruz looked him in the eye. "You couldn't carry out your plan to get rid of me ..."

Brume tipped his head to indicate Cruz was correct, but he admitted nothing.

"I just got it!" burst Lani, making Cruz nearly jump out of his skin. "The clue, I mean. A. Luben is Nebula spelled backward."

"Fifty bonus points to the young lady," cackled Brume. He wagged the gun. "We're wasting time. Let's go, Cruz."

Stepping out of the niche, Cruz saw Nyomie's jaw had gone rigid, a tiny vein, or rather, circuit, pulsing. Aunt Marisol's brow was creased so deeply he could barely see her eyes.

"Give me the cipher first," ordered Brume. "I know about that bio force field of yours."

Cruz shook his head. "No, not until we're out of here and I know they're safe."

Brume shifted the laser, aiming it at Aunt Marisol.

"Yes...I mean yes," surrendered Cruz. "It's yours."

Slowly moving toward Brume, Cruz reached into his shirt for the stones. He brought them out, then dipped his head so he could pull off the lanyard. As he did, Cruz brushed his hand against the front of his jacket, allowing him to grab something else, too. Cruz stopped a few feet in front of Brume, who'd held out his hand. Cruz extended his arm. His heart banging against his chest, Cruz opened his fist. The marble stones fell into Brume's waiting palm.

So did Mell.

"Mell, defense mode!" directed Cruz. "Target: the man holding you. Mell, sting!"

"Arrrrrgh!" screamed Brume as the bee sunk her stinger into his flesh. Flinging his arm out, Brume slapped at Mell. He hit her before she was able to get clear. The robotic bee spun out of control, smacked the wall next to him, and fell to the ground. "Nice try," growled the head of Nebula, shaking out his injured hand, "but it'll take more than a jab from a puny drone to stop me. Drop your pack, Cruz. Take off your jacket, too. You're leaving them here."

"But—"

"Do it. I don't need you pulling any more rabbits out of your hat."

Cruz broke out in a cold sweat. Without his comm or GPS pins, octopod, virtugraph, shadow badge, and tablet, he would have no gear to assist him with an escape attempt.

Brume was waiting. Cruz wriggled out of his pack and removed his jacket, setting them on the ground. A mini flashlight flew at Cruz, and he caught it.

"Now *move!*"

Crossing in front of the weapon, Cruz headed to far side of the chamber, where they'd entered. At the tunnel, he took one last look back at Nyomie, Aunt Marisol, Lani, Sailor, and Emmett. They'd gathered close, lips barely moving. Cruz suspected they were already brainstorming how to save him. It made him feel good, but he knew the odds were against a rescue. It was unlikely that he would ever see any of them again.

Cruz lifted a hand. *Love you, Aunt Marisol. Goodbye, Nyomie, Emmett, Sailor, and Lani. Thanks for the best year of my life.*

Clicking on the flashlight, Cruz stepped into the lava tube. Cruz and Brume began the hike up the spiral incline. Brume was hardly a man to be trusted, so Cruz didn't expect to survive long. But how much time did he have? A few days? Several hours? Minutes? There were things he needed to know, things only Brume could answer.

"You pushed me into the cave in Turkey, didn't you?" Cruz asked the man poking him in the spine with a gun barrel.

Brume chuckled. "Too easy."

"And my mother?"

"That was unfortunate. She forced my hand. I gave her plenty of chances to cooperate."

"Then you burned her lab."

"*Her* lab?" He grunted. "In that journal of hers, did she ever mention who funded her research?"

"She said you did, but—"

"That's right. If it weren't for me, she would never have discovered the serum. The formula was mine. She refused to accept that."

"How could she? You would have destroyed it."

"My money. My serum."

"*Her* work. And what about all the people it could help? You have a responsibility to the world—"

"Your mom had a responsibility to abide by our contract. That's how the business world works, Cruz. Look, I didn't get to be where I am without having to play a little hardball. I admit that, but I have people depending on me...I don't expect...you to understand." He was breathing harder. The passage was getting steeper. "You're a kid, but when you have...a family of your own—"

"I *had* a family," shot Cruz, his temper bubbling.

Brume did not reply.

As he passed one of the offshoot tubes, Cruz heard his aunt's voice in his head.

There are miles of lava caves in this volcano.

It gave him an idea.

"So...uh...Bryndis knows who you really are?" Cruz picked up his pace a little.

"No. I was careful to only communicate with her by message. She was too unpredictable. I couldn't take the chance that she might blab to you or one of the other explorers."

Cruz walked faster.

"Hold up...there," panted Brume.

Cruz ignored him. He kept going. He could see the next tube. A few more feet and he would be there.

"I said...hold up!"

Cruz ducked into the tube and ran!

"Cruz!"

The offshoot tunnel was thinner than the main one, the ground rockier and more steeply sloped. The best Cruz could do was a fast walk, keeping his elbows in tight to avoid brushing against the rough lava. He did have one advantage: light. Brume would have to slow down to feel his way through the dark passage, which would give Cruz time to gain a comfortable lead.

Taking a curve, Cruz dared to glance back. He saw a beam. *Dang!* So much for his edge.

He faced forward again. He had to pay attention, or he might go headlong into—

"Whoa!" Stumbling, Cruz clipped the side of the grooved wall with his upper arm. The stone tore his shirt. He felt the sting as it sliced into his skin.

Uh-oh!

A wall—dead ahead.

A bulge of hardened lava blocked his way. Cruz was forced to stop, his eyes darting around for a gap to climb over, under, or through. It was solid rock. He was stuck. One way in and one way out. Cruz spun around. Desperate, he plunged his hands into his pants pockets, but the only thing he came up with was a crumpled piece of paper.

Every problem has a solution. He heard his survival instructor's voice.

"Monsieur Legrand, I think I may have found the one problem that doesn't have a solution," whispered Cruz, his heart thumping.

Keep it together, Cruz. Manage your emotions. Stay calm. Focus on what's in front of you.

And what was in front of him was Hezekiah Brume!

Brume was coming around the bend. He'd attached his light to his belt, and the flickering ray cast eerie shadows on his shiny face. Huffing, he advanced toward Cruz. "A dead end," he snarled. "How fitting. It's clear you're not going to cooperate, so let's finish this now."

Cruz's OS band was flashing: *Cardio. Cardio.* The red line measuring his heartbeat had gone flat. He knew why. This was how Dr. Lu had communicated with her son when she was in the Synthesis hideaway on board *Orion*. Emmett was tracking Cruz through his OS band!

Nice try, Emmett, but too little too late.

Brume raised the laser.

Lifting his hands to protect himself, Cruz realized he was still clutching the crumpled page from his pocket. It wasn't much, but it was all he had.

He heard the laser power up.

"Wait!" Cruz waved the paper. "You need to read this."

"No more tricks, Cruz." Brume took aim.

"It's a letter from Roewyn."

"My ... daughter?"

"She's been helping *me*."

"*You?* Why would she do that? I don't believe it. I don't believe you."

"You don't have to. See for yourself."

Brume staggered toward Cruz. He was blinking rapidly, as if trying to focus. His face was red and puffy. Sweat poured off his brow. He took the note from Cruz. His lips mumbled along as he read. "'I've tried to

talk to my father ... refuses to listen ... make right everything my father hath done wrong.'"

Did he say 'hath'?

Brume looked up, his eyelids heavy. "Roewyn can't mean this ..."

"She does. She's been sending me these letters for months. I have them all back on *Orion*—well, except for the one written in jam. She even traveled to Jordan and India to find me." Cruz looked at the pistol pointed at his chest. "*She* saved my life."

Furrows cut through Brume's sweaty forehead. Cruz saw something in his eyes he'd never seen before, not in the classroom or even on a mission. Cruz saw uncertainty.

Brume put a hand to his jaw. "My face ... tongue ... feel thtwange."

Roewyn's note slipping from his fingers, the man dropped to his knees. He collapsed onto his side.

Cruz stared down at him.

Was Brume ...

... dead?

"Anaphylaxis." The word startled Cruz. Nyomie was marching toward him. "Probably an allergic reaction to Mell's sting."

"That's impossible. Her stinger doesn't have any venom."

"You sure?" Reaching for Brume's laser, Nyomie turned it off.

"Yes! No ... I don't know." He supposed Fanchon could have added it when she dismantled Mell's self-destruct mechanism. But wouldn't she have told him? It was probably against Academy rules, so she'd have to do it in secret—

Cruz stopped.

Behind Nyomie, another silhouette had appeared in the ghostly glow of flashlights.

He squinted as it came out of the shadows. "M-Mom?"

24

▶ "HI, CRUZER."

A new holo-video? The 3D high-definition image was so lifelike, Cruz could swear his mother was actually standing in the passage. His friends must have found a new journal in the chocolate fudge chamber, or maybe a holo-dome similar to his own. Cruz glanced at Nyomie, but she wasn't holding anything other than Brume's weapon. His adviser was now wearing a yellow hard hat. So was his mom, which, when you thought about it, was odd for a holo-video.

Could it be ...?

Could *she* be ...?

Cruz could hardly get the words out. "Are ... you ... real?"

His mother laughed, and gray-blue eyes with a few more wrinkles than he remembered crinkled. "As real as you are, son."

"She's real," confirmed Nyomie. "It was a big shock to us, too, when she appeared from behind that mirrored wall in the chamber. Uh ... Cruz? You okay?"

Cruz tried to answer, but his lungs were tightening. He couldn't seem to catch his breath. Everything began to spin. He felt his knees buckle. Someone caught him and eased him to the ground. His head was being cradled. Had he fainted? His hands and legs felt tingly.

"This isn't exactly how I wanted to break the news to you," he heard his mother's voice say.

A blurry face hovered over his. "Take a breath to the count of three, Cruz. In ... one, two, three, and out ... one, two, three," said his mom. "That's it. Let's do it again."

By the fourth inhale, she came into focus. Her hair was several inches shorter than he remembered, but everything else was the same—her smile, her eyes, the little cluster of freckles dotting the bridge of her nose. It wasn't a dream!

"Mom ... Mom ... Mom ..." Cruz couldn't stop saying it.

"I'm here, son. I'm here ... I've always been here, waiting until it was

safe to be with you again. I'm sorry it had to be this way. And I'm sorry it took so long."

Cruz tasted the salt of tears, both his and hers.

She hugged him to her, rocking him as if he were a baby. "I've missed you *so* much."

"Mom." Cruz clung to her, his mind a whirlwind of thoughts and emotions and questions, but none of them mattered. Right now, all that counted was that she was alive and all he wanted to do was hold on to her.

"Uh...I'm sorry to break up your reunion, but we do have a person in distress here," said Nyomie. "Petra, do you have epinephrine in your first aid kit?"

Cruz and his mom released each other. Wiping his eyes, Cruz sat up.

Nyomie had placed Brume onto his back, covered him with her jacket, and slipped a rolled-up scarf under his head. She was going through his pockets, no doubt looking for an epinephrine syringe like the ones the explorers with life-threatening allergies always carried. She wasn't finding anything. "He needs an injection to counteract the effects of the allergic reaction."

"Sorry, I don't have any—not even in my lab back in the chamber," said Cruz's mother. "I do have oxygen, though. I always carry that. It's vital down here." She quickly found an oxygen mask in her pack and gave it to Nyomie, who placed it over Brume's mouth and nose. Brume's face was swollen, and he had little welts on his neck.

"Cruz, I think *this* belongs to you." Nyomie was leaning toward him. She was holding the cipher. She'd found it in one of Brume's pockets.

Cruz slipped the stones around his neck. He tucked them into his shirt, relieved to feel the cool marble against his chest once again.

"So that's *him*," whispered Cruz's mom as they watched Nyomie take Brume's blood pressure.

"Yes." Cruz's voice was hoarse.

"I've never seen him."

"And I've seen him almost every day."

"Cruz, your arm—it's bleeding."

"It's nothing." It was true. He felt no pain.

"Let's bandage that. You don't want it to get infected. I'll get one from my kit." She passed him her water bottle. "And drink. You need to stay hydrated."

"Okay, Mom."

Mom. How strange it sounded. Cruz wasn't saying it in the past tense or to advance a program. He was saying it *for real*. For now. For what lay ahead.

Nyomie sat back. "The oxygen is helping, but his blood pressure is still too low, and his pulse is erratic. We need to get him to a hospital." She began putting away her first aid kit. "Cruz, if you take my pack, I'll carry the patient."

Cruz's mom drew in a sharp breath. "Nyomie, you can't possibly—"

"She can," broke in Cruz. "She's stronger than she looks."

"Maybe so, but it's not possible to carry *anyone* up the ladder all of you came down. That well is far too narrow. We'll have to walk out, and the shortest route is three miles."

"I see your point." Nyomie rubbed her chin. "I don't think we have that kind of time. Isn't there anything else we can do?"

"There *is* one thing," said Cruz's mom. She touched the torn sleeve of his bloodstained shirt. "But it's up to you, Cruzer. It has to be your decision."

Gray-blue eyes met brown ones. Her eyebrows went up. His went down.

Oh, no! *No!*

Giving the man a shot of adrenaline was one thing, but this? Had she forgotten who they were dealing with here? Brume had devoted the past eight years to tearing their family apart, and he'd nearly succeeded. The man was ruthless. Heartless. Relentless. Helping him would only give him another chance to hurt them. Cruz could think of a thousand reasons why he shouldn't help Hezekiah Brume but only one why he should.

Roewyn.

She'd sided with Cruz against her own father. Watching her, he'd learned that the right thing wasn't always the easy thing. And it sure wasn't always fair. Whatever decision he made, Cruz knew he would have to live with it for the rest of his life. He looked at the man lying on the ground. Cruz took a deep breath. "Okay, Mom. I'll do it."

She smiled, as if his answer had never been in doubt.

Cruz barely felt the pinch of the needle. His mother took a small vial of his blood and transfused it into Brume. Seeing the red liquid go into the man's arm, a thought occurred to Cruz. "Mom, my blood ... will it make him, you know ...?"

"Like you? No. Your healing ability is engrained in your DNA. Your blood will help boost his immune system but nothing more. And I can assure you there is no one else quite like you." Removing the syringe, she placed a small bandage on Brume's arm. "Now we wait."

Cruz was still trying to wrap his brain around everything. He'd expected to find Dr. Fallowfeld or another scientist at the end of his journey, not his mother! Here, of all places! He looked around the dark cavern. "Mom, have you been living in this volcano *all* this time?"

"No. I moved from the house on the point only last fall, once I knew you'd found my journal and had started searching for the cipher. I figured Nebula would tail you, and I had to be prepared for them to come here."

"I thought—we all thought—you didn't survive the fire in the Synthesis lab. Dr. Fallowfeld said he *saw* you die."

"Elistair had every reason to believe that," she replied. "The fire was intense, and I'd inhaled a lot of smoke, enough to kill a normal person—a person who didn't have the benefit of Tardinia Serum in her system. After the firefighters rescued him, I was able to make it from my lab to the secret entrance to the Archive. Fortunately, I have a few friends there who hid me and helped me work with the owners of this island to design and construct the lab and living space in the large chamber."

"How did you know Dad and I would move to Kauai?"

"I didn't. But I do know your dad and how much he loved it here. I had to choose a final destination for you to bring the cipher, and Ni'ihau offered the perfect solution: a private island where I could continue my work without being disturbed or discovered. No matter where your dad and you would have settled, the journal would have led you back here." She covered his hand with hers. "Luckily for me, you *did* move to Kauai, and it meant I could be part of your lives, even if you couldn't know it.

"Sometimes I would drive by the Goofy Foot or stand on the beach and watch you and Lani surf—from a safe distance, of course. It took every ounce of strength I had not to run to you and throw my arms around you. I almost did, too, on one of your hikes, but I spotted someone suspicious following you. That's when I realized Brume had eyes everywhere. It was too dangerous for me to ever contact you. One misstep could have ruined everything. I had no choice. I *had* to wait for you to come to me. It was the only way to keep your dad and you safe."

Cruz had a terrible thought. "What if you hadn't...?"

"Survived? I had a plan for that, too, thanks to my friends at the Archive."

Cruz put a hand to the stones. "Mom, Dr. Fallowfeld told me the formula doesn't even work. He said one of the toxins in the serum comes from a frog that's extinct..."

"That is true," she said. "I've been working on a solution and think I've found a substitute toxin from another frog that *will* work. It's a species that's endangered and rare in the wild, though, so the only way to procure the toxin is to go to the Amazon rainforest myself. Of course, with Nebula out there, I didn't dare travel, but now—"

"I could go with you!"

"That would be great, Cruz, except"—she tipped her head—"what about school?"

"We could bring all of the explorers—make it a mission, you know? We could go next year. Aunt Marisol could lead us, and you could assign each of the teams a search area. We know what to do. In Borneo, we learned how to spot animals hiding in plain sight..."

Grinning, she lifted a hand. "We'll see. One step at a time."

"That's what Lani always says."

"Smart girl, that Lani."

"And that's what Dad always says about Lani."

Her smile widened.

"Ohhh!" groaned Brume.

"He's coming around." Nyomie checked his vital signs again. "His blood pressure and heart rate are almost normal. His breathing has improved, too. I think we can take this off now." She removed the oxygen mask.

"Emmett Lu to Cruz Coronado!" The call was coming through Cruz's OS band.

He lifted his wrist. "Cruz, here! I'm with Nyomie, my mom, and Professor—I mean, Brume. We're okay."

Cruz's mom leaned in. "Emmett, are you on the surface?"

"Yes." They heard static. "We're at the rendezvous coordinates at Keawanui Bay. Wait, did you say you're with Brume *and* you're okay?"

"I'll explain later," said Cruz.

His mom bent toward his comm pin. "Emmett, it will take us a while to reach you. Maybe an hour or more. We'll need both the police and a medical team to meet us. Do you understand?"

"Copy that. We'll be ready. Emmett, out."

Nyomie was stretching across Brume to Cruz. "I almost forgot. Here's something else that belongs to you." She uncurled her hand.

"Mell!" Cruz scooped up the drone and inspected her for damage. She had a broken antenna and one of her forewings was a bit off. It looked like a hinge was bent. He gently set her on his forearm next to his OS band. "Mell, on. Are you okay?"

She flashed her golden eyes twice to signal she was.

It was a huge relief to know she wasn't seriously damaged, but he'd do a full diagnostic once they were back on board *Orion* to be absolutely sure.

Brume's eyes were open. He gazed at the trio hovering over him, tracking from Nyomie to Cruz to Cruz's mom. "Dr. C-Coronado?"

"Surprise," Cruz's mom said dryly.

Brume caught sight of Mell on Cruz's arm. Cruz saw him visibly shiver. The tables had been turned. And Brume knew it.

"Guess you were wrong. Looks like a jab from a puny drone *was* all it took," said Nyomie with a chuckle. "Okay, I think you're stable enough to sit up now. Fair warning: Try anything and I *will* break your arm."

"She can do it, too," warned Cruz.

Nyomie and Cruz's mom propped up Brume. He did look better. The swelling in his face had gone down, and the proper color was returning.

Brume took a deep breath and coughed.

"Drink." Nyomie handed him her water bottle and they watched him sip water. "Oh, and for the record, the young explorer here you've been chasing? He just saved your life."

The bottle slipped from Brume's hand.

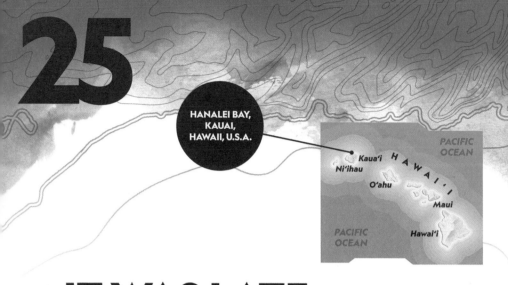

25

HANALEI BAY,
KAUAI,
HAWAII, U.S.A.

PACIFIC
OCEAN

Kaua'i
Ni'ihau

HAWAII

O'ahu

Maui

PACIFIC
OCEAN

Hawai'i

▶ **IT WAS LATE** afternoon by the time Cruz, his mother, and Aunt Marisol made it to Hanalei on the north shore of Kauai. Standing on the sidewalk outside the Goofy Foot, Cruz should have been exhausted. He wasn't. He was anxious and excited. Okay, hungry, too. But that could wait.

Lani was a few blocks away, spending the night with her family. Nyomie, Sailor, and Emmett were staying at Dr. Hightower's vacation house. In the morning, they would all meet at the airport, where *Condor* waited to return them to South America.

Cruz glanced up the street. It felt weird not to be searching for a Nebula agent behind every tree, light pole, and planter.

"Maybe you should go first, Cruz—you know, to prepare him," said his mother. She fiddled with her hair, pushing it behind her ear, then immediately tugging it back out again. "I wish I looked more ... Maybe I should clean up before—"

"You look beautiful, Petra," said Aunt Marisol, handing her a brush from her pack. "Besides, I've got dibs on the tub, and I plan on taking a looooong bath." She trudged up the steps to the apartment above the Goofy Foot, unlocked the door, and went inside.

Cruz's mom leaned in. "It's been a while since I dated, so my radar could be off, but did your aunt and Brume have a ... thing?"

"Yep. He fooled us all—her more than anyone." If Cruz's aunt felt anything like he had after learning Bryndis was Jaguar, it was going to take a while for her to get over it.

His mother looked up the staircase. "And then to see him being hauled away in handcuffs. Maybe I should—"

"Mom, *that* can wait," insisted Cruz. Turning her toward the door, he reached for the handle. "*This* can't."

She drew in a sharp breath. "I know."

"You ready?"

"No, but yes."

Opening the door of the Goofy Foot, Cruz marched in. He headed straight for the man behind the register. "Hi, Dad. Now, don't freak—"

"Cruz!" His father dropped a box of surf wax onto the glass counter. Some of the round tins spilled out and went rolling away. "What are you doing here? Why aren't you on *Orion*? Is everything—"

"Everything's fine." Cruz caught a tin before it dropped to the floor. "I'm with Aunt Marisol, Nyomie, Lani, Emmett, Sailor, and ..." He'd run out of air. "I have a surprise for you. But try not to lose it, okay?"

"Lose what? What's going on? Why would I—"

The bells on the door jingled. Cruz didn't look back, instead keeping his eyes on his father, whose jaw was falling open.

"Hello, Marco."

Cruz's father stood there, squinting like he was seeing a ghost and trying to decide whether he should confront it or turn and run. It looked to Cruz like he wanted to run. "Petra?"

"Yes. It's me." She put a shaky hand to the base of her neck. "My heart is racing ... I never thought this day would come ... yet, here we are ... me ... you ... Cruz."

Cruz's dad inched around the corner of the counter. He approached her cautiously, touching first her cheek, then her shoulder, as if to make sure she wasn't a mirage before wrapping his arms around her.

They hugged and kissed. Foreheads touching, the pair began speaking in rapid whispers, talking over each other, trying to catch up on years of conversations in minutes.

"But the fire..." said Cruz's dad.

"I hid at the Archive... then came here to set up my lab on Niʻihau."

"I was sure I saw you once... at Waimea," choked his dad, tears rolling down his cheeks. "I thought it was my mind playing tricks on me."

"It *was* me," she said. "I used to go there to think. It was never hard to spot you. With those wild shirts of yours, I could see you across the channel..."

His dad let out a laugh Cruz hadn't heard in...

Forever.

Tiptoeing to the door, Cruz flipped the sign. It was almost closing time anyway.

When he turned, his mom and dad were there to pull him into a hug. One arm around each of his parents, Cruz rested his head against his mom's shoulder. Long after they'd run out of adventures and stories and memories, the three of them remained standing in the middle of the store. Holding each other. Loving each other.

Letting the tears fall.

LATER THAT NIGHT, after three slices of pepperoni-and-sausage pizza with extra cheese, Cruz relaxed with his parents on the deck of their apartment. Cruz sat between his mom and dad in the porch swing that hung from the attic rafters. He gazed out past the fluttering palms to the tangerine sun sliding into the calm waters of the bay.

The trio gently drifted forward and back in the swing. Forward and back.

Cruz was ready to ask his mother the question that had been on his mind since his visit to the Archive. "Mom, if I don't get hit by a bus or something, how long will I live?"

Her face glowed gold in the setting sun. "It's hard to say, Cruzer. Like I said, you're one of a kind. The best answer I can give you right now is

you'll live longer than most people. But how *much* longer? Ten years? Twenty years? At this point, I don't know. I'm looking forward to doing more research."

"Maybe the Synthesis could help," said Cruz. He was thinking about how Jericho Miles had been the first one to save him from Nebula's initial attack. "I think things are different there now. You know my roommate, Emmett? His mom is the director."

"And his father is a curator at the Archive," she added.

How did she know?

Cruz was starting to make connections. "Was Emmett's dad . . . ? Is he one of your friends at the Archive?"

She shot him a coy look. "I'm not at liberty to say."

He was.

"I'm sorry I put you through so much, Cruz," said his mom. "I've often wondered if I did the right thing, creating the cipher and journal. I'm still not sure if it was all—"

"It was," said Cruz. "You'll see. When you complete the serum, it'll be worth it."

She kissed the top of his head.

Cruz bent his neck and slipped off the lanyard. He held the cord up and the trio watched the cipher slowly spin. It seemed to Cruz that his family had a lot in common with these little wedges of black marble. They, too, had been split apart and scattered, but they'd somehow found their way back to each other again. His family would never be as they once were. They would always carry the seams and scars of Nebula. Still, they had survived. They were together. Cruz knew he would never take that for granted. Not for one day. One hour. One second. No matter how long he lived.

Cruz lowered the cipher into his mom's waiting palm.

And let go.

CRUZ'S EYELIDS flew open well before

the sloth in Emmett's wildlife alarm clock was due to start squeaking. He knew right away something was different. *Orion* wasn't moving!

Cruz gently eased his arm from beneath a still-sleeping Hubbard. Slipping out of bed, he hurried to peek through the blinds of the porthole. "Emmett, we're here!"

They were back at National Harbor!

It was their last full day of school. This morning, Dr. Hightower would preside over the closing ceremony and their first year at Explorer Academy would officially end. The last two weeks had been a blur, studying for and then taking final exams. The faculty and explorers had been told Professor Luben had left the Academy early to handle a family issue. There had been an item on the news that Brume had been arrested for attempted murder, kidnapping, and art fraud, but they hadn't shown a photo of him, so no one had made the connection between Brume and Luben. Yet. Aunt Marisol and Professor Ishikawa had taken over conservation class, helping the students review the course material for the exam.

Meanwhile, Roewyn had called Cruz to tell him that her mother and grandmother were taking control of Nebula with plans to turn the company around. "It's a new beginning," she'd said on their video call. "Maybe for my dad, too. How can I ever thank you for what you did for him?"

"You just did."

Something told Cruz they would be friends for a long, long time.

"Emmett!" Cruz shook his roommate's shoulder. "We'd better get going. The shuttles are coming at nine, and we haven't finished packing."

"You go," croaked Emmett, snuggling deeper into his comforter.

Cruz showered, dressed, and fed Hubbard. He took the dog out to the meadow, then for a walk. Cruz had a few odds and ends to take care of. First, they headed to the bridge. Without the captain's help, Cruz never would have been able to retrieve all the pieces of the cipher. Of course, he couldn't reveal that in front of the crew. The best he could do was say, "Thanks for everything, Captain Iskandar. Have a good summer."

Raising his coffee mug, the captain gave Cruz a secret wink. "It was quite an adventure, Cruz. See you in September."

Cruz hoped so. He hadn't gotten his invitation from Dr. Hightower for next year. No one had. The Academy president was still reviewing their final grades.

Next, Cruz and Hubbard stopped at the tech lab to return Fanchon's virtugraph. He pulled the truth compass from his pocket. "It's an incredible invention, Fanchon. I'll send you all my notes, but from what I can tell, it works perfectly. Thanks for letting me test it."

Fanchon gently pushed the compass back toward him. "Keep it. A real explorer must always seek the one thing that matters most: truth. Speaking of testing things . . ." She leaned into a nearby cubicle. When she straightened, he caught sight of what she was holding and nearly dropped the virtugraph. "Is that—"

"UCC two-point-oh." Fanchon lifted the shiny black helmet. "It's passed all our lab tests. Now we need to assess it in real-world conditions. The job is yours, if you still want it."

If he still wanted it? Was she kidding?

"When do you want to go?" asked Cruz. "Lani and I aren't flying home until tomorrow. How about after the ceremony? Jaz could take us out in *Ridley*—"

"Whoa, whoa! I meant when you return to school this fall."

"This *fall?*"

"You'll need a full support team, like last time."

"But, Fanchon—"

"Go. Enjoy your break. It'll be here when you get back."

Only one task remained on Cruz's to-do list, and it was the most difficult one of all. Handing Hubbard's leash to Fanchon, he bent in front of the pup. "Be a good boy, Hub." The words caught in his throat. Cruz put his arms around the dog and held him close. He let his cheek linger against warm fur, as he inhaled the scent of strawberries and bacon. "I love you, Hubbard," whispered Cruz, a tear falling onto the Westie's yellow lifejacket. "I'll miss you."

Hubbard licked his ear.

Fanchon rested a hand on his shoulder. "He'll be here waiting, too."

On his way out of the tech lab, still drying his eyes, Cruz tapped

his comm pin. "Cruz Coronado to Emmett Lu."

"Just getting out of the shower. Meet you at breakfast."

In the galley, Cruz got a cheese omelet and toast, along with a glass of orange juice. Heading into the dining room, Cruz hesitated. Bryndis was at Team Cousteau's usual table. She was alone. The two had hardly spoken since Bryndis had dropped the bombshell that she was a Nebula spy. They'd attended class, as usual, and eaten together, as usual, but always with at least one other teammate present.

Ali, Zane, and Yulia were at Magellan's table. Ali saw Cruz and waved. Cruz waved back, then set his tray next to Bryndis's. He pulled out a chair. "Hi."

"H-hi." She sounded as nervous as he felt.

For the next five minutes, Bryndis swirled her Cheerios into a tiny tornado with her spoon. Cruz poked holes in his omelet.

"It looks like—"

"I was in the—"

They'd started to talk at the same time. Both let out an uneasy laugh.

"I was going to say that it looks like it's going to be a sunny day for graduation this afternoon in the courtyard," said Bryndis. "You?"

"I was in the tech lab earlier. Fanchon has a new UCC helmet."

"Really? That's great!"

"She's going to let Team Cousteau test it next fall." It was a dumb thing to say. Bryndis might not be returning. Dr. Hightower had agreed to let Bryndis finish out the term, but after that, nobody knew what would happen. They were still waiting for Dr. Hightower's verdict.

Bryndis glanced down. "Oh."

It was one tiny word, but it revealed everything. She *had* heard from the Academy president.

"You're not coming back next year, are you?" he asked.

She shook her head.

"I'm sorry."

"Are you?"

"Sure. What happened to you could have happened to any of us. We all trust the teachers and staff. How could you know what Dr. Vanderwick was up to? Look at me. I nearly put the journal right into her hands!"

"You did?"

"When it was broken, I was *this* close to asking her to help me fix it. I have an idea. After the closing ceremony, we'll go talk to Dr. Hightower. Sailor, Emmett, Lani, Dugan, and I will tell her how important you are to the team and that she *has* to invite you to attend next year—"

"No, Cruz. I appreciate it, but no."

"Why not? I know they'll do it, and Dr. Hightower—"

"Already said everything you just did. She said Dr. Vanderwick had done a good job of deceiving everyone, including her. She was willing to let me come back for a probationary period. I ... I turned her down. Going home was *my* decision."

"Why? I don't—"

"I just felt ... I mean, I feel like after everything that's happened, I need to be with my family for a while, you know?"

He did. Being surrounded by those you loved, and who loved you, was everything.

Bryndis stared into her cereal bowl like it was a crystal ball. "I might return, maybe the year after next ... I don't know."

"You'll be back," said Cruz. "Who else is gonna save me from crazy hailstorms in the CAVE? Besides, it's *örlög.*"

She looked his way, a dimple appearing on each cheek. "Destiny."

"EMMETT! CRUZ!"
Moving through the doorway into Bingham Auditorium, Cruz saw that the rest of Team Cousteau was already there. Dugan, Lani, Bryndis, and Sailor had saved the last two seats at the end of the row in the back section reserved for first-year students. The boys wove through the crowd to reach their teammates. It felt

weird to be among almost 150 explorers. When Cruz and the other recruits had arrived for training last fall, the older students were on campus for only a few days before leaving on their assigned ships. Cruz took the open seat next to Sailor. Lani and Emmett filed in next to him.

"Sorry we're late," Cruz said to Sailor. "Everest cam."

"An expedition going up?"

"From China." Cruz and Emmett had dropped their luggage off in their old dorm, the Mount Everest room, where they were to spend the night before leaving tomorrow. Their room featured a big-screen TV with a live webcam feed of Mount Everest. Cruz and Emmett had stopped to watch a climbing team begin their ascent. As always, each touched one of the colorful prayer flags that decorated the room and wished the climbers well. It was their tradition.

The faculty was filing in from the front of the room. They took up most of the first three rows. Cruz spotted Aunt Marisol in a poppy red blazer and pink floral scarf. She was between Monsieur Legrand and Professor Benedict.

"Hey, look, Professor Gabriel!" said Dugan. "He came for the closing ceremony."

"Thank goodness," said Emmett and Cruz in unison.

The Academy president, in her long white coat and matching pants, was crossing the stage to the podium. Everyone quickly found their seats.

"Welcome home, explorers!" Dr. Hightower's commanding voice filled the auditorium.

Claps, cheers, and whistles greeted her.

"I want to begin by saying how proud I am of all of you," she continued. "Whether through research, journalism, conservation, or rescue and rehabilitation, you all have made significant and lasting contributions to the world. I'm especially proud of our first-year explorers."

Puzzled, Cruz looked at Emmett, who lifted a shoulder.

"I was recently informed that their exploration efforts have led scientists to determine that the Danger Islands in Antarctica are home to more than a million Adélie penguins," explained Dr. Hightower. "This supercolony is believed to be one of the largest Adélie populations in the world. Thanks to our explorers, this area will soon be designated as a protected wildlife preserve."

Applause thundering around them, Cruz jumped to his feet with the rest of his class. He bumped fists with his teammates.

Dr. Hightower recognized other explorer classes, too: the third years, who'd created an initiative to recycle trash from the world's oceans; the fifth years, who'd helped rescue thousands of sea turtles caught in a storm in the Gulf of Mexico; the sixth years, who'd worked to protect China's bamboo forests for endangered species like the clouded leopard and the giant panda.

Dr. Hightower cleared her throat. "Now for the individual awards. We'll begin with the North Star."

Everyone in the auditorium swung to look at the last two rows. Cruz's face went hot. His heart began to pound. This was it!

"As you know, this award is presented to the first-year explorer who personifies the attributes we value above all others: respect, cooperation, and honor," said Dr. Hightower. "It is voted on by the entire administration, faculty, and staff. This year's recipient was a nearly unanimous choice. This explorer tackles every task with a can-do attitude and infectious energy. This explorer is described as fierce. Passionate. Brave. Yet this person is also a team player— honest, loyal, kind, and helpful. I, for one, cannot wait to see where this combination of courage and cooperation leads. Faculty and students, I am pleased to announce this year's recipient of the Explorer Academy North Star award is . . . Sailor York!"

The place erupted.

Sailor, however, had turned to stone. She was in shock.

"It's you! It's you!" shouted Cruz. He reached over and shook Sailor until she finally responded.

"Me?" Sailor slapped her palms to her cheeks. "Crikey!"

While Sailor stumbled her way to the stage, Cruz turned to console his roommate but saw it wasn't necessary. Emmett was clapping, too, the emoto-glasses a cherry blossom pink.

Sailor shook Dr. Hightower's hand, waved to the crowd, and made her way back down the aisle.

"Now for a special citation," said Dr. Hightower, raising her hands for silence. "The Rosalind Franklin award is given to an explorer who contributes to a major scientific breakthrough or discovery. This is not an accolade we bestow often, and in fact, it's been several years since we've had a worthy recipient, which makes this year even more remarkable because ..." She leaned into the microphone. "Ladies and gentlemen, we have a tie."

A murmur went through the room.

"That's right, we have *two* winners." Dr. Hightower gazed into the audience. "The co-winners of this year's Rosalind Franklin award are Emmett Lu, for his Lumagine Shadow Badge technology, and Lani Kealoha, for her Botanical Amplified Root Communicator."

Emmett's glasses, along with his face, went bright white!

The crowd applauded as Lani and Emmett made their way to the stage. Dr. Hightower hung a silver medal around each of their necks and shook their hands.

Once his friends returned to their seats, Cruz got a closer looked at Emmett's award. Dangling from a wide gold ribbon, the circular silver medallion featured Rosalind Franklin's face on one side and an etching of Explorer Academy headquarters on the other. It was incredible!

Cruz knew Emmett would treasure it forever. He did not, however, expect that Emmett would wear it forever. That night, as they put on their pajamas in the Mount Everest room, Emmett *still* hadn't taken off his medal. "Are you gonna sleep in that thing?" joked Cruz.

"I might."

There was a knock at the door. Cruz went to open it.

It was Nyomie. She had her clipboard. "Since you both have early flights in the morning, let's check you out now. Tablets, please?" She took their computers and removed their OS bands.

Cruz rubbed his bare wrist. It felt strange.

Nyomie took two cream-colored parchment envelopes off her clipboard. She gave one to Emmett and the other to Cruz. She raised an eyebrow. "Good night, explorers."

Once the door closed behind her, Cruz and Emmett stared at each other. They knew what the envelopes contained: their futures.

"You first," said Emmett.

Cruz peeled off the gold seal, lifted the flap, and took out the crisp parchment paper inside. He unfolded it, his eyes racing across the page. The hand-lettered cursive message was short—only a few lines to tell him what he'd been waiting to hear: that he'd be an explorer again next year! Last year, when he'd received his initial acceptance, Cruz had wondered if had he truly earned his spot at the Academy, or if it had been given to him because of his family connections. This time, he had no doubt. Cruz *knew* he belonged here.

"I'm in," said Cruz. He turned to Emmett. "Now you."

Watching his friend read his letter was pure torture. Fidgeting, Cruz searched the emoto-glasses for a clue, but the frames were transparent. Emmett's emotions were in turmoil. That was a bad sign. Plus, he was taking a long time to read only a couple of lines. Another bad sign. At last, Emmett looked up.

"Well?"

Without a word, he handed the letter to Cruz.

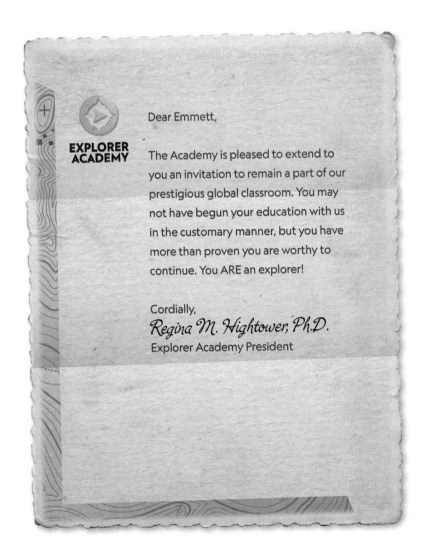

Dear Emmett,

EXPLORER ACADEMY

The Academy is pleased to extend to you an invitation to remain a part of our prestigious global classroom. You may not have begun your education with us in the customary manner, but you have more than proven you are worthy to continue. You ARE an explorer!

Cordially,

Regina M. Hightower, Ph.D.

Explorer Academy President

"Yay!" hooted Cruz. "I knew she'd ask you back. Didn't I tell you?"

"You told me." Emmett took back the letter. He eyed Cruz with suspicion. "Did you say something to her?"

"Uh … no." At that moment, Cruz was glad he was the only explorer with a virtugraph. Besides, it wasn't like he'd told Dr. Hightower anything about Emmett she hadn't already seen for herself.

There was another knock. This time it was Dugan, his pack and suitcase at his feet.

"Heading home, huh?" asked Cruz.

"Yep, my flight to Santa Fe leaves in a couple of hours. Just wanted to say goodbye."

Emmett came to the doorway.

Dugan nodded to the medal. "Nice hardware," he said, without a bit of envy.

Emmett beamed.

"Say, did you guys get your invitations for next year?" asked Dugan.

"We're coming back," said Cruz. "You?"

"Yeah. And I just saw Sailor and Lani. They'll be back, too. Looks like the whole team will be together again, I mean, except for …" He stubbed his toe into the floor.

The boys dipped their heads. Losing Bryndis was tough. But they would figure it out.

"Guess I'd better get going." Dugan slung on his pack. "Have a good break."

"You too," said Cruz, lifting his fist for Dugan to bump.

Emmett did the same.

Picking up his luggage, Dugan shuffled down the hall. "Oh, and Cruz, anytime you want to see the *sweetest* sand dunes in the world, let me know, okay?"

"Oh, so you want to visit Hawaii, huh?" Cruz shot back.

Dugan gave him a hefty grunt. "Later, Explorer Academy!" His words echoed through the stairwell. "Team Cousteau's the best! *Fortes fortuna adiuvat!*"

Chuckling, Cruz shut the door.

The lights flashed. Cruz and Emmett quickly got ready for bed. They slid under their covers seconds before the room went dark.

Plumping his pillow, Cruz turned on his side. "Hey, Emmett, since we're leaving tomorrow, you'd better tell me now."

"Tell you what?"

"The big secret."

"What big secret?"

"You know, what it means when your mom calls you Nou-nou."

"Ohhhhhhh no!"

"Come on, Emmett."

"Nope."

"I thought we were friends. You know me. I won't tell anyone." Silence.

"You swear?" Emmett's voice was small.

"Explorer's honor."

"I'm holding you to that. Okay. Nou-nou is French; it's short for teddy bear."

"Awwwww, that's nothing to be embarrassed about."

"Cruz, you promised—"

"I won't say a word. Not even to Sailor."

Emmett let out a happy sigh that filled the room. "I can't believe it. I won the Franklin award with Lani."

"You still wearing the medal?"

"Maybe."

He was.

"Of course, you do realize," drawled Emmett, "you and I... we still haven't aced time travel."

"There's always next year."

Emmett wasn't kidding.

Neither was Cruz.

▶ "CRUZ!"

Wearing a bright orange short-sleeved shirt, his dad had one arm around his mom's waist and the other arm in the air. His fingers were spread, signaling Cruz had five minutes before he had to go in.

Straddling his surfboard, Cruz lifted a hand in return. "Sorry," he said to the girl bobbing on the board next to his.

"It's okay," said Lani. "We've got all summer to surf."

"I meant about my dad's shirt."

She laughed. "He does have a traffic-cone look happening there. You want to come over tomorrow? You can take a look at my design for Mell's charging hub."

"Charging hub?"

"Didn't I mention it? You know how *Orion*'s always picking up trash from the ocean, right? I collected some of the glass and metal and made an upcycled charging station for Mell. It'll look like a beehive, only tinier."

"But she's—"

"Solar-powered, I know, but this way you'll be able to charge her at night, if you want. Plus, she's practically a member of Team Cousteau, so she ought to have a decent place to sleep instead of your pocket, don't you think?"

It was a good idea—a thoughtful one, too. "Thanks, Lani."

"Don't tell Mell, okay, *hoaaloha*?" She leaned forward, lying on her board on her stomach. "I want it to be a surprise."

"You do realize that she's a..."

Lani was already paddling out. She glanced back, a huge grin on her face.

She'd been teasing, of course.

Going onto his belly, Cruz swam out, too. He angled to his right so he wouldn't drop in on Lani. He took his time, wanting this final ride to last as long as possible. Seeing the approaching wave, Cruz aimed the nose of the board down and did a duck dive to let the break wash over him. Cruz surfaced to watch Lani ride the smooth curl in. She was an excellent surfer—better than he was. He wasn't jealous, though.

Cruz went out a bit farther. When at last he turned, the entire crescent-shaped inlet lay in front of him. The evening sun painted the edges of mashed-potato cumulous clouds pink and orange. Wisps of fog

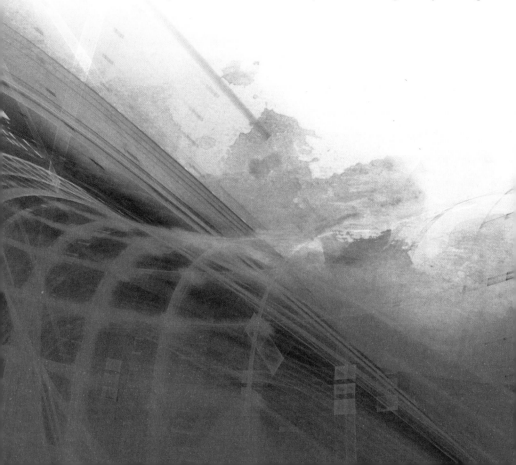

lingered in the deep green folds of the Hanalei mountains as braided waterfalls cascaded down their sharp peaks. In less than a year, Cruz had traveled to all seven continents on Earth but had yet to see a place more beautiful than this. Something told him he never would.

Cruz felt the oncoming swell. Pressing himself into his board, he stroked with the incoming surf as hard as he could. His mom and dad would be watching. Lani, too. He didn't know why he wanted to impress her. It had never seemed important before. Now it did.

Cruz's heart pounded against his ribs. This was his favorite part. He loved grabbing the rails, popping up, and feeling the powerful surge of water roll under him. Each time was a new test, not only of balance, but of will, too. Could he hold on? Could he master the wave? Could he ride it all the way in?

Cruz was up for the challenge. He was ready for whatever came next!

Almost time. Just . . . a few . . . more . . . seconds . . .

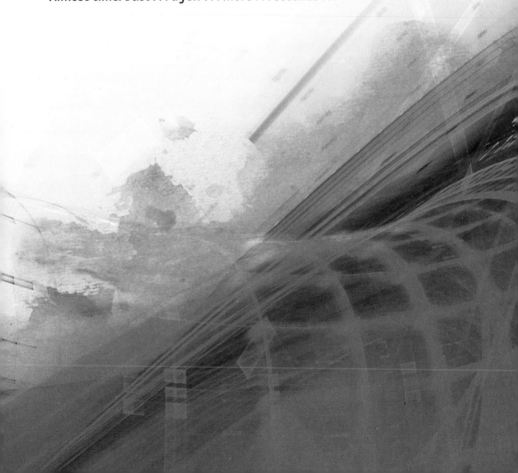

THE TRUTH BEHIND THE FICTION

The Explorer Academy recruits have navigated through the icy waters of Antarctica and searched for fossils in the sweltering deserts of Patagonia. They've invented technologies that bring them closer to understanding the natural world. And they've always tried to answer a big question: What else is out there just waiting to be explored? Real explorers from around the world are tackling this same question. Get to know these four National Geographic Explorers who are undertaking their own missions to protect the planet.

ARIEL WALDMAN

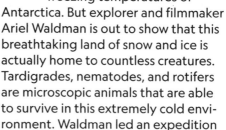

At first, it may seem like only penguins can withstand the freezing temperatures of Antarctica. But explorer and filmmaker Ariel Waldman is out to show that this breathtaking land of snow and ice is actually home to countless creatures. Tardigrades, nematodes, and rotifers are microscopic animals that are able to survive in this extremely cold environment. Waldman led an expedition to film these tiny titans, which are found under the sea ice, inside glaciers, next to frozen lakes, and in subglacial ponds. Her journey, sponsored by National Geographic and the NSF Antarctic Artists & Writers Program, led her to record microbial life in several locations. She descended below the ocean surface in a long metal tube used for observation, hiked up a glacier, and ventured to the stunning Blood Falls. With her work, Waldman hopes humans will come to better understand just how many incredible living things also call this planet home.

DIEGO POL

In the last mission of their first year at the Academy, the recruits use upgraded PANDA units to uncover a new species of dinosaur. Though paleontologist Diego Pol doesn't have a fictional PANDA unit, he does have a great deal of experience unearthing dinosaurs in Patagonia—a region with an incredible variety of animals from the Mesozoic era. With the help of his research team, Pol has discovered fossils of more than 20 new species of dinosaurs, crocodiles, and other vertebrates. One of his largest discoveries is *Patagotitan*, a 122-foot (37-m)-long titanosaur that was as large as a Boeing 737 airplane and weighed as much as 10 African elephants. All these discoveries help Pol to understand the evolution of reptiles like dinosaurs and crocodiles. As Pol says, "This is what paleontology is about: learning and reading these histories from the rocks . . . to put together this puzzle that is the history of life on our planet."

HEATHER LYNCH

Team Cousteau is thrilled when their fieldwork assignment leads them to an island full of Adélie penguins. Quantitative ecologist Heather Lynch has seen this incredible sight before. By using satellite imagery in her research, she discovered several previously unknown colonies of Adélie penguins living in the Danger Islands. There were 1.5 million penguins all together! This may sound like a lot of penguins, but unfortunately, penguin populations in the region have been steadily declining for decades due to climate change. That's where Lynch's work comes in—she incorporates statistics, mathematical models, satellite remote sensing, and biology to better understand penguin colonies. By surveying and counting penguins in the Antarctic, Lynch is finding out how to protect vulnerable colonies in the warming areas of the Antarctic Peninsula. She and her team created a free online database open to the general public that maps and counts penguins using remote sensing. It's a great way to get involved in the effort to preserve penguin populations.

RUTHMERY PILLCO HUARCAYA

Though Lani's Botanical Amplified Root Communicator (BARC) may not be a real-world invention yet, there are many scientists focused on restoring ecosystems by studying trees. Trees, which remove carbon from the atmosphere and lessen the negative impact of climate change, are key to the survival of countless species—including us humans! Like animals, trees and other plants have their own endangered species lists. Peruvian biologist Ruthmery Pillco Huarcaya leads conservation projects in the Osa Peninsula in Costa Rica to conserve these rare and threatened tree species. To restore these delicate rainforests, she and her team make inventories of flora, collect seeds, and grow threatened trees in nurseries. She has also worked with the Global Tree Campaign to analyze the conservation status of trees native to the Osa Peninsula. With these tree species cataloged, she can better understand how to preserve existing trees and increase their populations in the wild.

THE ADVENTURE CONTINUES...

33.8688° S | 151.2093° E

"M-MONSIEUR...L-LEGRAND!"

Hearing Cruz's voice blare through her comm startled Sailor. She nearly dropped her paddle into the icy water.

"I see," came the cool response from their teacher. "Alert your team."

"Um . . . ev-everybody," sputtered Cruz. "Cetacean sighting on the starboard side of kayak number . . . uh . . . uh . . ."

"Three," chimed in Emmett when it became obvious Cruz was too overwhelmed to remember which tandem kayak they were in.

Sailor grinned. She was excited, too, but knew better than to make a sudden movement. Cruz and Emmett were in the boat behind them. If she whirled around to catch a glimpse of the animal, she'd

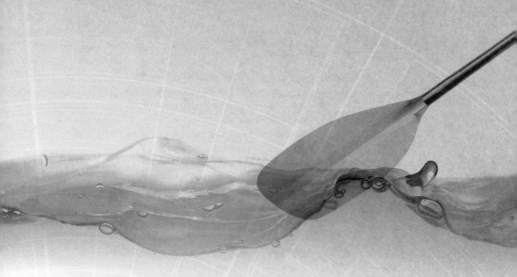

risk capsizing her kayak. Dugan, sitting in front of her in the bow, would kill her if she dumped them into the frigid Weddell Sea. Lifting her paddle, Sailor ever-so-carefully swiveled her upper body. The sight of a massive, steel gray body gliding through the mosaic of ice made her gasp. A whale was coming alongside their hull! Dugan stopped paddling, too. As the kayak slowed, the whale matched their drifting speed.

"*Magnifique,*" whispered Monsieur Legrand through the comm link. "Minkes can be curious, but it's rare to see them this close. They're among the smallest baleen whales, and quite fast. A minke can scoop, strain, and eat krill in less time than it takes for a humpback to open its mouth."

The whale rolled onto its side and seawater cascaded off its body. Sailor saw deep skin grooves, the curve of a long, tapered snout, and a single eyeball that seemed far too small for such an immense creature. Sailor stared into the eye. It stared back. The black pupil surrounded by a silvery blue iris seemed to be drawing her in. She leaned closer . . .

Looked deeper . . .

Face your pain.

Sailor jerked away, setting the boat rocking.

"Hey!" yelled Dugan. He slapped the water with his blade to keep them from flipping.

"Sorry, sorry!" Sailor sat up straight to help them regain their balance. Her heart was galloping, her head spinning. She was breathing fast. Too fast.

The kayak settled.

"You okay?" Dugan had glanced back.

"Uh . . . yeah," she rasped. "I'm just . . . cold."

"Better check your OS band. Your hide-and-seek jacket could be malfunctioning."

"Right. Thanks." But Sailor knew that what she was feeling had nothing to do with her coat. Fortunately, the minke was cruising toward the lead boat where Lani and Bryndis eagerly waited. It took a minute for Sailor's pulse and breathing to return to normal. It took her brain a little longer to recover.

One thing was certain. She couldn't let that happen again. Not here. Not now. Not ever.

It could ruin everything.

ACKNOWLEDGMENTS

From the moment Cruz first wrestled for his life in *The Nebula Secret*, I knew we were destined for a great adventure. Explorer Academy was a dream project, and I am grateful to my National Geographic family, who entrusted me with bringing it to life. Thank you, Erica Green, Jennifer Emmett, Becky Baines, Jennifer Rees, and Avery Naughton for your support, encouragement, and faith. Thanks to Eva Absher-Schantz, Scott Plumbe, and Antonio Caparo, whose stunning visuals so exquisitely captured the world of EA. A series cannot succeed without a dedicated team behind it, and mine is, simply, the best. It's been my great honor to work with Ruth Chamblee, Ann Day, Kelly Forsythe, Holly Saunders, Caitlin Holbrook, Laurie Hembree, Emily Everhart, Marfé Delano, Lori Epstein, Lisa Bosley, Alix Inchausti, Tracey Mason Daniels, Karen Wadsworth, John Lalor, Bill O'Donnell, and Gordon Fournier. I am awed and inspired by the explorers of National Geographic, whose passion for our planet sparked the series. Special thanks to explorers Zoltan Takacs, Nizar Ibrahim, Gemina Garland-Lewis, and Erika Bergman, who so generously shared their stories with me and their hearts with young readers. Thanks to my wonderful agent and champion, Rosemary Stimola, who has been with me since the beginning (far too many years to count) and her incredible team: Peter Ryan, Erica Rand Silverman, Adriana Stimola, Allison Hellegers, Allison Remcheck, and Nick Croce. I am also blessed with a fantastic cheering section of family and friends, especially my husband, Bill, who keeps the laughter and the chocolate chip cookies flowing. Last, but by no means least, I want to thank YOU, Reader! I am thrilled that you came along on the adventure. Something tells me that it is only the beginning for you. Wherever your path leads from here, may you always strive to discover, to innovate, and to protect.

Dare to explore!
Trudi